HEAD OVER FEELS

Rebecca Chase

Copyright

This ebook is a work of fiction. Names, characters, businesses, places, events and incidents are either the products of the author's imagination or used in a fictitious manner. Any resemblance to actual persons, living or dead, or actual events is purely coincidental.

Copyright 2021 Rebecca Chase

All rights reserved

Published by Rebecca Chase

All rights reserved. No part of this publication may be reproduced, distributed, or transmitted in any form or by any means, including photocopying, recording, or other electronic or mechanical methods, without the prior written permission of the published, except in the case of brief quotations embodied in critical reviews and certain other noncommerical uses permitted by copyright law.

To C, you took me to my first match and introduced me to the wonderful world of rugby. Thank you.

Chapter One

Beads of sweat slid down Sophia's chest. She stilled her trembling fingers long enough to pull down her skin-tight dress to a respectable length. The hem slipped from her hands. The scarlet material clung to her curves, daring her to accept its challenge and wear it beyond the confines of her bedroom.

She cringed at her reflection in the mirror. Graham would smirk when she wore anything revealing. Maybe her ex-boyfriend had been right, she wasn't sexy, and the dress wasn't her style. But her job meant the world to her, and Sophia refused to risk the wrath of her boss over a dress. Why did she have to dress up for the art exhibition anyway? She was never required to wear more than jeans and a jumper while running activity sessions with bereaved children.

She loved working for The Jameson Foundation, and the work she did, the charity changed lives, but the essential fundraising events tested her limits. They ensured major donors saw the importance of their donations and gave a little more. But Sophia was a support worker, not a fundraiser, and these nights left her empty.

But the demands from her boss still rang in her ears,

"You will be serving food to funders and giving a speech. Wear something smart but demure. It's an art exhibition, not a formal dinner. There will be creative types whose money matters to this charity. Don't wear that ugly brown thing again."

There hadn't been time to buy a new dress. The red dress, borrowed from her housemate, caught her eye in the mirror.

I look like I'm trying to get laid. Not that anyone would want to sleep with me, or that I'd let any guy get close enough to try.

The dress did something special to her body. Sophia admired her boobs in the mirror. The scarlet material stretched comfortably across them, cutting below the flush of a fading summer tan. She rarely showed her body off, but the plunging neckline made her want to arch her back while puffing out her chest, and the scarlet colour brought out the natural red highlights in her brown hair.

Her pulse thrummed, and her breath caught in her lungs. Sophia reached for the hem again.

"What's up?" Nicky, her housemate, poked her head around Sophia's bedroom door.

Sophia yanked at the scarlet fabric, but it continued to grip her upper thighs like the hands of a horny man on a crap date. Sheer willpower wasn't enough to make the dress, that had moulded itself to her curves, move lower on her legs. Would Olympic class tugging help?

"Don't you dare ruin my dress. I never fail to get laid when I wear it," Nicky exclaimed, striding into the room, her blonde bob bouncing as she walked. She appeared in the reflection in the mirror. "You look fantastic. The funders will be eating out of your hand.

Your arse looks amazing." Nicky gave Sophia's bum a quick pat.

Sophia's face creased in annoyance at her inability to allow even her best friend to touch her. She stared at their reflection, remembering how unlikely it was that they became friends on the first day at Bristol University seven years earlier. Nicky was a firecracker; slim, petite and feisty as hell. She was everything Sophia wasn't, but their friendship had never been stronger. They were lucky to have each other.

"I know she's your boss, but I don't see why Tasha decides who wears what. If you're going to wear a dress at least pick one that makes a statement," Nicky said, but Sophia was distracted by her globe like boobs.

"I look like a sixteen-year-old desperately attempting to dress to impress the bouncers so they can get into a club," Sophia smirked.

"Are you saying I have no class?" Nicky jested.

"No," Sophia sighed. "You're shorter than me and slimmer, it doesn't look indecent on you. The trashy dress suits you," she teased.

"Thanks. Maybe I shouldn't let you borrow my dress." Nicky rolled her eyes, but there was a grin on her face. "You can attend the exhibition in that hideous polyester thing your mum gave you years ago for graduation instead."

"Sorry, Nicky. I'm an awful friend. I throw myself at your feet, begging for your mercy. Can you ever forgive me?" Sophia attempted an awkward bow.

Nicky straightened the wide shoulder straps that came down to form the suggestive neckline. "Stop flashing those Bambi eyes at me. I can't be angry when you look at me like that. You look beautiful and not cheap or trashy. But let's ask a man's opinion. Oi, Ryan!" she hollered in the direction of the corridor. "Come here; we need you."

Before Sophia could protest, Ryan swaggered into the room. He'd styled his blonde hair in surfer waves. Sun-kissed skin shone from his naked chest, and baggy shorts rested casually on hips that drew her eyes to his perfect V lines. Nicky's fuck buddy was the sort of guy who starred in your fantasies yet possessed the intelligence of a Labradoodle puppy.

Ryan was the first guy she'd had in her bedroom in years. Sophia shrunk, shy in her outfit as he shrugged. "I'd do her but lose the underwear. You don't need anything under that dress if I remember correctly." He winked at Nicky

Sophia winced. *I can't go commando.* But before she could protest audibly, Ryan seized Nicky and swept her over his shoulder. Nicky laughed and squirmed as they headed out the door. Jealousy and embarrassment heated Sophia's face.

It wasn't that she fancied Ryan, more that he was a reminder of the things she wanted; a gorgeous guy slinging her over his shoulder and anywhere else he wanted. *And yet I won't let guys get close.* Nicky regularly told her she was beautiful, but she couldn't believe it. The blame for that lay with Graham.

What had her colleague, Jack, and the only male she had in her life said? "If you want to be confident, then do something that scares you." He'd struggled to come out to his conservative parents until he was in his late twenties and they'd refused to accept him as part of the family ever since. He'd understood what it was to be scared.

"This scares me," she whispered to her reflection. But Ryan was right; her underwear made the dress bunch at her hips. She would look better without it, and maybe going commando would boost her confidence and make her feel sexier. *It's worth a try.*

Nicky's bedroom door slammed shut. Within moments the laughter turned into declarations of need.

Sophia sighed as she raked up the hem of the dress, reaching underneath to grab her black cotton underwear. No one had come close to making her moan like that. Even when she'd had fun with her favourite vibrator, she hadn't uttered a peep.

There's something wrong with me. Sophia's ex-boyfriend, Graham, had suggested as much, reminding her constantly of her faults.

He would hate this.

The rarely released rebel in her rose angrily. Graham could piss off, along with his controlling behaviour that she knew damaged her self-worth. She yanked down her underwear and tossed it in the wash basket.

Sophia headed out her room and padded down the corridor, heels hanging from her fingers. Muffled offers of pleasure accompanied moans from Nicky's room; they were promises that Sophia had never experienced first-hand. Ryan's words resonated through her as she drove to the art exhibition, sexual acts she'd only imagined filled her. "I'm going to taste every part of you tonight, and I'm not going to stop licking you until you're screaming this place down."

Sophia avoided the sharp elbows and handbags worth

more than her salary as she moved through the crowd of guests, a silver tray of hors d'oeuvre between her hands. Art wasn't her thing, and the pieces paled into comparison when she could watch those attending the exhibition instead. They barely noticed her as she handed out food, swiping bite-sized pastry parcels with their veiny hands while boasting about their importance and achievements. Portly men who chanced a canapé from the serving plate, while eyeing their unimpressed wives, spoke loudly, "I really shouldn't. According to my wife, I'm supposed to be watching my weight." They followed up their reasoning by ramming a third and then fourth spinach and feta parcel into their gobs.

Force a smile and get on with it.

At least the venue was stunning, albeit chilly. The grand cathedral stood in the centre of town. Its beauty took Sophia's breath away. If it hadn't been for the event, she would have been investigating every nook and cranny or better yet, at home in her fleece pyjamas.

"Aren't you a sexy minx?" A man with ruddy cheeks and a throbbing nose wedged himself between her and the exit to the busier cloisters. Hidden from her view was the grand entryway into the spectacle that was the central part of the church. Sophia imagined the gentry, centuries ago, bowing in worship as they continued their debauched lives in private. The cloisters were off to one side, arranged as a square with a garden situated in the middle. In the summer, the smell of herbs and well-tended plants ruminated around the maze of paths. Rumours told of bodies hidden below the cloisters. No one had found the door to the crypt. It was probably a way to make money from tours, but Sophia had been fascinated with the building since she'd first visited it.

Tonight, there was no opportunity for adventure. The cathedral beckoned her to discover more of its mysteries, but she couldn't escape the irritating stranger.

"Would you like something to eat?" Thrusting the plate in front of him, she attempted to divert his attention.

He ignored the canapés and leaned closer.

Bloodshot eyes loitered on her chest. "Is everything here on offer tonight?" Alcohol wafted from his breath into her face.

She pursed her lips, swallowing the bile, and hid the grimace threatening to replace the plastic smile that had served her so well that evening. Even guys she was attracted to weren't allowed in her personal space, let alone men like this. Nicky said her barriers to physical contact were too high, but it was the only thing that stopped her getting hurt again.

"I'd pay handsomely for the right item," he said. His sausage-like fingers moved closer to the tray and what was beyond it.

She recoiled, searching for an escape. What was wrong with this guy? The other guests were mostly polite, and some were great champions of the charity's work. At the other end of the corridor, Tasha stared her down with a warning look. In the briefing before the event, Tasha had demanded that she keep the guests entertained at all costs, but Sophia wasn't about to sell her morals for a quick buck. *She shouldn't push me like this.* But Tasha had never liked Sophia. *She'll make my life hell if I disobey her.*

Drool gathered in the corners of the letch's mouth. Sophia's muscles primed in fight or flight as he moved in.

✲✲✲✲✲

Why did I come here alone? Aidan's stomach knotted, but he kept his pace to the cathedral. A mesmerising and foreboding sight, the gothic building loomed through the dusk like a warning. It was as if something was going to happen tonight that he couldn't predict or prepare for.

He shook it off. The evening was a promise to John, a friend and a former mentor who saved him from a life of anger and sadness. Unfortunately, it was also another night going stag. A woman on his arm would have eased the obligation.

Bianca was the last significant woman in his life. She loved to hang off his arm at events. He reminisced their explosive bedroom antics and the flick of her tongue across her lips. Once upon a time, the memory of what else she did with her lips would have required a not-so-subtle shift of his trousers, but now it left him cold. Unfortunately, he couldn't trust Bianca Tandy. While her impulsiveness was attractive, over time, it became dangerous. She forced her position in his life, attempting to drive everything and everyone out.

Inside the building, the cold numbed his face, but it couldn't dull the memories of her. He'd executed their break-up in public and away from valuable things. He'd feared her taking a golf club to his car or manhood. If anyone questioned him, he'd said it ended because they weren't compatible. In truth, the nail in the coffin of their fling was the day he discovered Bianca was lying about being on the pill, desperate to hogtie him for good. Babies weren't something he wanted, and it had cemented his decision to finish with her. Despite all that,

Aidan didn't hate her. He didn't even know her. That she hid most of her true identity worked well for both of them. Aidan had no intention of sharing his true self with anyone, especially not a woman. *You can't commit to long term.*

Don't think about it. But the emotional scars of his possible illness were there every day. He hadn't had a diagnosis of the hereditary Huntington's disease yet, but only because he refused the tests. *I don't want to know my future.* Huntington's was a death sentence. He'd watched his dad die from it and knew the suffering that would come from testing positive. *I want to live for now, enjoy my life, enjoy women.* Long term relationships weren't for him, and as a result, it was easier not to let anyone in. No one should have to suffer because of him.

Aidan shook himself. *Don't do this to yourself. Get through this event and then go to a bar and see what the night brings.*

Taking a deep breath, he turned full circle to admire the beauty around him. The architecture displayed a mixture of violence and grace that spoke to his past and soul. Today, he was an artist showcasing his work, but by the weekend, he'd be an artist of a different kind. He'd use every ounce of strength and aggression in his muscles as he battled adversaries. Power, adrenaline and brutality would roar through him as he sprinted around a rugby pitch to the chants of thousands of fans singing his name.

A cackle of laughter drew his attention. His eyes caught those of a perky blonde woman at the end of one of the corridors. The make-up caking her face didn't hide that she was a little older than his thirty-five years. If she was trying to catch his attention with the bounce to her walk, it worked. *Maybe she can make the night interesting for you.*

"Hey there, sexy. I'm Tasha." A giggle sprang from her ruby red lips. "You are hot! I bet you get that a lot."

"Umm…"

"I get it a lot, too."

Confident women were usually a turn-on, but she was off the scale. Her intensity was like kryptonite to his flirting skills. Wild eyes were upon him, and briefly, she reminded him of Bianca. It wasn't a good thing.

"Fancy a date sometime? Unless you don't think I'm attractive," she squealed.

"I err…" He stumbled through his words, trying to keep up with her machine gun comments and questions.

Bottle blonde hair was flipped in his direction, whipping him in the eyes.

"You think I'm ugly, don't you?" she said with a pout.

"Actually, I was—" he attempted.

"Oh, you're Irish. I love Irish men," she moaned. He got that a lot, his accent was impossible to hide. Seduction dripped from every pore as she slithered closer. "I can prove to you that I'm beautiful all over, although it's my bedroom skills that you really need to experience."

Aidan remained silent. He had the chat-up lines, he always did, but there was something about her that made him nervous to say them. What would he be talking himself into? He didn't want to lead her on.

"Call me. You don't want to make me angry now, do you?" the woman growled, slipping what he presumed was her business card into his trouser pocket and attempting to stroke his crotch at the same time.

Aidan flinched at her unwelcome advances. She'd made his penis jump back inside his body. *You need to find safer people to talk to.*

Tasha's spiked heels barely made a noise as she departed. He turned in the opposite direction, ramming into a soft woman's form. *Watch where you're going, Aidan, you fool.* Scarlet flashed in front of his eyes and he accidentally hip barged her away.

With quick, strong reflexes, he wrapped one arm around the front of her waist and stopped her hitting the floor. The dress clung to her curves as she hung like a rag doll in his arms, her legs flailing in mid-air. The tray she'd been carrying clattered to the floor, muted by the dull roar of chattering guests.

Everything turned to slow motion as the hem of her dress slid up her thighs. Aidan's crotch stirred. The awkward angle was a bonus as it offered him the best view of her clothed bum. It was a struggle not to stroke his free hand along one perfectly formed cheek. Did it feel as good as it looked? An outraged voice cut through his imaginings.

"For fuck sake. Will you put me down?" The scarlet beauty wriggled in his hands, the waves of her chestnut hair cascaded down her shoulders. He held her firmly against him. The scent of coconut filled his lungs, and his stirrings increased.

"I think what you mean to say is 'thank you'," he whispered in soft Irish tones. The woman in his hands froze momentarily before resuming her bid for freedom. What was the safest way to put her down without her falling? Her efforts gave him an unexpected thrill as she tried to wrestle herself free. Her skin-tight dress climbed higher.

I want to see her face.

Aidan stood straight, forcing her vertically against his chest. She squealed enough to make him pull back. She stumbled.

His adrenalin surged as she spun, glaring at him. He admired the defiant way she lifted her chin to meet him. Her dark eyes narrowed.

His responding arousal was intoxicating. He shifted uncomfortably, hoping it didn't show through his chinos. It pulsed with every flutter of her eyelashes.

Flushed cheeks and red, moist lips caught his attention. The spotlights in the cathedral highlighted the gold strands of her hair, matching the flecks dancing in her eyes. She struggled with the hem of her dress while reaching for the plate that was still on the floor. Flustered, she tripped and nearly fell off her heels.

His reputation with women was well earnt. Friends and foes had bandied about the word shameless alongside his name on more than one occasion. She wasn't like his other women though, her shoulders slumped forward, and she repeatedly fiddled with her clothes as if uncertain of herself.

"Why would I thank you?" Her hiss was barely a whisper. "Your massive body was in the way."

There was something about her that turned him devilish and ready to tease. Maybe she could make his evening less of a chore. He would gladly take her home that night. He'd enjoy bringing out more of that fierce attitude and obliterating her shyness in the bedroom. "You noticed my body then?"

"It's impossible to miss." Her tone was laced with exasperation, but the hint of a smile teased the corners of her mouth. His grin stretched further. What was it about her that appealed to him so much? She was the opposite of ladies like Tasha; dignified, funny and not forcing an agenda on him. *I'm actually having fun.*

Her gaze dipped, looking down his body and pausing at his crotch. Did she know she was staring? Her eyes widened, and her mouth dropped open in surprise before transforming into a small smile. What did her reactions mean? He was hooked on working her out.

"I have eyes as well, although I wonder which of us is admiring the view more," he replied with a wink.

"I don't know what you mean," she stuttered, but her eyes flicked back to his crotch, and she blushed as red as her scarlet dress.

He forced his laugh down. Laughing wouldn't help him seal the deal, and he wanted her. There was a beauty radiating from her, but it was more than that. She'd sparked his interest. Was it the way she'd attempted to hide her cute freckles with make-up or her awkwardness at their interaction? She was a challenge that made him want to play his best game. She would be in his bed by the end of the night. He'd bet his rugby career on it.

CHAPTER TWO

Sophia gasped for breath. What was happening? She'd gotten away from the old letch who'd attempted to cop a feel of her boobs and instead found herself in the path of one of the most attractive men she'd ever met. *All those years spent avoiding men and I jump straight into the hands of a gorgeous one.* But it was looking into his eyes and seeing something mysterious, maybe a softness, that attracted her further. His touch had her nerves sparking her to life. Electricity jolted her awake for the first time. *It was never like this with Graham.* A deep need ached in her belly, one she didn't want to let go of. Like a flash she recalled Graham standing over her, calling her frigid because his touches didn't turn her on. She'd trusted him for a while, even loved him, how could a stranger nearly floor her just because his dick swelled when he looked at her?

Lust at first sight. Nothing more. Get yourself under control.

Her knuckles were white, where she clenched the serving plate. *That guy is too hot for you, and what about his teasing? You can't trust him.* Yet her stomach fluttered when she caught him staring. His musky scent, with tropical undertones, filled her lungs. It was impossible to concentrate while he stood in front of her. Her eyes lingered on the swelling below his belt, his lips, his thighs and especially his hands.

Oh, his hands. The plate nearly slipped from Sophia's grasp again as she remembered how firmly he'd held her. She wanted him.

But I don't even know him.

"I have to go," Sophia bolted down the corridor, Nicky's nude heels, that she'd insisted went with the dress, clacked against the stone with her retreat.

The Irish stranger called out. "Wait, I didn't get t-"

The sound of her heels drowned him out, not that they could compete with the volume of her thoughts. *Stay and spar with him.* She shook her head as she implored the cathedral ghosts to drag her to the underworld and away from the situation she didn't have the confidence for.

"Fucking Nicky and her fucking dress," she cursed. Her breasts bounced as she hurried away. *This wouldn't have happened if I'd worn my brown trouser suit.*

For the next hour, Sophia handed out food, smiling and laughing with a charm she didn't usually possess. Was this what happened when you fancied someone? She sought out the sexy stranger in the crowd, and every time she found him, he was laughing and telling stories as his soft baritone carried across the cathedral's acoustics. His blue eyes twinkled in the low lighting.

Willing herself to be calm, she attempted to control her desires.

You're a powerful woman who rules her own body

and not the other way around. It was an ineffective mantra. Her body was responding to him. Instead of looking away, when she glanced in his direction, he'd return her gaze with the same intensity he'd displayed when he'd caught her staring at his crotch. Her face burned, revealing her attraction.

I'm ridiculous. It wasn't like in her twenty-eight years she hadn't touched a guy's cock before. But Graham had never had this effect on her. Sophia attempted to scrub away the memory, but a shiver danced across her naked arms. Nibbling her lip, she imagined what it would be like to lick the tip of the stranger's penis.

A sour-faced Tasha clicked her fingers in Sophia's face as she walked between groups of funders, a reminder that Sophia needed to get back to work. Sexual fantasies swirled as she offered canapes to anyone who'd take one.

Time dragged on. It was made worse by the throb of the pads of her feet, but when the crowds thinned, and the guests headed for the presentation, Sophia took a quick break. She limped down the corridor, her hatred for the heels renewed. The cloisters of the cathedral were a distraction from her blisters. The architecture was powerful yet graceful. The elegance of the walls stilled her. Stone formed an awning above her; it was as if she was in a stone forest, hidden from the sky. The cathedral was a cold building on a dark October evening, especially now that her adrenalin and lust were ebbing.

A chill ran down her spine as she paused at one of

the donated paintings she'd missed before. It wasn't like the traditional watercolours and oils displaying local scenes that she'd seen that night. This painting was captivating. There were depths to it beyond her reach, mocking her lack of understanding. In the image, differing shades of blacks and greys built up around a path. The uneven trail was surrounded by trees, leading into a dark wood. Clouds hovered. Slithers of light still teased the edges of the branches as if a hint of the day remained, but night was coming. Something unseen loomed in the background of the scene, a storm maybe? Dense clouds obscured the ripples of light and promised something foreboding or menacing. There was one figure in the painting. It was in the distance and surrounded by trees.

Sophia stared. Was it supposed to be a real person, or did it represent something else? The figure was the only colour against the trees, decked in a scarlet red and standing alone. It was significant, the crux of the painting, and in its simplicity, it formed an unfathomable mystery. What though?

The smooth caress of an Irish brogue caught her off guard. "Do you like it?"

She nodded thoughtfully.

"What do you think it means?" The words formed on what she already knew was a beguiling mouth.

The mysteries of the painting eclipsed her earlier embarrassment. No longer did she fumble for words around the Irish stranger. The first genuine smile, since she'd arrived that night, touched her lips. "It's beautiful but, and this sounds weird, the painter's pain grips me. It's hard to explain, and I can't do it justice."

"You're doing fine. Please carry on."

The image reflected her loneliness and struggles. *Has the painter suffered as I have?*

Sophia tried not to overthink how easy this chat between them was. There was no denying the stranger was jaw-droppingly handsome, but it wasn't debilitating her as it had earlier. Instead, she spoke without fear of judgement. "The darkness suggests suffering, but there are glimmers of light. I can't decide if the light is hinting at hope for the future or lost hope. Then there's the lone red figure in the distance. I think it's a he. I'm wondering if he's lonely, is he suffering through the darkness or is he causing it? Or is he becoming free, moving further from the darkness and suffering? There's an overwhelming sense of loss, but the loss of what?"

Sophia turned to the quiet stranger. His sapphire eyes took her breath away. They weren't pinning her with lust or displaying his amusement. Instead, they looked through her. His brows furrowed. His thoughts were as indecipherable as the painting.

"Sorry," Sophia whispered, "you must think I'm weird."

"No, it's not that, it's just—"

"And sorry for earlier," she hurried, "I didn't mean to be rude. You caught me off guard."

"You seemed a little flushed before, and I wasn't sure if it was something I said or did..." That cheeky smile of his resurfaced. Her cheeks reddened.

"So, the painting," she said suddenly shy and gestured back to the canvas trying to change the subject.

His soft laugh surprised her, and her tension eased. There was a freedom to him when he laughed like he was a little boy without worries. In the twinkling lights of the cloisters, she vowed that her new mission would be to hear that laugh again. "Go on then, what about the painting?"

"There's a lot of beauty there, but the suffering makes it painful to look at."

He stepped closer. A tingling of desire in her core rushed over her.

"Still," she joked, "I'm not sure I'd pay £3,000 for it."

His responding chuckle brought out her smile although she wasn't sure why. All remnants of anxiety had disappeared. *Am I glowing?*

"I'm guessing you've never heard of the artist?"

"Is he famous?" Shrugging, she read the name on the card next to the painting. "Aidan Flynn."

"He's not necessarily famous for his art, but in some circles, he's considered a bit of a celebrity."

"Do you know him? Did he explain the meaning of the painting to you?" She mused over it, fighting the blushes that betrayed her excitement. This was the longest she'd spoken to an attractive guy in years.

"Yeah, you could say that. I think the artist would be impressed with your understanding, although you've missed a couple of bits."

"Like what?"

"Close your eyes for ten seconds and then look at the painting again. It's amazing what extra things you see."

"You're kidding me, right?" Sophia eyed him suspiciously.

"Come on. It will be fun," the stranger teased. "I'll do it too, and then we can both look silly."

She waited for him to do it first, rolling her eyes at the ludicrousness of it when he couldn't see her.

"I heard you roll your eyes," he said, making her smile.

"Fine," she sighed and closed her eyes, amused. *One, two, three—*

A hand clamped aggressively onto her bum cheek.

*****

People had viewed Aidan's work numerous times, but no one had versed its detail like her. *She speaks the true meaning of my painting and my mind so easily as if she understands the deepest parts of me. Maybe she's suffered too.* She wasn't just beautiful, but intelligent and funny, too. She'd bewitched him.

Aidan hesitated in telling her he'd painted it. If she knew he was the artist she'd want to learn the truth behind it. Was he ready to open up to a stranger about his dad? It would lead to more questions and long-held secrets. *Best to hide it a little longer.*

He opened his eyes, needing to see her again and readying himself for further truths from her analysis of his painting. But she was rigid. A fog of anger came down like a blind over his eyes. His muscles tightened, and adrenalin ripped through him at the sight of a drunk, ruddy-faced, pig of a man mauling her arse. Had he been the man from earlier, when Aidan had walked into her?

Aidan had come across men like him before. Frequenting clubs was a precursor for it, but it was her reaction that shocked him. Aidan had witnessed ladies shouting insults, slapping the guys before storming off, but she stood there frozen, tears prickling her eyes.

"Excuse me," Aidan said sternly, as he grabbed the collar of the man's jacket. He outmatched the drunkard in strength and agility. Aidan pulled the man to a corner, where he bit back his rage. A charity art show wasn't the place for a smack-down as much as he wanted to destroy the guy. "What the hell was that?"

The toad-like man wobbled, his eyes protruding too far from their sockets as he stared at Aiden in silence.

"You don't deserve to breathe the same air as her, let alone get close enough to touch her," he snarled. "If you do anything like that again I'll crush every bone in your body. Do you understand me?"

The guy nodded. Aidan pursed his lips and blew the tension from his body, quelling his anger. He was relieved he hadn't been out of control. "I get it, you're horny, and she's hot, but you can't go around molesting women. You need to apologise to her. Now!"."

The man shook and, for a split second, Aidan pitied him. But the fear on the face of the woman who had brought his painting to life remained with him. He had no regrets as the man shuffled up to the beauty in scarlet.

I don't even know her name.

She inched backwards, but the panic on her face was softening, replaced by surprise. Her gaze flicked to Aidan when the man apologized and shrank away into the crowd. Then, much to Aidan's disbelief, she smiled.

A member of staff encouraged Sophia and Aidan in the direction of a side room for a presentation by the charity's CEO.

Lightly touching her arm, Aidan fought the barrage of questions he wanted to ask and the savage need pulsating in his pants. "You're gorgeous," he whispered, his voice deep and his lips brushing her ear. He turned on the charm that served him so well before. His gait relaxed, and his smile turned to the lazy one that made women lick their lips in expectation. "I should tell you my name because you'll be screaming it all night. What time do you get out of here?"

"Seriously?" she replied, stunning him into silence. "And there was me foolishly thinking you weren't a prick."

"No, wait..." But he didn't have a comeback. She had the measure of him again.

"When will I learn?" she mumbled striding away.

*****

Sophia shook her head. Did he think that all it would take was a crap chat-up line and she'd be in his bed? His charm had endeared her to him, but what if he only fancied her because of her dress. Nicky had too many stories of guys' lines. But there was something else. *You ran away because you're scared. What if he does want you for your body? Would that be so bad?* Cocky guys typically left her cold, but when she'd talked to her Irish stranger there had been little lurches in her stomach, a yearning to touch him, smell him and taste him.

But why him?

Did hearing the action between Nicky and Ryan go to my head? She hadn't trusted any guys since Graham. The prospect of being hurt wasn't worth putting herself out there. Who was to say the stranger would be any different? *You were just talking, nothing more.*

Striding in the direction of Ray, her CEO, who was drumming up passion for the charity, she continued her inner monologue. Ray was an expert in inspiring people and drawing money from their wallets and tonight he'd transfixed the crowd. He chose his moment and introduced the members of his team. One by one, they pulled on the heartstrings.

Suddenly it was Sophia's turn. *You need to focus and remember that this is your job, not a pick-up joint.* She stepped up to the microphone.

"The Jameson Foundation changes lives. It touches the hearts of those who are suffering and in need," she said to the crowd.

Sophia spoke with gusto as she shared the story of a little girl who she supported.

"Most seven-year-olds spend their days playing in the park or watching TV but not this little girl. She was struggling with pain that most of us will never understand. Milly's mother had died from terminal cancer twelve months earlier. Milly was struggling under the weight of her grief. Every day was worse than the day before, and she was desperate." When Sophia talked about the positive change in Milly, because of the charity's support, a smile broke out on her face and on the faces in the crowd. The speech was from the heart. She was good at her job, and with every word she spoke her passion was evident.

Pausing, she willed herself not to look in the crowd for the Irish stranger, but it was futile as she fixed on him instantly.

The intensity in his eyes made her breath catch. During her years as a support worker, she'd developed a talent for reading people, but he was a mystery to her.

Closing with an impassioned plea for support, she stepped away from the microphone, leaving Ray to push the money message one last time. Adrenalin eased as she moved to the edge of the stage and stared anywhere but at the Irish stranger.

"Play it cool," she whispered, sweeping a hand casually through the waves of her hair. "Don't look in his direction."

But she was drawn to him. She gazed at his face.

"Sorry," he mouthed to her. Worry lines had appeared across his forehead.

"Thank you," she mouthed back.

A jolt of happiness hit her belly. She was his only focus. His eyes were wide, and a grin lifted the corner of his mouth. *Down girl. An apology doesn't make him the man for you.* But a quiver still reached her core.

People surrounded her as schmoozing replaced the presentations. An onslaught of questions came her way, fired at her until she struggled to draw breath. The crowd had closed in on her, blocking her viewpoint, and any opportunity she had of seeing her stranger. Minutes ticked by. Would she get to speak to him again?

Finally, an hour later, after regaling the group with stories and exhausting their questions, she found an escape route. Disorientated, she searched for him, but he was gone. Her heart sank. Emptiness consumed her as her desire dwindled before disappointment replaced it. She shivered, the chill covering her as she excused herself from her colleagues and went in search of things to tidy.

Shirking off her heels, she eased her bare feet onto the stone. The silence around her was a sigh of relief. An empty corridor offered her the opportunity to be alone with her thoughts, and she took her time to find the discarded glasses from the dark cloisters of the cathedral.

At the back of a window ledge, she spied a forgotten

champagne flute. As she reached for it, the aroma of tropical fruits intertwined with a musky scent that wafted around her, sending blood rushing through her limbs. An ache reached her crotch, but she resisted the urge to whimper.

Her Irish stranger's presence and smell were already etched on her mind and body. "Hello again." His voice was deep behind her, his Irish brogue strong.

A moan caught in her throat. His breath crossed her naked shoulders. They had to be on the cusp of touching, and she imagined a sliver of light separated them. All she had to do was step back to feel him, but instead, Sophia inched to the side to give her space to turn.

"Don't." His husky yet gentle command encouraged her to move back in front of him, and she remained in her original position.

"Please touch me," she whispered. *Did I say that aloud?*

He toyed with strands of her hair. Lips brushed against the pulse point behind her ear, causing a shiver that had nothing to do with the dropping temperatures of the corridor.

"I'm sorry about earlier, you just…" His words faltered, and she waited, her body taut. His breath tickled her neck. *I need to see him.* But she remained still to give him space to speak. "There's just something about you. I couldn't think straight. You're a sexy, beautiful, intelligent woman, and I haven't been able to stop looking at you all night."

Heat radiated through her body, and her breathy sigh surrounded them as his hands gripped her hips.

"You don't mean that," she said, devoid of conviction. "I'm not your type."

His devilish laughter had her quivering. "I'll stop if you want me to, but you are my type. If you keep trembling like that, I'll have to turn you around so I can show you how much of my type you are."

Shivers consumed her body, expressing more than just her desire. What if her fear of getting hurt stopped her from being with him? Would the pain from her past win again?

"Please," she uttered. Maybe if he made the first move, she could push past her fears. What would it take for him to turn her around and kiss her?

"Please what?" His voice was gruff.

She willed herself to speak. "Don't stop."

His hands travelled across her bum. The stroking of his palms against her sensitive form caused whimpers to fall from her lips. It was a sound that hadn't left her mouth before. Hungrily he pulled her back into his chest. Hardness pressed against her.

Sophia tried to clear her head, but clarity fought with the lust that saturated her body. A bead of sweat ran down between her breasts. But there was something else; dampness in her knickers rubbing against her. Her limbs were like jelly. What was happening? The agonising ache, the overwhelming longing that she'd never believed in. *I can't be wet, surely?*

"I've been wondering all evening if you were wearing knickers." One of his hands crept round to her front, touching her through the scarlet dress. He paused. Was he waiting for her consent?

"Please," she murmured again. Gently he cupped her, the heat from his fingers joining that already radiating from her core.

"So, there's no attraction between us then?" he

asked playfully.

She longed for him to tease her more, verbally and physically. "None at all," she replied, her words staggered. His fingers caressed her intimately again.

His growl had her weakening further. "Not even when I do this?"

Soft lips brushed across the curve of her neck, and his hand moved up the front of her body. It edged closer to her chest and her sensitive, erect nipples. Holding her breath, she held tightly to the last bit of control she had over her body.

She moved the palms of her hands against the cold stone wall, submitting to the need he drove through her. Starvation for more of him overwhelmed her, and his gentle sucking against her skin only temporarily held off her yearning for greater satisfaction.

Suddenly, both hands were teasing her, pausing in front of her breasts, daring her to act. Sophia arched her body and pushed her breasts forward into his hands while her bottom pressed against his erection.

"You are incredible," he whispered between needier kisses. The sound of his suckling against her neck was as intoxicating as the movements themselves.

Silently she urged his palms against her nipples as she rocked her body softly against his.

A noise in the corridor stopped him. He rubbed himself once more against her as if he was trying to imprint his body onto her memories.

"Goodbye, Sophia," he whispered.

Suddenly her back chilled, his body no longer joined to hers.

She turned to say something, anything. Although the heat from where her Irish stranger had touched her remained, she was alone.

Chapter Three

Sophia remained frozen, facing the wall, confusion carved on her face. Desperately she clung to some essence of her disciplined self, but he'd shattered her control. On shaky legs she returned to the event, nearly walking into John, one of the charity's trustees.

"Hello, Sophia." John was a kind older man who cared deeply about the work of the charity. The significant crow's feet that had formed at the edge of his eyes gave away his recently retired age and reminded her that he'd brought his wisdom to many a meeting. "Your talk moved me. It reminded me of the differences this charity has made. I'm proud to be a small part of it."

"Thank you. Although I don't think it's a small part. We couldn't survive without your support," she said sincerely.

"Oh, stop trying to make an old man smile," he laughed, his eyes crinkling again. There was a tinge of a local accent and the respectful air of a gentleman when he spoke. "I have to say, I've barely been able to keep in my excitement tonight." He invited her into a secret. "Seeing my protégé here was a dream I never thought could be realised!"

John's wistful smile beckoned her curiosity.

"Who was your protégé?"

"Aidan Flynn."

Sophia stepped back in surprise. Where had she heard that name already tonight? Of course, Aidan Flynn was the artist of the mysterious painting! Maybe John would be able to answer some of her questions.

"He's a fantastic rugby player and artist. Let me show you his painting." They walked to the artwork as John's fatherly tones told some of Aidan's story. "I was Aidan's rugby coach when he was a teenager. He was an interesting lad, shut people out, probably because of what he'd been through, but when he played rugby, he came alive.

"Discovering art transformed his life. I like to think I'm one of the reasons he took up painting. Oh dear, that sounds like I'm blowing my own trumpet," he chuckled, "but I am proud. He donated one of his pieces for the exhibition. It's quite powerful."

John led her to the creation that had enthralled her earlier that evening.

"I love this painting," she sighed, seeing more depths to it than she remembered. Even with all the layers of pain it encapsulated, there was something she couldn't grasp, meaning at the tips of her fingers.

"It's not my favourite," Tasha bellowed as she bounded up to them.

Instantly Sophia was filled with the misery that accompanied the presence of her attention-seeking boss. John quickly said his goodbyes and dashed off.

"Did you see him, the artist? He was here tonight. So hot. I wanted to rip his clothes off and use my tongue as a paintbrush and his body as the canvas. Look at him." Tasha thrust her phone in front of Sophia, smacking it against her nose with her child-like impatience. "I found a photo of him online. He's in his rugby strip."

Sophia gasped. Her Irish stranger was giving a cheeky grin to the camera as he proudly displayed his emerald green kit. The shirt followed the contours of his torso, and the matching shorts were tight enough to showcase what she'd remembered against her.

"I'd sell my nan for a night with him. It's only a matter of time before I give him the fuck of his life. He insisted on taking my number."

Sophia couldn't believe it. Aidan Flynn was the rugby playing artist, and he'd requested Tasha's number, not hers. Sadness crept up on her, bringing a wave of tiredness. Now that he was in Tasha's sights, Sophia would be less than a distant memory.

"Game over," she whispered to herself as she trudged away.

*****

Aidan meandered home. *I shouldn't have left the event. Why did I disappear before getting her number?* The darkness swallowed his sigh. The heels of scantily clad ladies clicked past him. He couldn't distinguish their slurred catcalls from their heckling. An aroma of sweat and alcohol reached his nose. But the obtrusive nightlife didn't obliterate the smile that transformed his lips when he thought of *her*.

Options of what to do next tried to hold his focus, but his attention drifted. Seeing Sophia, lying next to him as sunlight filtered through his window and lit up her naked body, was his objective. The recollection of her big brown eyes and wet core made his cock stir.

Aidan had experienced more than his fair share of women. As a minor celebrity, through his international and club rugby playing, he'd had stunning women flocking in his direction. These women had made a career out of faces that were perfected by make-up and surgery. Men idolised their bodies, but none of them had made such a sudden and intense impact. *Sophia is above them all.* There was something innocent and yet naughty about her. A contradiction that he wanted to delve into. Perceptive abilities and mesmerising beauty had combined to distract him and intimidate him all evening. *Was that why I rushed off?*

The curve of her breasts had made him salivate with hunger as if he was on the verge of wrapping his lips around a strawberry that dripped with melted chocolate.

He wouldn't settle until she was whimpering against him. Her moans would keep him rigid for hours.

But it was more than that. It was the way she spoke about his art; no one had seen it as Sophia had. Her musings weren't because she was trying to impress him as an artist. Instead, she'd searched for meanings, delved deep to find the truth. What she said mattered. It would be a risk to show her his other work, but he wanted to. Would she find the true meaning in those pieces? Would she locate his depths? People told him he didn't have any and yet he wanted her to see the real him. But what if she found out his fears about Huntington's?

He was torn between seeing her again, for what could only be a fling, and carrying on life as before. A guy without a future can only have flings, yet he wanted her to see the true him. That was his reason for leaving. *You're scared by how much you want her to like you.*

The earthy scent of fresh rain filled his lungs. It

reminded him of practising his kicks in playing fields. Hours spent trying to perfect his skills and be the best or to hold off the pain in his life. It had worked. He was the best or had been before he retired from the International team. Years of pain, injuries and sacrifices had been pushed down inside of him like his hands now pushed deep into his pockets. Failing to reach his goal wasn't an option.

I can't even focus on my rugby match this weekend. I need to see her again. Nothing else would make sense until he did. He'd work everything else out later, but now he needed to be close to her. How though?

"I need a plan!" he shouted. Pigeons flocked to the skies, braving the rain just to flee the fool who was running out of options.

*****

Sophia slumped in front of her laptop, her feet cold against the kitchen floor. *Please let me sleep.* For hours she'd lain in her bed, tossing and turning, her pillows thumping against the bedroom door, thrown with grunts of frustration.

Even when rubbing her eyes, Aidan's body teased her thoughts. The fitted long grey-sleeved t-shirt and black chinos he'd worn at the exhibition had fed her fantasies. It was a simple outfit, but every time she closed her eyes it conjured up images of her ripping it from his body before she traced his naked skin with her fingertips. The aching between her thighs wouldn't abate.

In the haze of insomnia, she'd considered speaking to someone but snores now drifted out Nicky's room. There was no one else to offload to. Sophia didn't have many friends, and although her mum was a bit of a night owl, she was busy enjoying her new life with her husband in their Spanish villa.

Besides, what would I say to her?

"Hi, mum, how're things? Yep, it's ridiculously late, but I'm fucking horny. I'm as surprised as you are. This has never happened before. I met a rugby playing artist, and I can't stop imaging what it would be like to straddle his lap and ride him slowly as his hands grip my arse and his mouth explores my nipples."

That wouldn't be well received by her previously glacial mum whose lectures during Sophia's teenage years had always focused on the dangers of men. "Your education is your only priority. You need to stay away from all men. They may seem charming, but they're only after one thing, and as soon as you give it to them, they'll dump you quicker than yesterday's potato peelings. I've been there." Sophia wasn't allowed to forget her mum's "mistake".

But Sophia had always behaved. She was sensible to the point of boring. Most weeks she didn't even get horny.

I can't say that anymore. Sophia would have laughed if she wasn't frustrated by her inability to gain satisfaction. She'd tried every toy in her small collection, but she was consistently on the brink of orgasm with no relief. *But I'm not ashamed.* That was a bigger surprise. All this time she'd rolled her eyes at Nicky's sexual exploits or hidden away from men she considered might be attractive, but her appetite for Aidan eclipsed fear and shame. *How can I want someone I barely know?*

Before she let herself debate the consequences of her actions, she typed "Aidan Flynn" into Google.

A smile toyed with her lips as she studied the image in front of her.

She pushed herself back in the shoddily made kitchen chair, nearly rocking it off its legs.

Get a grip!

But it was pointless because seeing those bright blue eyes brought a familiar response. The memory of Aidan's messy hair and his lips against her neck left her breathless and needy. She slid her hand towards the waistband of her bed shorts. Arousal pulled her hand lower. As her fingers brushed her bikini line, it was his hand she imagined.

"What are you looking at?" There hadn't been a footstep or a squeak yet suddenly Nicky was behind her, gawking over her shoulder.

"Fucking hell, Nicky," she screamed, pulling her fingers from her knickers. "Don't creep up on me like that!"

Her heart thumped so hard it could have shattered her ribs.

"Keep your knickers on, honey, I called your name a couple of times." Sophia perched in front of the screen, willing her heartbeat to slow. Thank goodness Nicky hadn't realised exactly where her knickers were heading. "What are you doing up at three in the morning?"

"I could ask you the same thing," Sophia replied testily.

"I woke up famished. Sex always leaves me starving." Nicky wrestled with the chair before sitting.

"Who's the guy?" she asked, motioning towards the laptop screen. "He's hot."

Sophia's shaky finger moved to minimise the picture, but Nicky stopped her. "How come you're so fidgety? I promise I won't judge. I was googling hot firemen this week."

A creak of the kitchen floorboards caused them both to turn. Ryan must have been hungry too, or lonely.

"Why are you looking at Aidan Flynn?"

Sophia shuffled in her chair as Ryan grabbed the seat next to her and dropped into it. Pinned between Nicky and Ryan the smell of sweat and other odours she didn't want to consider crept into her nostrils.

"You've heard of him then?" Nicky asked.

"Yeah," Ryan flipped his hair. "He's an awesome rugby union player, well he was. He plays for the Bulls, and he used to play for Ireland."

The highlights of Aidan's rugby career continued to echo around the room until Nicky butted in. "Soph, why are you looking at him in the middle of the night? He's gorgeous, but he doesn't look like-"

"Like?"

"Ummm, he doesn't look like your type. He couldn't be less like Graham," Nicky said, stumbling through the words unable to make eye-contact with Sophia. "I mean, he isn't geeky, and I suspect the worse he could do is break your heart rather than, anyway…"

They were both uncomfortable at the mention of Sophia's ex-boyfriend. Graham had destroyed Sophia's trust in men with his emotional abuse and cheating. Nicky rarely brought him up. She'd never liked him but hadn't let it impact her relationship with Sophia. Nicky had been her rock, and Sophia was eternally grateful for her love and support.

"Aidan was at the exhibition tonight. There isn't anything to tell," she replied casually.

"Oh, you're wrong there."

Sophia and Nicky turned astonished to Ryan. The light from the laptop gave his face an eerie glow.

"Don't you know?"

"Know what?" they asked in unison.

Ryan leant back in the chair, balancing it on two feet and smirked. "There's lots I could tell you about Aidan Flynn." It was a rare occurrence that he was the most informed person in the room. "I'll tell you if you make me pancakes!" He folded his arms across his chest, triumphantly.

"Pancakes? In the middle of the night? You're not at the Ritz."

"Those are my terms. If you want to learn everything about Aidan Flynn, then I get pancakes."

"Fine," Sophia replied.

Ryan jumped up, gyrating around the kitchen. Boxers rested precariously on his hips while his cock threatened to peep out and give her a show.

Sophia chanced a glance. "And put that penis away. No one needs that in their life."

"I do." Nicky grinned while bouncing up to join him and together they bopped and shimmied while Sophia giggled at the stove.

Aidan's photo remained open on the computer screen as they tucked into some of Sophia's finest pancakes. Syrup slid down Ryan's grinning face covering his chin.

"Time to spill the beans, Ryan."

"Can't I enjoy eating a little longer?" he pleaded.

"Talk, sticky face!" Sophia waved her knife in his direction.

"Okay," he said, wiping his chin with his finger and slowly licking the syrup off, his eyes focused on Nicky.

"Oi, you can play your sexy games later! Tell me about Aidan Flynn, or I will use the knife somewhere lower."

"You're scary when you want something," he said, cupping his manhood uneasily. "Right, listen up, ladies. Aidan Flynn is a rugby player, originally from Dublin."

Sophia rolled her eyes. Ryan wasn't sharing anything new.

"However, he isn't just known for what he does on the pitch."

"He's a very talented artist," she huffed.

"I didn't mean that," he said, as his fingers danced over the keyboard. "He's a player off the pitch, too. He's dated, allegedly, a shitload of women, including a lingerie model, two actresses, some reality TV babes and several glamour models." Pulling up press photos, Ryan evidenced the women he was referring to.

Stunning blondes stared back. *I'm never going to be in the same league as these women. I'm not great in bed. I couldn't compete with Graham's exes, and they were bedraggled students, not sex goddesses!* "There's meant to be a video of him and Bianca Tandy, a glamour model, screwing. I've not found it yet, and I've scoured the internet."

Sophia froze, all the night's excitement drained from her. It was getting harder to ignore the obvious; Aidan had been bored at the exhibition, he'd played her, and she'd made it easy. Shame colluded with her sadness. Her mum had taught her not to be easy with guys.

Ryan finished with a smile. "The guy is an idol."

"I'm not sure this is what Sophia was expecting,"

Nicky said, cautiously glancing at her. Sadness was adding weights to the corners of her mouth and dragging them down.

"He's got a history of fighting too. There was an alleged bust-up with his former coach, Mick Daniels, at Bath, a team he no longer plays for. Coincidence? And there's been scuffles on nights out."

Sophia's face sank into her cupped palm.

"In his defence, I don't think he's as bad as the media make out, and no player comes close to his skills on the pitch. Well, until the end of last season. He's missed every conversion, like a penalty in football, this year and he may get dropped soon."

Nicky stood slowly. "Let's leave Soph alone, Ryan, I think she's tired."

"I've said the wrong thing." The proud face melted with genuine concern. Eyes flicked apologetically between Nicky and Sophia. "I'm sorry, Soph. Like I said I don't think he's as bad as they say. He just likes women, sex and excitement."

"Come on, let's go." Nicky tried to distract him, dragging him off his chair, his boxers precarious once more.

"Goodnight, Sophia. Don't let the bastards get you down," Ryan added as an afterthought as he left the kitchen.

Nicky's hand rested on Sophia's.

"I'm an idiot. Why did I let myself get taken in by him? Was I an easy alternative to boredom?" Sophia moaned. Nicky would never judge her, but still, Sophia didn't share the detail of what had happened. It was her secret for now. *I don't want anyone else's opinions to get in the way of how I feel, yet.*

"Don't stress, he might be a complete arsehole, but he might be what you need, a guy to give you those experiences you've missed out on. Either way, be careful," she said softly. Nicky had been caring for her since the day they'd first met, and Sophia's troubled break-up with Graham had sealed their friendship for life. "Get some sleep, okay?"

Sophia nodded before Nicky shuffled out of the room.

Taking one last look at Aidan's photo, she remembered the look of awe he'd given her when she talked about his painting. There had been more intensity in his ocean blue stare than in the picture itself. *It doesn't stop him being a dickhead, like every other guy, though.*

Closing her laptop down, she felt a chill for the first time since he'd touched her. Autumn rain slapped the windowpane, and eerily mirrored her mood as she wandered to her bedroom.

Chapter Four

"He was all over me," Tasha's shrill voice arrived through the office door before she did.

Sophia tried to like Tasha when the charity had first employed her as a manager and Sophia's boss. She'd made unsurmountable efforts, practically milking a soya bean herself to provide the perfect soya milk coffee. But Tasha's hostility toward Sophia had grown since her first day.

"I'll be his Tasha beast between his sheets," she screeched.

Janet, the team assistant, caught Sophia's eye. "Did you meet Aidan Flynn, too? Was he very attractive?" she asked softly.

Sophia glanced at Tasha, planting the well-practised plastic smile on her face. "Yeah, we said hello, nothing special. He was alright. You should see his painting."

"Alright?" Tasha's voice could shatter glass. "His body was like something out of a porno. When he took my phone number, I almost came!"

"Tasha!" Janet blanched.

"Hold on," Jack, the fundraising manager and everyone's gay best friend piped up. "I saw you talking to him, Sophia, and the chemistry between you...wowzers! I had to fan myself. He couldn't stop staring at you."

"No, you must be wrong. I'm sure Aidan barely knew I was there." Eyes wide she pleaded with Jack for silence, but it was too late, Tasha was already glaring.

Tasha's mouth tightened. "Where is my report? Or are you too busy boring everyone about last night to finish it? By the way, you really should make more effort at work. You look like shi-, you don't look good, sweetie."

An expletive-filled rant teetered on Sophia's well-bitten tongue, but Janet distracted her. Her permed grey curls bounced up and down in excitement. "I forgot to say. There was a message on the phone this morning, left at five this morning!"

Sophia raised her eyebrows. Janet was usually the epitome of efficiency, and yet she hadn't mentioned this until midday. "It was from Aidan Flynn."

"He must have lost my number," Tasha declared, smirking at Sophia. Sophia fought the temptation to roll her eyes.

Janet shifted awkwardly, her brown polyester dress audibly catching on her tights. "The message was for Sophia."

Sophia's head whipped around so fast she jarred her neck. "What?"

"He wants you to go to his house this afternoon and pick up a donation cheque."

Wrath radiated from Tasha. "What?"

"I said—"

"I know what you said, Janet," Tasha spat. "But she's not going. I'm the manager here. I'll go."

A wistful smile appeared on Janet's lips. "He even described her doe eyes.'"

Sophia wanted to blush and giggle all at once, but her excitement was cut short by Tasha's shout.

"I'll take care of it. No more arguments."

"Sophia is going," Jack insisted. He and Tasha both had the same level of superiority, and he was sticking his neck out by vetoing Tasha's decision. "Aidan asked for her." Jack usually reserved his stern tone for contentious fundraising meetings. "All donations are important to our charity. I'm the Fundraising Manager. It's my call."

Tasha's hands balled into fists; a tantrum was imminent. "But the report!"

Sophia lifted her chin. "I finished the report this morning. I emailed it to you a couple of hours ago."

"Excellent," Jack announced victoriously. "That's sorted then. Get your things ready and off you go. Actually, hold on, let's work on your make-up first, you look like hell, love."

Sophia allowed herself a smile. Jack was not one for chatting make-up; work was his priority. He probably wanted to remind her of the processes when collecting a donation.

"Must have been the worry about that urgent report," Jack joked, as he took her by the shoulders and steered her towards the toilets.

*****

The sun stretched through the kitchen window, glinting off the granite covered island. Most of the time Aidan loved his home, with the little cottage down the lane for his mum, but today he couldn't settle.

"What's wrong with you, honey? You've been in a fidgety mood since you returned from training," Aidan's mum said, tapping a teaspoon against her mug. She'd taken a break from gardening, where she was at her happiest. The hollow metal of her teaspoon acted like a soundtrack to Aidan's yanking of the kitchen drawers. *I built this house from a crappy old barn myself and I should know where everything is.*

"I'm fine." *What am I looking for anyway?*

"Then stop pacing like a caged tiger and stop banging those drawers. I'm your mum, remember? You can tell me anything." Piercing blue eyes stopped his search. "Is it because of the Bath game tomorrow? Hopefully, you won't see Mick."

Mick had been the only man his mum had dated since his dad had died. When Aidan had played for the Bath team Mick, the coach, had wheedled his way into their lives, encouraging his mum to share the pain of her loss and then using it to get her to sleep with him before she was ready. He'd dumped her afterwards, breaking her already vulnerable heart. During a training session, Mick had laughed in Aidan's face. "I'll do it again, and she'll take me back. Your mum is easy." Aidan had punched him. The newspapers had painted Aidan as a petulant player whose bad attitude made him impossible to manage. He was kept on the bench until the Bull's manager had bought him out of the contract. If it hadn't been for the Bull's, he wouldn't have scouted for international games. The bad reputation hadn't gone away though.

Aidan had barely thought about the Bath game or Mick since he'd met Sophia. The way she'd talked about the charity's work had opened his eyes to a world he'd forgotten and what she'd said about his art made his hand ache. *I want to paint again.* She'd inspired him.

His cock juddered, it didn't want to be left out. During their moment in the cloisters, Aidan wished he'd slid the hem of her dress up her legs and run his hand across her naked thigh. Would a stroke of his thumb make her shake with lust against him?

His fantasies paused as uncertainty loomed. It had been like that all night. Was Sophia genuinely attracted to him? If he'd brushed her sensitive nub with his finger, would she have writhed against him? If he had his chance again, he'd tease her, test her. Aidan longed to take his time with her, have her whimpering as he-

"Are you sure you're okay?" his mum asked. He'd forgotten where he was. Light shining off the golden bell-shaped lampshades brought him back. The house was a classic Cotswold cottage, yet it had industrial design touches. History was present in the materials used, but Aidan had a love of modern features. *Like my life, although that's more of a clash between past and present.* Soft furnishings combined with curved tables and sharp edges. Glass and light were everywhere, which gave the place an airy, open feel.

The smell of freshly brewed coffee wafted around him. This was home.

"Sorry, yes." Usually, he'd save his fantasies for his alone time, but he couldn't get Sophia out of his head. "Don't worry. Mick Daniels doesn't bother me, and he shouldn't bother you. I'm not getting into a fight with him again. But if he comes near you, if he thinks he can insult you-"

"Sweetheart," she interjected, handing him a fresh mug of coffee. "It's okay; he won't. And I can't have you getting in trouble again for my mistakes."

"It was his mistake, not yours." He wiped a smudge

of mud from her cheek. She was wearing her sturdiest jeans and a fitted plaid shirt; her gardening wear. "He used your vulnerability and your kindness against you when you were dating. Mick Daniels is a bastard."

"Aidan, language. Let's not talk about this anymore. I do have something else to ask you, though." He noticed the tone immediately. It was the one she used when broaching the subject of his health. His mum rushed on before he could leave the room. "Dr Sampson called me. He thinks it's time you had the test for Huntington's disease."

Aidan hunched his shoulders, even the name of the disease sickened him. "He shouldn't be speaking to you about any of this. It's my decision, and I would prefer not to know. We've been over this."

"But it's stopping you from living."

"In your opinion. I'm doing okay."

"But if you got the test done and it came out positive, you'd be able to get medical help. Please, Aidan," she begged.

"Mum," he softened. The conversation brought raw memories of his dad's final years. His dad's cruel comments or fixations over not having things how he wanted them were particularly hard to deal with. His mum had shown endless patience, although Aidan had heard her cry many nights when she thought he was asleep. "It doesn't matter what they might be able to do. I watched dad die. I've seen exactly how I'll suffer if I'm tested positive. I can't do that. Please, let's drop it. I want to enjoy my life."

His mum nodded but based on his previous experience he knew that wouldn't be the end of it.

"Maybe you should go for a swim and work some

energy off."

He pushed a hand through his hair before wiping it down his face. The action reminded him of Sophia's breasts against his hands. Maybe it was his brain protecting him, pushing away his painful conversation and replacing it with something that brought pleasure. It worked. Her return made his body ache. Sophia was the perfect distraction.

"Good idea." Stretching his muscles and powering his sex-starved body up and down the pool would help. "And if anyone calls for me send them my way."

"Who would be calling for you today?" She eyed him suspiciously. "Not Bianca? I thought that mingy witch was out of your life."

Stifling a laugh, he smiled at his mum. She was usually the epitome of politeness, but not when it came to the women from his past. "She's long gone. But you never know who's coming around."

The coffee cup his mum held to her face wasn't big enough to hide her curious smile.

Weaving through the corridors, admiring the photos of his rugby victories and his range of paintings he headed in the direction of the pool room. He was crap at keeping things that counted from his mum. *How can Sophia matter already?* Would she respond to the garbled answer machine message he'd left in the middle of the night?

He had to see her again.

*****

The rumbling of Sophia's old car down the rutted dirt track that, according to Jack's map, led to Aidan's converted barn had her bouncing against the worn fabric of her seat as her seatbelt pushed against her chest.

It's no big deal; I'm just picking up the donation and leaving. It will be fine. But the butterflies in her stomach protested in memory of the night before.

Her mouth dropped as she parked in front of the house. Leafy plants stood tall outside the front door of the classic Cotswold stone barn. The windows reached high up the one storey building, shining bright and large. Nothing was hidden from view, which was ironic considering the owner was brimming with secrets. The barn sat comfortably in the middle of large, manicured yet fading gardens. The late summer, stretching through September, had taken its toll.

Sophia stepped up to the door, wobbling slightly as her heels crunched against the gravel. She forced her hand to the iron door knocker, trembling as her fingers touched the cold metal.

She yanked her hand back.

Don't be a coward.

Taking a deep breath, she gazed at the building. The work to make it magnificent shone from the highlights in the stone. Lavender tickled her nose while the last flush of sun reminded her of warm summers spent playing with the neighbours while her mum worked all hours.

Trees swayed, accompanied by the melodic sound of a trickling stream and chirping birds. A soft breeze sent shivers dancing down her bare legs

Stop procrastinating. The urge to see Aidan warred with her fear of them being face to face. What if something happened? What if it didn't? Straightening her plaid skirt and shifting her top distracted her shaky hands. With her eyes closed, she reached for the door knocker once more.

"Can I help?" A soft voice from behind a trimmed fuchsia bush startled her. Sophia's car keys nose-dived to the ground as a lady walked across the grass to meet her. "Oh sorry, I didn't mean to make you jump, but you've been standing there an awfully long time. Let me get those." The lady bent down. Her silver and blonde hair sparkled in the sunlight and brought an attractiveness to the delicate features of her face. The electric blue shirt and the tie that kept her hair tidy matched the colour of her eyes. She made gardening wear look stylish.

"Thank you." The jangling noise of Sophia's keys being returned to her hand brought her to her senses. "I'm Sophia."

"Nice to meet you." The lady's smile glowed as she shook Sophia's hand. But the wrinkles above her high cheekbones and the tired hands betrayed a weariness too. "I'm Kate. Are you here to see Aidan?"

The warmth in her eyes was familiar. "You're Aidan's mum!"

"Yes, I am," she replied proudly. "How do you know him?"

"I don't really. I met him at the art exhibition last night, the one for The Jameson Foundation. I work there."

"Such an important organisation," she said distantly. "I didn't know Aidan had got involved. I'm glad he's supporting it. He's caring and loving. He could change lives if he…"

The pause stretched for an age.

"If he?"

"Oh nothing, ignore me. The ramblings of an old

woman." Sadness touched the edges of her smile.

"Not that old, surely? You must have had Aidan when you were very young."

"You're too kind. I was twenty-six, and his dad was thirty-four. Our families found the age difference a little controversial at the time." She chuckled. Her words were a glimpse into a happy past. "A long time ago now. Anyway." Quickly Kate became business-like. "Aidan's out the back, but he'll be easy to find. I'd take you, but I don't want to stomp my muddy boots onto his lovely floors. I hope you'll cheer him up; he's in a funny mood."

Sophia stifled her "oohs" and "ahhs" as she followed Kate's directions. Someone had spent a lot of time creating a comfortable, stylish and attractive home. The original beams and exposed stonework honoured its history while the expanses of glass displayed the panoramic views of the surrounding countryside.

She imagined last night's pancake party happening in Aidan's house. A giggle escaped her lips as she fantasised Aidan enjoying her pancakes and chasing her around the kitchen while thrusting in his boxers. *Don't think about it; he's not the guy for you.* The wistful smile remained though.

A glass door at the end of a corridor blocked her journey. With a push of the handle, she opened herself up to a rush of stimuli that shocked her senses. Water splashed, heat frizzed her hair, the smell of chlorine made her nose twitch her, but none of it compared to what she gazed upon. *Oh, God.*

Aidan powered up and down the pool; his back,

arms and the rear of his head on show. His firm body cut through the water, strength emanated from his biceps causing waves to thrash and flee away from him as he pushed through. Muscles contracted with every sweep of his arm, his shoulders flexing with each stroke.

An athletic arm arched, his elbow aloft before his hand sliced the waves of the pool. Sophia froze. He conquered the water that splashed then rippled to the edge of the pool. Aches ran down her body. Her body reacted in ways she couldn't control. It was happening again. The throbbing from her crotch was a warning, but she couldn't tear her eyes away. Sophia's fantasies of running her finger and then tongue down his back added to the feast.

With his evident strength, he could easily lift her against a wall allowing her to wrap her limbs around his naked torso.

"I can't do this," she whispered, taking one long last look before bolting.

*****

She's here. Aidan's eyes stung with chlorine, and his deep breaths hurt his chest, but still, he sensed her.

It was as if the heat from her stare seared his flesh, even as the cold water created a protective layer around his body. *I haven't swum this hard in years.* But he wanted to show her how well he performed. When her eyes fluttered closed at night, he had to be the man she dreamt of.

His confidence faltered as he noticed she was leaving. Was she disappointed? Aidan wasn't a big rugby player, but he was strong and muscular, and women adored his agile form.

"Wait!" he shouted, water rushed into his mouth, the ensuing coughs hiding the desperation in his voice. The waterline peaked above his pecs as he stood on the tiles of the bottom of the pool. Droplets of water trickled off his shoulders before joining the rest of the pool with a *drip-drip* noise. Sophia stopped, her shoulders sagging.

His pulse raced as she turned. He'd memorised everything about her and yet now she was finally in front of him, she took his breath away. Aidan's gaze followed her curves, pausing at the hips he remembered holding, his hands twitched in anticipation. With deep sighs, Sophia's breasts moved slowly up and down. The familiar sensation of his jolting cock stole blood from his brain.

"Why were you were leaving?"

Sophia faltered. Her gaze flitted around the room, looking at everything but him.

"I didn't want to disturb you, I mean, disturb your swimming," she said quickly.

"You weren't disturbing anything." His palms went to the edge of the pool directly in front of her feet. He fixed her with a stare as he pulled himself up and out, but her face reddened, and she quickly broke eye contact. Water slid down his naked body. He stood in front of her, not close enough to touch. His muscles continued to burn from the swim, but they competed for his attention against his growing erection.

Her eyes struggled to meet his. They repeatedly dipped, trying to see more of his body, almost as if controlled by an unwavering force. He grinned when her eyes finally lingered on his. He hoped she wanted him as much as he wanted her.

"You look tired. Didn't you sleep well last night?" Aidan asked, causing Sophia to flinch. He'd hit a nerve.

"Aren't you cold? Maybe you should get dressed," she replied.

"I can't get naked in front of you." He stated. Her dark brown eyes widened. He caught her looking at his crotch before looking away. Aidan nearly pumped his fist triumphantly into the air.

They stared wordlessly at each other. Sophia's teeth tugged at her plump lower lip, which made him crave a kiss from her. Would she taste sweet? How would the rest of her taste? Sophia was a mystery he was aching to uncover.

His old Irish team swim shorts couldn't hide his erection much longer. The green material clung to his thighs. They were roomy, but soon he'd be straining if she carried on staring at him like that.

"Don't you have a towel you could put on? You might get cold or something?" Sophia responded hesitantly, fiddling with her blouse, pulling the bottom of it down. All she succeeded in doing was pulling it tighter against her breasts and giving him a view that made his body hum.

"There's one over there." A lone finger casually pointed to the corner of the room, eyes never leaving hers. "You can get it for me seeing as you're concerned."

Golden flecks appeared to crackle inside her eyes.

"I couldn't care less to be honest," she replied with a cheeky smile. "But I thought that you'd want to give your best performance tomorrow, seeing as you're playing Bath. Aren't the Bulls and Bath meant to be massive rivals?"

"Did you Google me?" She rolled her eyes, but the

grin didn't waver. "I'm flattered you're so concerned about my "performance"."

She huffed at him but continued to stand her ground. He stepped closer, and she met him head-on.

CHAPTER FIVE

"Shouldn't I be collecting the cheque for the charity?" Sophia whispered, her thoughts blurred as he neared her.

Aidan's body radiated heat. He held her hips gently at first. She relaxed. Being close to him seemed right, but why? Aidan's head dipped, and she took the hint; closing her eyes and pressing her lips forward, she waited.

The thud of her heartbeat was the soundtrack to nothing. There was no brush of his lips against hers. Gingerly, she opened her eyes and found him studying her with his darkening blue ones. *Please don't let him be playing a game with me.* Did it matter if he was? She was fed up of waiting for things to fall into her lap.

I want him.

Easing out her tongue, she licked his top lip with just her rosy tip. Suddenly his lips were on hers, hungry and urgent.

With a quiet moan, her eyes drifted closed, and she immersed herself in the kiss. The taste of her strawberry lip balm merging with the chlorine that still clung to Aidan's lips surprised her, but it didn't stop her. Nothing could. His sensuality eclipsed her nerves. It barely satisfied existing needs; instead, it opened her to more unmet cravings.

Aidan bit and sucked at her, ferocious in desire. His

hands travelled round to her bum; kneading it and claiming it. She kissed him back just as hard.

Her hands reached around his neck, desperately pulling him closer. *I don't want this to end.* His tongue parted her mouth, and she beckoned it in as his hands continued to caress her bottom.

"More, please," she whimpered into his mouth, but fears flared too, gravitating to Graham. Kisses with him were because she was trying to divert him away from pushing her further than she was ready to go. At a family event, he'd drunkenly demanded she drove him home because he was poorly. When they'd got in the car, he'd clumsily shoved his tongue down her throat and pawed at her clothes just as her mum had come out the house to say goodbye. He'd denied it had happened the next day.

Initially, Graham had agreed to develop the physical side slowly. She'd needed to get to know him before she lost her virginity to him. But the more Sophia had revealed her insecurities, the more knowledge he'd had to manipulate her. Her pleasure hadn't been an essential part of their relationship, and if she didn't do what he wanted, he guilted her, made sly insults and added to her anxieties. Her inability to trust guys was one of the reasons she'd hidden away from them until now. *And because I've believed Graham's comments. How do I know Aidan won't manipulate me? Why would he pursue me when I'm not his type? How can I be enough for him?*

Aidan pulled back, and concern etched his face. "What's wrong? Am I getting you wet?"

The water from Aidan's swim was damp against her, making her white blouse transparent, but that wasn't the wetness at the forefront of her mind.

Humour was her defence. "You have no idea." She was wet beneath her skirt, and it was because of Aidan. She couldn't let what had happened with Graham get in the way of seeking pleasure.

Aidan elicited a low growl before grabbing her face between his hands and kissing her hard. Sophia's barely varnished nails grazed his neck before stroking up to his dripping hair, her thumbs rubbing against his scalp, fingertips gliding across his skin. His groan echoed in her mouth.

His hands moved again as he tried to get closer, gripping her bum and pulling her against his hardness. Her body hummed, the strokes of her tongue against his the result of pent up need. Her crotch pulsated as it rubbed against him. Sophia tried to align their bodies, grinding against him, desperate to have him against her core. Aidan throbbed and grew with each movement.

Needily he pulled her skirt up her thighs, revealing more of her legs and giving him greater access to her body. Aidan's fingers dipped beneath the fabric, stroking the bare flesh of her thighs. His hands urgently moved higher. Thumbs brushed against the bottom of her knickers, touching the already wet lace that blocked him from her skin. Her murmurs of 'yes' egged him on.

His hands moved higher, thumbing her through her knickers, pressing the lace to one side.

The faces of the women Aidan had been with flashed in front of her. Even during the most sensual experience of her life, she compared her ugly and replaceable face to their internet shots. Fear surged, and her body tensed. Graham had made it clear she wasn't enough. Aidan would realise the same.

Sophia jerked away, unwilling to be a conquest that he ditched for another easy lay.

The visible shock and then hurt across his face stuck in her chest. Sophia waited for him to say something, but Aidan didn't question what was happening or pull her tighter. His hands fell to his sides, and sadness crossed his face before a mask quickly replaced it.

"I'm sorry," she whispered.

"For kissing me?" he asked.

"No, I..." she faltered, exposed and embarrassed. *I don't trust him, and I'm too inexperienced.* It wouldn't take long for Aidan to see what Graham saw. She wasn't the kind of woman men wanted to stay faithful to. *I can't offer him what he needs.* How could she explain that to a man like Aidan?

"It doesn't matter," he stuttered. "The donation, what you really came for, is by the front door."

Before she could explain, he dove into the pool. Water flew into the air as he disappeared beneath the surface.

Tears pricked her cheeks. Aidan's reaction was the reminder she needed. *I'm not sexy enough for him.* She needed to stay away from men, or she'd get hurt. It was the only way to keep her heart safe. *I don't want to go through what I went through with Graham. I can't face that again.*

Stepping away from him, back through the maze of corridors and out the house, she swiped the brown envelope as she left.

As she gunned her engine and took off down the driveway, she looked in her rear-view mirror at the house fading into the distance and vowed, "I will never return here."

Sophia pulled over and parked haphazardly on the side of the road not far from Aidan's house. Sorrow hit her in waves.

Graham had been the only guy she'd trusted, and it had taken years to get past his actions. He'd guilt her for spending time with her family or refuse to speak to her because she'd met up with friends. Gradually he stole from her the things she liked about herself until she wasn't sure who she was anymore. It was a toxic relationship, but knowing that now didn't bring her confidence back.

Aidan is a playboy but does that mean he's toxic like Graham? Do I like him because it can't mean anything?

Sophia veered between opinions and decisions. How could she trust her judgement when it came to guys?

To top it off she'd been unfair to Aidan, and pushed him away without explanation. Graham would have taken away his affection if she'd done that to him, his form of punishment. Is that what Aidan had done or had he been embarrassed by the rejection? He'd tried to hide what was going on, and pretend he didn't care. But she'd wounded a guy who, in the last twenty-four hours, had made her smile, protected her and sent her into a state of arousal more intense than she'd ever experienced.

Clumsily, she swiped at the tears spilling from her eyes, adamant that he was better off without her. *I'm better off without him too.*

Still, she hated being alone. What would it be like to wake up with someone, not just for sex, but for more? Sophia ached for someone to hold her through the nightmares that startled her awake in the early mornings, leaving her crying and empty. Pushing down a sob, she considered what it would be like to have a guy to come home to after a long day at work. Comforting grieving children took its toll, and it drained her. Was it too much to want someone to love her, someone to move the earth for her?

But I'm afraid of being hurt. Aidan was a player, but would he destroy her confidence, and make it impossible to trust new people again? Graham had gone to great lengths to destroy her belief in herself and others. If Nicky hadn't supported and cared for her, building her up and helping her find value in herself while keeping Graham away, then who knows where she would be now.

It was too late to go back to the office, but she spied her phone on the seat next to her and remembered her promise to call Jack.

The incessant ringing at the other end was like a tiny hammer hitting an out of tune bell within her skull.

"Hey, babe," Jack's voice echoed down the phone. "How did it go? Has he declared his undying love yet?"

Sophia forced a laugh.

"That bad?" Jack asked. There was no fooling him. "Well, at least it was worth it for the charity."

"What do you mean?" she asked. Confusion beckoned her headache closer; she needed rest.

"The bank transfer, the donation. Surely Aidan told you?"

"Told me what? I've got the donation in an envelope right here." She turned the envelope over in her spare hand. It was A4 size and had a rigid board inside; the type used when you want the contents kept safe and flat. It was unnecessary for a donation. Something else caught her eye, a handwritten line near the flap. "Please be careful with the contents as they're important to me."

"I have no idea what's in your envelope, but Aidan has transferred five thousand into the charity's account this afternoon. That man is not only jaw-dropping sexy but generous. You need to make him yours," Jack joked. "So, what's in the envelope? You have to open it."

"Probably a note to go with the money. I'm sure it's nothing important." But she didn't believe it. Something about it unnerved her. Why would someone write that on a donation, what else could be in there?

Stop overthinking it. For all you know Aidan is playing games with you. But tossing the envelope onto the passenger seat didn't stop her staring at it.

"I'm going home. I've got a headache."

"You're not going to tell me what's in the envelope? Sophia, honey!" Jack paused, but she didn't take the opportunity to fill the silence. Eventually, he continued, "Sorry, I'm too nosey for my own good. I need some excitement in my life. I wish a guy would look at me the way he looked at you last night. You go home and rest."

"Will do. Bye, Jack."

The memory of Aidan's pained face reared. But he could have any woman he wanted. She was sure there'd be another beauty in his bed by nightfall.

Meanwhile, I'll be alone forever, and it's my fault.

*****

Aidan lay in bed. Another night where the early hours teased him and the clock brought him closer to daylight. Sophia must have opened the envelope by now.

"Why hasn't she called?" he asked the darkness.

It was rare to be confronted by a woman who didn't

fancy him, but it happened. Sophia had liked him, and her behaviour suggested she wanted him. So, why did she pull away? He thought back to his behaviour that afternoon. Did he show off too much in the pool? *You were cocky, maybe too cocky.* The women he met usually liked that. *But Sophia isn't like those women, that's one of the reasons you're attracted to her.* He was going around in circles.

There was no pride in his rugby prowess anymore either. His slipping performance on the pitch reminded him of the other person weighing heavily on his mind. Aidan had managed to avoid another call from Doctor Sampson after his swim. The answer machine message had included a reminder that as a doctor, he had a Hippocratic Oath to keep the privacy of his patients. If Aidan's tests came back positive, he'd ensure no one knew about Aidan's illness. But things had a way of getting out, Aidan had seen it with plenty of sports stars before. The coach was looking for an excuse to move him from the bench to permanent retirement.

Aidan's thoughts drifted back to Sophia.

Embarrassment still flitted around him from the way he'd rubbed himself against her like an inexperienced teenage boy and the near fumble when she'd told him he was making her wet. He didn't get like that around women. There was an innocence to her that he hadn't experienced in a long time.

The memory of her panicked recoil when he'd run his hand beneath her skirt brought sickness to his stomach, but there was no point going over it again. Sleep wasn't coming and revisiting the moment wasn't helping. Aidan grabbed his phone as he shuffled towards the art studio. Drawing had helped the previous night, and maybe it was what he needed now to drown his thoughts.

Sketching a picture of Sophia had been cathartic. Attempting to recreate her beauty into something tangible, even on a piece of paper, had been near to impossible, but it had brought him calm. The sketched sparks in her deep eyes had unleashed a thrum of arousal that had remained with him until she'd rejected him by the pool.

There was silence throughout his home; not even a ticking clock disturbed his late-night wanderings. Recalling the nights when he was younger, anxiously pacing around the house where he and his mum had barely survived, saddened him. It hadn't only been because of an inability to manage his emotions, although watching his dad sink into depression while fighting with bouts of uncontrollable aggression was terrifying. Doctors said his dad's behaviour was due to Huntington's, but that didn't always make sense to a confused and scared little boy. Losing his dad and watching his mum struggle through each grief-filled day had left him broken. He'd roamed their small flat to ensure his mum was safe and still with him. The fear he might lose her wasn't logical or based on anything but his inability to cope, and his grief. It had been like a stone in his gut that had refused to soften for a long time. Has it softened?

Even now, there was something imperative about wandering in the night. A slight chill resting on his naked skin had him shivering, his tight black boxers weren't enough to keep him warm. It was like he was the only person alive. The creaks of the old place reminded him of the future waiting for him. It was his safe space for now, but for how long? Were his bouts of rage the start of his Huntington's symptoms? Maybe they were due to a lifetime of anger brought on by fear of his future. *But I don't need help; I'm okay.* He knew he was lying to himself. The obvious thing would be to get help, get tested, but what if he tested positive? He'd watched his dad die and couldn't bear to die like that. But Huntington's wouldn't give him a choice.

He paused and tried to bring calm back to his mind. A hum surrounded him. It was probably from all the electricity needed to charge and sustain his gadgets, but his artist's brain romanced it and imagined it was the life force of the house.

Moonlight shining through the broad windows guided him around his home. He didn't need the lights. Finally, he reached his art room and stilled. He was his true self here, and no one's judgements or words truly mattered when he was in his sanctuary. It was a mess his mum wanted to tidy up, but no one was allowed in here without his permission. Scraps of paper covered in sketches and swashes of paint lay haphazardly on tables, seats and the floor. It was an expression of his busy and cluttered mind, and the only place he could let it out freely. On the pitch he was celebrated by thousands of fans, it often brought out his cheeky persona, but here, in his room, surrounded by paintings and a rainbow of colours he expressed his depths. At one point he'd gone through a phase of painting the walls, using them as his easel. That had been an attempt at recreating his dad's face through abstract design. It was a mixture of reds, yellows and oranges. It was as if flames licked up the walls.

He flicked on the light switch, and the surge of light

temporarily blinded him. He snapped his eyes closed and breathed deeply as an attempt to bring calm to his uneasy soul once more. With his eyes open, he took a seat in front of his easel. Aidan was ready to unload onto the paper what was churning inside.

The pencil eased his cluttered thoughts. It glided as if ruled by a part of him he didn't control. Earlier stresses faded as he feathered the soft waves of Sophia's hair. Even in pencil form, her beauty astounded him. There'd been stunning women in his life, but they didn't compare to her.

How did she become the only woman I want so quickly? What would she do if she knew about my dad and my future? The women in his past had been flings. They weren't with him for long enough to get hurt. If they got too close, then he ended it. *I can't be with anyone who might feel obligated to stay with me if I get ill. I don't want to burden anyone or watch them suffer like mum did.* A long-term relationship might involve children too. No child deserved to suffer what he had. There was a possibility they'd contract Huntington's. It was best if he continued having flings and nothing else. But what did that mean for Sophia?

A vibration startled him. His phone glimmered with a text from a number he didn't recognise.

His breath caught in his chest.

Hi, it's Sophia Mitchell, from the charity. Thank you for the drawing. I can't describe how incredible your work is, you have fantastic skills. I hope you win your match today.

Aidan called her immediately, as his heart thundered with a mixture of joy and anxiety. Drops of sweat rolled down his chest while he waited for her to pick up.

CHAPTER SIX

The phone vibrated.

Why is he calling? It had taken Sophia half an hour to compose her text, and now he wanted to talk? She stared into the glow of the screen as she accepted the call.

"Hello?" She whispered.

The soft sighs of his breathing accompanied a snare drum solo sounding from her heart. She traced the sketch she'd found in the envelope with her fingertips. *I usually hate images of me.* But she couldn't stop admiring Aidan's creation. She'd been adamant they would never speak again, but then she saw the drawing. He'd made her beautiful, but he'd shown her flaws too. She had a tiny scar above her eyebrow where she'd itched too hard when she had chickenpox as a child. He'd included that. Aidan hadn't filtered how she looked but created the real her. That meant something she couldn't explain. *It was enough to make me text him.* But what now?

"You're too good for me." The Irish accent made tingles sprint up and down her spine.

"What?" she stuttered.

"Sorry, hello, I meant to start that better." He swallowed loudly. "I wanted to say I should have behaved better earlier. I shouldn't have been a dick when you pulled away. I can't apologise enough. Are you okay?"

The vulnerability in his voice gave her pause. "I'm fine. I had something on my mind," she replied. *It was a little lie, but he didn't need to know that.*

"I should have been more respectful, I just... Are you sure you're okay?"

"Yes, sure. I promise." She needed to move the conversation on before she splurged her fears. *I can't tell him we're moving too fast, because he'll laugh at me.* "Did you draw that picture of me?"

"Yes, I couldn't do your face justice, though. By the way, there's something you should know."

"What?"

"I would have said it's impossible, but you sound even more gorgeous on the phone."

Sophia rolled her eyes and laughed. "You're such an Irish charmer."

"You're lucky that I'm charming after you sent me a text in the middle of the night. I need to be well-rested for the game tomorrow. You could have destroyed my chances of winning."

"Shit, I'm sorry. I'll go."

A deep chuckle filled her phone's earpiece.

"You bastard, don't tease me like that!"

"Okay, scout's honour, I'll be good to you. But how good do you want me to be?" His voice dropped. "Or do you prefer it when I'm bad, Sophia?"

Aidan didn't need hands to turn her on. Her crotch ached when he growled her name.

"So, the match today then?"

His laughter revealed he recognised her not so subtle change of subject. "I am teasing, you know. If our conversations make you uncomfortable, you'll say? I'm not great at being serious or at reading people even face to face, but I'd never make you do anything you weren't happy with. I can come across as a bit of an arse, but I can't help but try and make you laugh or turn you on."

"Which you're very good at," she conceded with a smile, sharing an embarrassing guffaw when she heard him cheer. "I shall let you know if push me too far."

She was enjoying the banter. Nicky was her only other banter buddy. Sophia was too busy trying to shut people out, especially guys, to laugh with them like this. *But why is it comfortable with him?* Maybe it was his confidence or his humour.

"Good. So, you were asking about the match?"

"Are you going to win?"

"Of course, we're awesome. However, Bath have annihilated us before. Maybe I need something to motivate me. Any thoughts?" Charm formed behind his words; it was like a soft change of pitch in a love song.

She feigned ignorance. "I could promise you a smile if you win?"

"I would like more than that."

"I'll buy you a drink."

"Are you asking me out?" he teased.

Her smile never faltered. "You wish."

His laugh wrapped around her like the snuggly duvet. "Yes, I do. I wish for a lot more, but I'll settle for a drink. Meet us at a bar after the game?"

"Okay." Staring at the picture again, she pushed away the numerous reasons not to do it. "Although I've heard you're not as good on the pitch as you used to be."

Aidan's silence stretched on. Her chest tightened with each passing second. *Have I upset him?* Absentmindedly she crossed her fingers.

"Maybe we should make our bet more interesting as you're so confident," he whispered huskily. "If I score a try, you give me a kiss, *and* I get to paint you."

Fear bubbled inside her. She gazed at the drawing and focused on the light freckles smattered across her nose. *I didn't realise they'd been visible beneath my make-up.* She loved her freckles, but Graham said they were ugly. It was meaningful that Aidan had included them. Her smile on the paper gave the air of cheekiness, yet her eyes carried depth. People rarely noticed her cheekiness, but Aidan had. Graham had often mentioned she was dull, joking she was as deep as a puddle. It was only after they broke up that Sophia wondered if it was reverse psychology. Had he been trying to get her to prove him wrong and try something she wasn't ready for?

That's enough about Graham. She stared at the intricate pencil marks. *Aidan saw these things in you from one night.* What would he create if she posed for him?

"Okay," she whispered.

"Good, well that's decided. And when you pose for my painting, you have to be naked," he teased.

"Hell no! I'm not posing naked for you."

"Okay, maybe I should paint you in what you're wearing right now. Which is...?"

"I'm not telling you." But she looked down anyway. *How would I describe it to turn him on?*

Aidan's laugh was wicked. "Ah, it was worth a try. I'm sitting here almost completely naked apart from my tight black boxers." She elicited the tiniest sigh. "And talking to you has made me rock hard."

"I'm not having phone sex with you," she replied.

But I want to. I can't believe I'm thinking that. The corners of her mouth came up in a smile as her hand slowly slid down her stomach towards the thin elastic waistband of her knickers.

"Okay, okay. I should probably get some sleep," Aidan replied.

"Yes. You've got a game to win."

"And a try to score."

"You're certain I'm going to kiss you? Pride comes before a fall," she teased back. *I feel like I'm glowing.* "You'd best get your beauty sleep because you need it."

His laugh came over her in waves of pleasure. He spoke quietly, "Will you tell me one thing, even though I sound like a perv? I promise I'll do another drawing for you."

Taking a deep breath, Sophia looked down at her nightwear. "I'm wearing a pair of teal lacy knickers and a t-shirt that says "*Lucky*" on it."

"You read my dirty mind, and my cock is very grateful, I think it's trying to do a jig for you." Sophia's face hurt from grinning, but she continued to beam. How could he turn her on and make her want to laugh at the same time? "I wish I was getting "lucky" right now."

"You're cheesy, Aidan." *Best not tell him how much I like his cheesiness, he's cocky enough as it is.* Sophia dropped her voice, attempting to be a little serious. "Thank you again for the drawing. Good luck for tomorrow."

"Thank you. I like knowing this match is for you. I'll text you when I know what bar we're heading to. But if you get nervous, I'll understand. Sleep well, Sophia."

"Goodnight, Irish."

"I can't believe we're spending our Saturday afternoon in a sweaty pub." Nicky grimaced.

"What do you mean? I've got rugby on television, beer in my hand and two beautiful women next to me." Ryan beamed. "And against all predictions, the Bulls are beating Bath with only ten minutes left of the match!"

Sophia smirked as she stared at the television. Her heart raced every time Aidan had the ball. Would she regret her promise?

Ryan continued. "I can't believe Aidan Flynn is playing so well. This is the best he's played since his International days!"

"Maybe he's found a new good luck charm," Nicky winked at Sophia.

"He hasn't scored a try yet… Has he?" Would she ever understand rugby?

"He hasn't scored a try in over a year. But today it's not from lack of effort. He hasn't worked this hard in years. I can't imagine the pummelling he's had."

The match was a fight of skill and strength, a spectacle of horror and thrills. The players were like warriors battling for the fate of thousands. Bodies launched into each other, leaping through the air with the force of war tanks before smacking to the ground. Aidan had been crushed more than most, but he refused to stay down, continuing to slog after every flooring. Her pulse raced.

"Can we go into town for a night out tonight?" Sophia asked Nicky tentatively, like a teenager asking to go on her first date. *I have a promise to keep*. The Bulls were trampling Bath in points and performance. "I'll need to change into a dress first, though."

"I usually have to drag you kicking and screaming into town."

Soon I'll be face to face with Aidan again. Am I ready?

"Do you want to get drunk too?" Nicky rubbed her hands together with glee.

Alcohol was a necessity for courage. Sophia's skin tingled in anticipation.

"I'm going to have to keep an eye on you," Nicky added. The words had a double meaning. Nicky was protective but never overbearing, sacrificing her fun on many a night out to ensure Sophia was safe.

"Shush, Flynn's going for a try again and with ten seconds remaining!" Ryan had taught them that even after time had run out, the game wasn't over until the ball was down. If Aidan dropped it or missed his try, the game would be over.

Excited Sophia spilt her ice-cold water in her crotch. It did nothing to cool her enthusiasm; nerves were building. *He hasn't scored yet, that's a good thing, isn't it?* The consequences were both tempting and terrifying.

She was glued to the television screen. Aidan hurtled down the right of the pitch. There were no teammates to support his challenge; he'd grabbed his only chance. Legs beat down as he searched for a path to the try line. Bath's players had spied his actions and were shouting a battle cry.

Surely this can't be for me. But the display of Aidan's tenacity suggested otherwise.

In the pub, conversations stopped mid-sentence as the crowd turned to the television screen. A try like this from anyone, especially Aidan, was as epic as a royal firstborn.

"Shit, he's in trouble now," Ryan winced.

Three gigantic players charged towards him from different angles. They bore down on him, ready to crush him between their behemoth bodies.

One attempted to grab him. Aidan turned. Gripping the ball tightly against his chest with one hand, he slammed against the guy, shoulder barging him away and giving himself time to run. Stumbling slightly, the crowd gasped, but he regained footing. His legs pushed on as he pelted down the pitch. Was he going to do it? He darted and zigzagged to confuse the two ogres heading his way. Their nearing bodies created a vice to pin him. But he was too quick and ran gazelle-like between them.

Sophia's heart was in her mouth. As one, the crowd in the pub witnessed another player, of monstrous proportions thundering toward Aidan. No one else was close.

"His nickname is 'The Destroyer,'" Ryan whispered between grinding teeth, speaking about the giant Bath player. "He destroys bodies and careers."

Still, Aidan sprinted, exhaustion hidden.

'The Destroyer' ran at him with hands ready to toss him in the air if his extensive shoulder action didn't break his bones first.

Chipping the ball over the giant's head at the last minute threw confusion onto the face of his opponent. Aidan didn't pause for breath. He ran for the ball, sprinting past 'The Destroyer' who stopped before realisation hit him and he turned to chase Aidan. They were metres from the try line.

Ryan was jumping up and down, joined by the rugby fans surrounding them. "Come on, fuckin' move it! MOVE IT!"

Aidan dived for the line with 'The Destroyer' at his heels, ready to take out his legs.

Everything slowed as he flew, his legs high as he clutched the egg-shaped ball close. Aidan sailed across the line and slammed the ball down triumphantly.

The pub erupted, the crowd on the screen went wild, Bulls' players screamed to the skies in triumph. There were whoops and hollers, and fans shouted Aidan's name in exhilaration. As the pub turned into an end of battle carnival, Aidan performed a sexy winning dance. His cute bum wiggled, and his arm swung as if he was doing a lasso, but it didn't last long as his teammates barrelled him over.

Sophia laughed, although her nerves itched. Heat covered her arms and tingles reached her scalp as she moistened her lips with her tongue. *I'm going to have to keep my promise.*

Destiny was coming for her, and she couldn't wait.

"I can't believe it!" Ryan was in awe of Aidan's performance. "It's the best I've seen him play. Shame he got punched in the face."

Aidan's face had taken the brunt of 'The Destroyer's' failure. After finishing his celebrations, he'd received an unprovoked thump. It was the trigger for an all-out war between Bulls' and Bath players, a red card for 'The Destroyer' and a lot of blood from Aidan. The spectacle had secretly enthralled Sophia.

Everyone's eyes fixed on the screen, and they waited to see what would happen to Aidan. Maybe he'd cancel the night out. Suddenly, he appeared for his after-match interview.

"Still looks hot," Nicky commented, a sympathetic glance in Sophia's direction.

One eye was partially closed. His face resembled a patchwork quilt with bruises surfacing in a variety of colours. Dried blood crusted on the edge of his lip.

"Aidan, that was an incredible performance, especially the last minute. I would say a return to form, but I think that it ranks as one of your greatest matches of all time. How are you feeling?" the television interviewer asked.

Aiden's body may have been a little broken, but his voice was still smooth. "Thanks, Jim. I'm knackered, but I enjoyed myself. It was tough, they gave a good fight but credit to the whole team. We pushed hard, did what we had to do, and it was a great win for us."

"What brought on this change? The recent rumours have been that you might get dropped. Was that your motivation?"

"You shouldn't believe everything you read about me, Jim." He looked directly into the camera. "I made a promise to someone, and I always keep my promises."

He's winding me up even now. Sophia blushed, and laughter bubbled in her throat. *I hope his fat lip hurts.*

"You weren't trying to settle old scores then? Was your promise to a certain person here today?" He meant Mick Daniels, Aidan's old coach. Ryan had filled in a bit of background about the rivalry between the teams.

With a laugh, bereft of his natural charm, Aidan brushed off the comment. "Let's not rake up the past. Let's just say I owed someone the chance to see how well I perform. I brought my best performance today, and I intend to reap the rewards."

Sophia shifted in her chair and offered a loud sigh. Her fringe fluttered in the air.

"One more question before I let you go and enjoy your celebrations. What does the future hold for Aidan Flynn? What you displayed today suggests retirement is a long way off, or will you be one of those player-coaches who does it all, even making mascots of your wife and kids."

It was a light-hearted question, but Aidan froze. It was only a split-second response before his mask appeared, but a white pallor covered his face beneath the array of bruising. His laugh was awkward and unconvincing. "I have no idea what the future holds for me, Jim. I'm enjoying the game. Besides, a wife and kids aren't part of my long-term plan. Maybe you *should* believe what you read about me, after all."

Sophia sucked in a breath. Was he joking? It was a harsh reminder that she didn't know him. Maybe he was what the papers suggested: a guy who fooled around, liked to screw glamorous women and who had no intention of settling down. She wasn't thinking long term, but she didn't intend to be a one night stand either. *What am I getting myself into?*

*****

Aidan slammed his fist on the sink before tossing water across his face, cleaning off dried blood. His anger was like lava; it seared his insides, daring him to erupt in violence. He fought to keep it below the surface. Why had Jim asked that question about wife and kids? The game had been a major 'fuck you' to his enemies and critics, but anger eclipsed celebration.

Sophia will be judging you. Another wave of wrath hit him.

The game had been for her. Aidan had never given a fuck what his women thought of his playing before. They never cared. As long as they were on the arm of someone who looked good and had money to spend, they were happy. If they pressured him in any way, he'd replaced them with another fame-hungry woman.

His hatred of himself clawed against his skin. He'd wanted to impress Sophia, but the interview had made him out to be a "fuck 'em and leave them type". *Maybe that's who you are; a bastard who doesn't give a shit.* The maudlin attitude was driving his confidence away. Was he experiencing one of Huntington's diseases' mood swings?

Aidan's hand formed a fist so tight that it turned his already pained knuckles white. Pulling his arm back, he readied to punch the wall. Adrenaline splintered his body.

"I don't think that's a good idea, Aidan," called out the familiar voice of Doctor Sampson from behind him.

Aidan's tightly formed fist froze. *Don't turn around. Don't let him see your rage.*

"Who let you in?" Aidan grunted.

"I saw your mum in the corridor."

Aidan snapped back, "You didn't tell her why you wanted to see me, did you?"

"No, I told her I wanted to congratulate you. It was true. You played a fantastic game today."

"Don't bother with the niceties, doctor. You're here for more than that. Say your piece and get lost." Aidan didn't hate the man, but it aggravated him that the doctor refused to take the hint. The doctor couldn't change Aidan's mind about taking the test.

"I'm here because I'm worried about you. You've been cancelling your appointments and avoiding phone calls. And call me Alex. I've known you for over twenty years. I care about you," he replied. The empathetic tone was like nails down a blackboard to Aidan.

Aidan turned. "It comes down to this, Alex," he spat his name. "I'm not having the test. I haven't wanted it for years, and nothing's going to change that. Coming here isn't going to make any difference."

"But you're thirty-five, the age your dad's symptoms started to show." The doctor was a good man, but he wasn't welcome. Alex stroked his beard before he spoke again. "Besides, it's not just about the test. I need to check you're doing okay. I've been your doctor since you moved to England and I think it's important to do a check-up. I'm aware you have team doctors, but I know your history. It's not wise to shut me out."

"I know how old I am and what that means, but I'm not getting the test," he replied. "You should go." What had changed? Was it the pregnancy scare with Bianca? Was it his increasing anger, which was scaring him? Maybe it was because this winter would be twenty-five years since his dad died.

"Have you had any symptoms? Your mum is worried. I've been hearing from her a lot at recently."

"It's none of your business, and it's none of hers either. It's my life. Please leave me alone."

"Fine. I'll go. But I'm keeping an eye on you, and I'll be here when you need me. All you have to do is pick up the phone, not even for the test if you don't want it. If you need someone to talk to, I'll be around. I'm not just a doctor for the body."

The doctor slipped out the changing rooms.

The rush of energy left Aidan, and he dropped his hands to the basin. The cold ceramic diverted him from the pain in his calloused hands. It had been twenty-five years since they laid his dad to rest and moved to England. Pain from watching his dad shout at him, push him away and reject him blistered his heart, but he shut it out. *You can't deal with that now. Don't let the sadness catch you.* He'd worked hard to avoid dealing with the past, and he couldn't let it win now. *I should be celebrating.*

His phone vibrated with a message from Sophia.

Great game! You were amazing. I hope you're okay and not too damaged. See you in town tonight.

The smile on his face was as uncontrollable as his rage had been. How could the simple message fill him with ecstasy?

"Am I hooked?"

Chapter Seven

Sophia struggled under the unwarranted attention of the stranger near the dancefloor. *Where is Aidan?*

The music thumped and lights beamed sporadically across the darkness of the club.

"You must have fallen from Heaven because you're an angel," the bearded hipster said with a wink. His manicured lumberjack beard and coiffed hair suggested he wouldn't be able to satisfy her without regularly checking himself out in the mirror. The memory of Aidan's well-formed body leaping out the pool had her gaze flickering around the club. Had he found someone else to entertain him? *Maybe the bet is off, and I won't have to kiss him after all.* It wasn't relief that followed that statement, but disappointment. *I want to kiss him.* Nervous anticipation made her skin tingle.

"Can I have your number?" the hipster asked. It was a casual request like he was ordering chips at a late-night takeaway.

"Ummm, no." She folded her arms across her chest.

"But I'm as good as life gets. I've completed half marathons, I'm well-travelled and let's not forget, I'm hot as fuck. I could be going home with any number of women tonight, but I chose you, you're the lucky one." There was barely a pause for breath. "Even If you have a boyfriend, he couldn't compare to me."

Sophia sighed. Shouldn't Nicky have bought their drinks by now? The hipster's eyes suddenly bulged out of his head. His mouth was so tight that she couldn't see his lips, and he cowered. Sophia stepped back uncertainly.

Hands appeared from behind and rested on her hips, clutching her gently. She readied her elbows. The night was turning into feeding time at the zoo. It was time to dismiss another lothario.

Suddenly, a familiar musky scent enveloped her. Aidan's provocative aroma that held touches of tropical fruit permeated her senses before penetrating her body.

"Sorry, mate," the hipster uttered from beneath his perfectly designed beard. *Do hipsters have special beard scissors and beardy barbers?* "I didn't realise she was yours."

Did she want to belong to someone? The stranger's departing walk distracted her. Skinny black jeans gripped his legs so tightly that it looked like his cock might be trying to jump back inside his body when he wiggled away. The grinding bodies on the dancefloor quickly swallowed him up.

Sophia swayed as Aidan's hands melted into her curves. Her black chiffon cocktail dress skimmed her breasts and hips, and her belt gripped her at the waist. The beautifully styled outfit showed enough of her chest to tease. Casually, Aidan stroked his thumb up and down her hip. *I want more.* Gently she eased back and rested against his broad form. There was a safety in his body. She sighed her anxieties away.

"You had quite the effect on him," Sophia teased.

"Not as much as you did. You've been breaking

hearts for the last ten minutes." Aidan's lips found the soft flesh behind her ear. At the brush of his mouth, tingles raced through her body. Aidan bunched the material of her dress in his hands as he caressed her curves.

"You've been watching me?"

"Now I sound creepy."

Sophia laughed freely. From anyone else, she might have been spooked to learn she'd been watched, and her reactions studied. But she liked that Aidan had been her voyeur. What else had he noticed while observing her?

"Well done for the game today. That score was incredible. I hope your face is okay." She didn't turn around, scared of breaking their spell.

"I was a bit nervous before I saw you tonight," he said so quietly she nearly didn't hear him over the music.

"Because of your face or because of the kiss?" she ventured. *Or because of the interview.* She hadn't forgotten what he'd said, but had wondered at his subtext. It reminded her of the painting and Aidan's hidden side. There was a mystery there, but what would it take for him to explain?

He pulled her tighter against him and for a minute they danced, learning each other's rhythm and rolling their hips to the beat. It was a slow swaying of limbs interspersed with subtle grinding as heat radiated from his body into hers.

As he spoke, his body stiffened. "I guess I'm scared about making a mistake, of hurting you and pushing you too far." She froze for a beat. That wasn't what she expected him to say. Maybe he sensed her response because he began to pull away, but she quickly reached for one of his hands and placed it across her heart.

"I'm scared as well," she replied. "But my heart isn't beating fast just because of fear. It's excitement too. I want this. I will stop you if you go further than I can handle."

"And if you stop me I won't disappear like at the swimming pool," he said softly. *He's still worried about it, even after we talked last night.* Aidan took her fingers and positioned them on the pulse point at his wrist. "Can you feel how hard my heart is beating too?"

"Yes," she replied before holding it up to her lips and kissing it gently. They continued to dance, skin to skin, limbs entangled as they touched each other's bodies. At the sensual connection, they were in their own world in the middle of the bustling bodies.

Sophia breathed his musky scent again; it filled her lungs. The tingles were back, and goose pimples appeared on her arms when his lips brushed her neck.

"I didn't realise you had such a quiet side, or am I meeting Aidan in his seduction mode?" she inquired, swaying with him.

"Seduction mode for me usually means cheeky quips followed by a toe-curling kiss," he replied, amusement filling his voice.

"Interesting…" she said. "I look forward to that later, because I like cheeky Aidan as well as this version of you."

Aidan's laugh was like a nip of whisky on a wintery day. Warmth coated her insides.

"And I have a bet to collect on," he replied. The butterflies in her stomach fluttered frantically. *I want a kiss.* "You look beautiful tonight. I'm afraid I can't say the same about me, the bruises are particularly bad."

She moved her head to look, but he held her in place.

"Are you scared I won't fancy you anymore if I look?" she teased. After their late-night conversation, she knew to stop him if she felt uncomfortable. It gave her the freedom to embrace her cheeky side without fear of unwarranted consequences. "Or are you scared I won't want to kiss you anymore?"

Humour was the only thing distracting her. They'd built up to the kiss for too long, what if it wasn't as good as she'd imagined?

The rumble of his laugh electrified every nerve in her body.

"If that's the case then I guess we'll shake hands and go our separate ways. You'll always have that awkward moment at the cathedral when I made an arse of myself to remember me by. Maybe you'll realise you've made a lucky escape," Aidan joked. *But is there a trace of truth behind his words?* She kissed the pulse point at his wrist again before turning around. Bruises covered his face, but in the darkness of the club, it wasn't as bad as she'd expected.

"It's worth the risk. Wouldn't you agree?" *Please say yes.*

He stared into her eyes and wrapped a couple of strands of her hair around his finger. It wasn't tight, but she still felt a pull at her scalp. Her body hummed in anticipation.

"I was hoping to get to know you better, but I can't think straight when I'm around you. When you're in front of me, I want to kiss you-."

"Then, why don't you? A bet is a bet." Something was holding him back.

She licked her lips in anticipation. Aidan tucked a finger in her skinny belt and pulled her closer. He bent his head to her neck. His mouth found her pulse point, and his kisses caressed her skin.

A moan escaped her lips.

"Aidan, please kiss me properly," she said in his ear. "Don't be scared you'll break me, or hurt me. Just kiss me."

He looked up and stared intently at her. In the bustling club, they froze. It was as if silence surrounded them. Why did this kiss seem more important than any other?

Sophia licked her lips before rubbing them together, waiting for something, anything.

"Please," she mouthed soundlessly.

Aidan's mouth met hers.

Days of uncertainty culminated in one of the most passionate kisses she'd experienced. Their embrace was as much a battle of wills as their conversations. Aidan kissed her fiercely, wincing slightly, probably from the pain in his lip, the result of his earlier pitch altercation. But the pain didn't stop him.

"I can't keep my hands off you," he said between panting breaths.

Sophia's arousal surprised her. Her growing wetness was becoming an irrepressible physical reaction whenever he was close.

With his finger, Aidan reached underneath one of the thin straps of her dress. His skin was coarse. Sophia trembled as he stroked her, causing her to rub against him. He was hard. Her head lolled, her eyes closed in bliss. Her tongue flicked out of her mouth, and with a sigh, she licked her lips.

Enticingly Aidan edged her backwards, manoeuvring her until they were in a darker part of the club. Music pulsated through her body, but dancing was the last thing on her mind.

It was as if they were the only people in existence. Sophia studied him. *I need to remember him in case our moment slips away.* He continued to move her backwards, only stopping when he'd pinned her against the wall that enclosed the dancefloor.

They stared at each other in silence. Aidan's eyes were dark as he took her in. His chest heaved with each breath.

"I don't want you to stop," she said before wrapping her arms around his neck, pulling him close into her. A glimmer of light couldn't slide between them.

Aidan cradled her face between his palms, and they nipped at each other's lips. She tested his control. As her lips brushed against him, she smiled against the supple caress of his mouth. Fervent kisses quickly replaced gentle ones. She dismissed the possible repercussions of their public display. Their tongues delved into each other's mouths, Aidan's massaging hers, working to build a fire that would burn throughout her body. They both fought for control. It was a clash of spirits to see who'd cause the most pleasure and make the other cry out, as desperation for ecstasy took hold.

It was his swelling erection rubbing against her that brought her first moan. As if spurred on, he reached for the soft flesh of her bottom and kneaded it. Aidan lifted her slightly and aligned their bodies. His murmurs frayed her control. *I need more.*

Suddenly a shadow appeared behind Aidan. Aidan eased Sophia down and turned. A beast of a man confronted him.

"Excuse me, mate. This isn't that sort of club." A

local accent formed the bouncer's words. His grimacing face suddenly lit up. "Aidan Flynn! You're a hero. But even you can't get down and dirty here."

"Sorry." Aidan relaxed his hold on Sophia. He adjusted his clothes with one hand while holding her with the other. "Got a bit carried away."

"No worries." The titan winked. "Just calm it a little."

Oh God, I'm still quivering, but I'm not freaking out. Their making out session had been reckless, but she'd wanted it to continue.

"Sure, thanks," Aidan replied. The swaggering bouncer was already forgotten as Aidan turned to her. "I should probably buy you a drink and then sit far away from you. I do want to chat with you, too. I want to get to know you, but sitting away from your body is a necessity."

"Good idea," she replied breathlessly. "That was hotter than I was expecting."

"Tell me about it," he replied, shifting his trousers awkwardly, drawing attention to his dick.

She glanced down, it was starting to twitch. "Please stop staring at him like that," Aidan responded referencing his erection. "He's hard enough as it is."

Half-heartedly, she punched him in the arm, but he caught her hand, holding it and threading his fingers through hers.

"Luckily, you're talented at rugby and art because you're not as funny as you think you are," she teased.

"I haven't even shown you where my biggest gifts lie yet," he replied quickly.

"Shut up and get me a drink," she said just as fast.

He beamed back. "Anything you wish, my lady.

And what is your heart's desire, other than me, of course?"

She rolled her eyes, but laughter bubbled in her throat. "Surprise me."

"Oh, Soph, that's the entertainment for later."

She smiled despite herself as he winked, grinned and bounded towards the bar.

*****

Sophia's stomach ached like she'd performed a thousand stomach crunches, but she couldn't stop laughing at his quips. The hope he'd pin her to the sofa if she asked him to kiss her abs better was never far away. *I can't believe I'm sitting with a local hero and learning he'd not arrogant, stupid or a dickhead.*

How am I so calm around him? Maybe it was the alcohol or the fogginess brought on by unharnessed arousal, but she didn't want the night to end.

Glancing at Aidan, she realised he only had eyes for her. Ladies walked past, pouting and sticking their chests out, but he barely noticed. Some looked like they were going to fall into his lap with flailing arms and legs. No matter who they were or what they tried, he shooed them away. The women didn't look like her, at first, she'd been jealous, but every time Aidan ignored them, her confidence rose a little.

She resisted the urge to launch her body across the glass table and into his lap. This conversation was meant to be the opportunity to get to know each other.

"Are you enjoying your drink?" he asked.

Sophia scrunched her nose saucily as she sipped her Sex on the Beach cocktail. The irony of his choice of drink wasn't lost on her.

She crossed her legs, squeezing her thighs tightly together. Having him so close, while her normal inhibitions were suckered away by alcohol, had her imagining grinding against him.

Aidan's darkening eyes observed her trembling legs through the glass of the table.

She sucked harder on her straw. Her lips were raw from the ferociousness of her nibbling. Sophia owed it to herself to drag him to a quiet corner and let him use his tongue, his thumb and any other part of his body to gratify her longings. *But I want more than physical. I need to know what this is.* She shook her head as her internal battle continued.

"Okay," she replied, attempting to break the spell of desire coursing through her. "You wanted to get to know me better, so I'm letting you ask me anything."

Aidan opened his mouth, his eyes dancing mischievously.

"Nothing rude, though," she added quickly. "At least, not at the moment."

He grinned cheekily.

The music continued to pulsate through her. Occasionally, colours flashed across the dancefloor and lingered on Aidan's face. Aware of people around them they were world's away from the bodies gyrating against each other as the beat of the music thumped through the club.

No one else matters.

Finally, words broke the silence that was an unknown entity between them.

"Why when men tried to talk to you earlier were you like a rabbit in the headlights? What's in your past?

Did someone hurt you?"

Chapter Eight

Sophia's gaze dipped to the surface of the glass table between them. Slowly she shredded a red paper napkin, breaking it into perfectly torn squares. Aidan had found something that reached deep into her psyche. He wasn't just a sexy body with a smart mouth; he was disarmingly insightful, too.

Aidan's warm hands settled around hers. His skin was rough, the match must have taken its toll, yet he was spritely considering his energy must have been flowing out of him like water through a colander.

"Soph," he whispered, easing into her thoughts and encouraging her to look at him. No one but Nicky shortened her name that way, but it was the second time he'd done it that night, and she liked it.

A softness had replaced the fire in his eyes. They creased at the edges as he implored her to share her secrets. *Can I trust him?*

"I get scared sometimes," she finally said, hating the fragility in her voice.

"Of me?" One eyebrow raised while the other curved slightly, he looked like a puppy who'd been told off but wasn't sure why. "I'm not going to hurt you. I could never be violent to a woman."

"I mean, I get scared of being hurt emotionally.

Although, don't for one second think of me as some delicate rose," she challenged him. "I'm not sure if I can trust men, I don't know if I can trust you. I don't want to be heartbroken again."

"Again?"

She faltered, drawing back her hands, annoyed that he'd picked up on the slip of her tongue. "I've heard things about you that surprised me. I should probably stay away from you, but I don't want to. I want. I want you."

"That's honest," he replied bluntly.

"Never mind. I'm drunk."

Sophia swallowed loudly. The silence between them was lasting too long. *I shouldn't have said anything.* "Maybe I should go."

Suddenly he removed the torn serviette from between her fingers. Aidan wrapped his paws protectively around her hands and cocooned them.

"Look at me, Sophia." Lifting her eyes, she stared at him through the ends of her fringe, captivated by his eyes, even as anxiety attacked her stomach.

"I'm not going to pretend to be something I'm not. I have a mischievous side. I'm not perfect, I get into trouble, and I love sex."

I'm not enough for him. He's all about sex, and I don't know how to satisfy a man. Graham had called her frigid more times than she could remember. Aidan's thumbs stroked her hands as if he sensed she was seconds away from escaping.

"But," he continued "that isn't the only version of me. I reckon you're the same. We both have many dimensions to who we are. I'm not just a bad boy rugby player; I'm also an artist. I created the painting that you saw depth in the other night."

"You're also the guy who made a sex tape with a glamour model." The words and judgement were out before she could stop them.

Aidan's shoulders stiffened.

"You've been reading up on me." His solid chest moved slowly with his sigh. "Yes, I did make one, although it's not how the gossips reported it. She wasn't some one-night stand. Bianca and I were sort of seeing each other. One night we were messing around. I thought it would be interesting for our personal use."

Aidan leaned closer, locking her eyes with his. He was offering her a rare opportunity, Aidan without his mask.

He gently stretched out her hands with his fingers. His thumbs stroked her skin and made circles across her palms. Against her control, Sophia stretched her pelvis forward, subconsciously inviting more of him. Beneath her longing lay her insecurities. She had no allure. She couldn't compare to someone like Bianca Tandy.

"Bianca has been trying to improve her celebrity status for some time. I suspect the tape "leaking" was part of that ambition. I stopped the tape getting beyond the buyer. You can trawl the internet for eternity, but I guarantee you won't find it."

The stroking continued. Sophia's skin tingled, sensitive under his thumbs. It was as if there was a lone nerve that connected her hands and crotch. Aidan was teasing that nerve gently, but she could feel it as sensitively as if his thumb was against her clit.

"Sophia, honey." She couldn't meet his expectations, let alone his eyes. "Do you have anything else to ask me before we head back to the dancefloor?"

"Wife and kids?" she blurted out. "They're not in your long-term plan. You said to the interviewer."

*****

Aidan sat quietly, as explanations sped through his head. He wasn't ready to divulge his medical issues before he'd explored what was between the two of them.

"A wife and kids aren't part of my long-term plan, and they never will be." His words were brutal, like an icicle wedged in the throat. With one swallow, it could slice her gullet.

"Not even if you met the right person?" she questioned. "You might meet someone and fall in love and-"

"It's not who I am, and it's not what I want." Attempting to soften his face and voice a little, he beckoned her closer. "Come here, Soph."

Aidan encouraged her to stand and led her to perch on his knee like she was riding him side-saddle. The softness of her arm curved around his neck. It brought comfort even in the middle of the strained conversation.

Their faces were inches away from each other. Sophia turned to look at him, but the seriousness of their discussion seemed to have diluted her earlier passion.

"I don't want to hurt you. You've been hurt, and I want you to tell me about that someday. That the guy must have been the biggest fuck up in the world." He forced himself not to wince in guilt at his next sentence. "But I don't make promises I can't keep, and I expect you don't either. I can't predict what will happen between us."

Sophia smiled half-heartedly. Aidan nearly growled in frustration at not being able to read her.

"But," he said, holding her closer, "I promise to try my best not to hurt you."

Lifting her chin with the tip of his finger, he stared into her eyes. "Okay, Bambi eyes?"

That distant smile was on her lips again. Aidan couldn't figure her out, and it made him want to examine her closer. He was used to wrapping women around his finger; in life and the bedroom. But Sophia was different.

"Okay," she agreed.

Kissing her long and hard, he revelled in how soft and inviting her lips were. A murmur left his mouth when she relaxed into him. He was comfortable with her in a way he couldn't understand.

"I can't get enough of you," he said eventually.

Smiling sweetly, she appeared happier than she'd been for the bulk of their talk. Aidan sensed a smile resting back upon his lips, mirroring hers.

"Seeing as you don't want to talk about the fuck-up guy who broke your heart," Sophia stiffened, and he cursed himself for killing the moment, "We should talk about what you owe me."

His kisses eased the lines in her forehead that her furrowed brow had created. The intimacy of his actions surprised him.

"You've forgotten already. How could you?" he teased. "As I recall you owe me a naked posing session for my painting."

She wore a smile as she tried to swipe him. Aidan reached for her hand, kissing the inside of her wrist. The sweet smile turned to brazen lust. Her eyes dilated, and his body responded instantly.

"It doesn't take much, does it?" She grinned, wriggling against his hardness.

"Not when I'm with you."

Sophia's smile was a combination of triumph and confidence. It was as if she learnt for the first time she had a skill she never believed possible.

"I didn't promise naked modelling. I didn't promise anything, and I only make promises I can keep." It was a playful dig.

"Okay, not naked modelling, but I do want to paint you. What do you think about modelling for me in what you wore to bed last night?" Sophia's mouth screwed up to the side of her face in what he'd already established was her thinking pose. "Until I rip it off you with my bare hands, lick your nipples with the tip of my tongue and make you come with my fingers."

Even in the semi-darkness of the club, he could see her blushing, her chest frozen as she held her breath. He sighed in relief. *She still wants me.* The need to please her was overwhelming, but he hid it with humour, unsure how to manage it. His vulnerability when with her surprised him.

"We should dance," she suddenly stated.

"I'm going to have to find a way to stop your unsubtle changes of subject," he joked.

"But first," a flash of seriousness touched her face, "I need some air. I need to step outside alone."

"Alone? We're okay, though?"

"Yep, but I need a moment. Just some fresh air; sober up a bit."

Aidan's chest tightened, panicked that she might have realised he'd hidden his truths. "You're coming back, though?"

Slowly she stood, already forcing distance between them. Her shoulders dipped under the weight of their conversation.

"Yes, I'll come back."

"Promise?" Aidan didn't want to be vulnerable, but he was scared.

"Promise," Sophia replied decisively, pecking him on the lips.

He cradled her face between his hands and pulled her between his knees. Tilting her face before kissing her hard, he marked his territory. Every ounce of passion and intensity he had filled the kiss, ensuring the memory was enough to bring her back to him. Edging open her lips, parting them with his tongue, he explored her mouth. Sweet alcohol from her cocktail lingered on her tongue.

His hands were restless, journeying from her face down her shoulders, before continuing lower, stroking her body and tickling her hips. Desperately trying to recreate their moment on the dancefloor, Aidan grabbed her bum. The softness of her eyelashes fluttered against his face.

A mixture of jasmine and vanilla graced his senses. Her intoxicating perfume fused with his thoughts and left him hopeful that her fragrance would linger on his skin all night. Their tongues were urgent as they sought a connection, something to hold off their mounting need for a little longer. Finally, when he realised, she was just as greedy as he was, he relaxed. He released his grip of her bottom. The kiss softened, their mouths brushing against each other.

Aidan nipped at her lower lip one last time before their mouths parted. Both of them were breathless.

Aidan rested his forehead against hers.

"Promise," she repeated between breaths.

As soon as she pulled away, a coolness replaced the warmth she'd brought. Instantly Aidan missed it, missed her.

Sophia turned and smiled reassuringly before walking out the front of the club to the chill-out area. His eyes didn't leave her body until she was gone from his view.

Stepping onto the dancefloor to join his teammates, he breathed deeply.

What's happening to me? I'm never the vulnerable one.

Aidan tapped his foot nervously as he stood on the edge of the dancefloor. The baseline of the music beat through him, swelling through his body before it slunk away only to be replaced by another beat, and another throb. His eyes repeatedly flicked to the doorway. Suspense lingered longer than Sophia's perfume.

Forcing his hands into fists before stretching them, again and again, helped him take control of his bubbling anxiety. It was a technique John had taught him as a teenager for dealing with anger. It gave him focus and his energy a safe place to reside.

What were his motives with Sophia? He didn't do the chasing. Women always came to him. *Should I be running away from her instead?* What if she got hurt because of him? He cared about her. He wanted to heal the damage done to her and keep her demons away. Confusion raged as his hands repeated their fist action.

He relived their moment on the dancefloor, remembering pinning her against the wall and her soft moans. She'd met him head-on, surprising him. *Maybe-*

"You alright mate?" A voice cut into his musings.

Kong, his teammate, waved a hand an inch from his nose. The guy was hairy and unkempt with dark brown hair that was in desperate need of a cut. Tufts sprung out from his chin, forming a messy beard. Kong was tall, built like a giant granite god. Looks were deceiving, though; he was one of the kindest, softest guys in the world. A rare gem, looking for a woman to settle down with, not just a shag from a rugby groupie.

"Why aren't you celebrating? It's the best win we've had in ages," Kong asked.

Aidan smiled, but happiness was absent. He needed to see Sophia again. What if she didn't want to stay with him. Was avoiding telling her the truth a mistake?

A hand squeezed his bum cheek. Aidan turned, holding his breath, she must have sneaked back in. Instead of seeing Sophia, he found himself staring at the wild lime green eyes and spider-like eyelashes of Bianca Tandy. Her thigh-skimming black latex dress barely held her in. Long, platinum blonde hair slapped her arse while she drunkenly wobbled in front of him. That level of effort meant she was intent on snaring a rich idiot tonight.

When he'd first laid eyes on her, eight months ago, he'd thought she was stunning. She'd been so individual, with flawless beauty that stopped him in his tracks and a body he wanted to exhaust. He'd spied her pretending to pole dance in a club one night. It had been impossible to ignore the way she'd gripped the pole, as her legs wrapped tightly around it and her stomach muscles taut as she pulled herself up before springing off and into his path.

When he woke the next day, with her body sprawled over his, he realised his judgement had been clouded by alcohol. Orange tan had layered his sheets, and he continued to find her acrylic nails hours after she'd gone. Her face up close and without make-up betrayed the beginnings of a tired and detached existence. Bianca was a testament to the fakery you could create with a bit of money and the motivation to bag yourself a rich man.

"Hey, sexy." Her hands were already making their way underneath his shirt. "You deserve the fuck of a lifetime for your performance on the pitch today."

He removed her hands but didn't let go of them unsure what she might try. Sex was all she offered, and that had been fine in the past. But that wasn't enough for him anymore, and it hadn't been for a long time. He'd only recently started to realise why. Aidan had missed the sex-on-tap initially, but that had faded. His attraction to Sophia fuelled his brain and body infinitely more. He'd spend hours in her company, if she let him, listening to her talk about her job, hobbies or her other passions. She was intelligent, caring, and even now, he was seeking her out. *Where is she?*

"No, thanks," he replied frostily.

"Don't tell me you're still angry about the sex tape? You shouldn't be. Your body looked hot and the way you screwed my brains out, fuck yes!"

Bile rose to his throat. "Is that why you sold it?"

A cackle cut through him as if she'd slashed him with a shard of glass. "As I've said, someone stole it."

Lifting her leg, she tried to rub her foot against his crotch. Aidan watched her stumble on her leopard print six-inch stiletto heels. If he hadn't had hold of her hands, she would have face planted, hitting the sticky floor. Bile pushed against his throat once more as he caught the stench of sweat and cigarettes radiating from her body. Watching her was like watching himself in Sophia's eyes. It made him hate himself that bit more.

"You're wasted," he spat the accusation at her. "I've told you before that it's over. Leave me alone. Go home, Bianca."

"Go home to a cold empty bed? I'd rather you were in it. We always had lots of fun when we'd been drinking. Remember skinny dipping-"

"I'd rather not remember. What I liked was that I didn't need to make any effort with you. We're not friends. We're not anything." He hated the cruelty of his own words, but he loathed seeing his past in front of him even more.

Bianca hurled herself at him. At the impact of her cigarette smoke kiss, Aidan froze in shock before heaving her away. Anger sparked, he breathed deeply through his nose. Sucking all air from the club, he tried to rid himself of her smell.

"You still want me, I know it." A voice more edgy than seductive made him realise her confidence was slipping.

Both his hands pointed to his groin, framing it for her.

"Look, Bianca, nothing is going on there. My dick is soft, and that's the first time it's been that way all night."

"I don't believe you. You want me. I know you do," she replied uncertainly, stealing several looks at his crotch.

"I want what you can't give me. Please leave me the fuck alone."

Fever hit her eyes. "You're going to regret this. Make sure you read the papers over an early morning wank tomorrow, that's if you can get your dick up."

She stuck up a middle finger in his direction before she spun on her toes and marched away. Aidan didn't watch her go.

The incident reminded him how much he'd hated being a spectacle for gossip-hungry leeches in the Bianca days. Temporarily he wondered what her threat might involve, but he quickly became distracted. Why hadn't Sophia come back? Had something happened to her?

Aidan said a short goodbye to Kong before striding to the club's exit. His heavy heart raced as a cold sheen of sweat settled on his body.

The rain was falling, and it brought a chill that reached deep inside him. Beads of water collected on his skin while drizzle clung to the strands of his hair. The musty smells reminded him of autumns filled with damp washing that never dried in the hovel he once shared with his mum.

Looking blankly at the faces around him, he searched around the entrance. Aidan pushed people aside as he caught sight of black dresses and long wavy hair. Shrieks and yells filled his ears.

She's gone.

He continued to dodge cigarette smoke that clouded his vision. His heart thundered in his chest.

"Everything ok?" The familiar bouncer stared down at him suspiciously.

He must have looked like a typical drunk, freaking out people while he tripped over his own feet, but it was panic that controlled his actions.

"Have you seen a woman? She's about this high," he said, using his hand to direct the bouncer's eye line to the top of his chest. "Black dress, long hair, it's a kind of brown colour with red and gold strands. She's beautiful, big brown Bambi eyes..."

Words were falling out of his mouth as if there was a stuck tap in his brain.

"The one you were with earlier?"

Maybe Sophia had slipped to the loo when he wasn't looking and was now clambering around the levels of the club, trying to find him with the same desperation that was plaguing him.

"Yep, that's the one. Have you seen her?"

"She jumped in a taxi about five minutes ago. I think she was crying."

Aidan walked away. His fingers trembled as he tried to call her. The sweet tones of her answer machine message faded his remaining hopes.

She couldn't have found out about his Huntington's, could she? What else had happened? *I've lost her for good, and I don't know why.*

Chapter Nine

Sophia struggled through sore eyes to see the numbers on her watch. Fresh tears blurred her vision.

6.09 am

She'd managed three hours of fitful sleep between the sobbing. Fear and hurt combined aggressively before sorrow filled her heart. Did caring about someone always result in suffering? It wasn't worth it. At least her humdrum life hadn't brought gut-wrenching agony.

He told me that he'd try not to hurt me yet within ten minutes he was kissing Bianca. Sophia sobbed loudly, not bothering to wipe away the tears that were soaking into her duvet. Closing her eyes, she attempted to blank out the images that repeated on a loop in her mind. But she couldn't forget.

Last night she'd gone outside to get some air and process what Aidan had told her. It wasn't like she wanted marriage, but she wanted to believe they might be more than a meaningless fling. She'd already invested her heart. Unfortunately, carefully weighing up her options while flush with alcohol was like trying to identify the planets in the solar system with a microscope.

Fears of other people's judgements no longer existed

with Aidan on her side. He was coaxing her to discover her true identity. She'd owed it to herself to see where their thing was going and fuck the consequences.

On re-entering the club, Aidan's and Bianca's hands were entwined while she flirted with him. Sophia had watched from the side, waiting for him to walk away, but he'd held Bianca tightly. And then, as Sophia deliberated stepping closer, they kissed. It wasn't like the way he'd kissed Sophia. Instead, there was a raw passion. *They were equals in a way I'd never be able to be with him.*

Aidan wasn't hers and had no intention of being so. Everyone that watched his interview heard him say he didn't want marriage and kids. Maybe he just wanted to fuck whoever he wanted when he wanted.

The memory of her ordeal, of bolting from the club, tears pouring as she threw herself into the first empty taxi, was too much.

Sophia meandered to the lounge. There was no point lying in bed waiting for exhaustion to knock her out. Picking at the worn fabric that frayed at the arm of the old sofa, she let the mindless chatter of some Netflix show desensitise her to her sadness. Slowly it lulled her to sleep.

Hours later, Nicky's feet padding down the corridor woke her. A bucket hung limply from Nicky's hand, and her face was ghostly pale.

"I may have drunk too much last night."

"May have?"

"Okay. I drank like a squaddie on leave." Nicky slipped onto the sofa and held Sophia's hand under the blanket. "What's going on, Soph? You look like you've been crying. Is it Aidan?"

"I didn't mean to ditch you last night," Sophia replied.

"Don't worry about that. Ryan and I hung out with the other players on the team. What happened?"

Familiar pain crept inside Sophia when she repeated the story of her night.

"This isn't me. I don't do stuff like this. I do the right thing," she rambled. "I've kept all these rules for myself about not sleeping with someone too quickly. And I've tried not to comment about how it can't go anywhere because 'a wife and kids aren't in his long-term plan.'"

"Oh, honey."

"But still it wasn't enough. Bianca's hand was on his dick! She's everything I wish I were; confident, beautiful and with no inhibitions or fear. She reminds me of Kelly."

"We'll talk about Kelly another time, but let's focus on you for now. You're incredible. You care so much about other people; the kids at the charity, me, even your mother and her judgements."

"But…"

"And you're beautiful. I know you don't believe me, but you are, and men look at you like you're something. I'd kill to have your eyes and your arse."

"But…" she tried again.

"And who cares about Bianca? The way your sexy rugby player looks at you makes every other woman jealous, even me."

Sophia squeezed her hand. "Huh? You?"

Nicky squinted at her. The hangover was winning. "Yes, but not because I want Aidan. It's Ryan's loving gazes I want. He treats me like a ball of wool that's there for him to paw like an excited kitten."

Sophia sighed long and hard, her fringe flopping around her forehead.

"And when it comes to the rules maybe you want to give them up because they never meant that much to you. Your mum forced her judgements on you. She made you think rules mattered more than how you felt, and that has stopped you from living." Nicky finished before her head plopped back onto Sophia's lap. "Thinking hurts. What did Aidan say when you confronted him about Bianca?"

"I didn't. I ran to a taxi and came home. Aidan might not know I saw him."

"And he didn't call?" Frustration crept into Nicky's voice.

"I turned my phone off after I texted you to say I was heading home. But…"

"But nothing." Nicky fought to drag her body to a vertical position. "Give the guy a chance. I'd beat the shit out of him if he hurt you. I'd take on the whole of the Bulls team. Give him the chance to explain himself and don't worry about the wife thing. You've barely kissed!"

Sophia's skin prickled with excitement as she remembered their kiss in the club. She'd not experienced anything like that before. She sat on her hands to stop her fingers caressing her lips at the memory.

"Sitting up wasn't a good idea," Nicky muttered, her mouth downturned as she flopped back down.

"Don't you dare puke on me," Sophia warned. "By the way, where's Ryan? He's normally breaking things when left on his own this long."

"He went to the shops to get me some paracetamol and coffee. He said he was going to force a bacon butty on me too."

"It might be what you need."

"Do you want to see my stomach floating in this bucket?" Nicky threatened as she pushed the bangs of her bob to the side.

Sophia grimaced as she shook her head. "What's going on between you two? Friends with benefits not working anymore?"

"The sex is amazing, and it always has been. The things Ryan can do to my body just with the palm of his hand…"

"I don't want to-."

"The volume increases tenfold when you're not here." Even hungover, Nicky was trouble. "But I want more than amazing sex. I want dates, and I want to be his girlfriend."

The front door slammed.

"But don't tell him," she begged. "It would ruin everything."

This relationship stuff isn't easy for anyone.

"Ladies, you have to see this."

Ryan tossed a Sunday tabloid in front of them. At the headline accompanying Bianca's picture, Sophia shouted, "Fuck the fuck off!"

*****

"Aidan, I don't understand how this is happening! How can she get away with these lies?" Aidan's mum's voice rang out across the kitchen.

"You can't deny the title is good, *'My Sex Romp Threesome with Angry Aidan and The Destroyer'.*" Aidan jested.

"Aidan Liam Flynn, this is not the time to joke."

Anger had defined him when the paper landed on his doorstep. There had nearly been the hole in his kitchen wall to prove it. But time had passed, and John had been his listening ear. Calm reigned once more.

"Why did she do this to you?"

"I don't understand why she does anything, mum. She said something as she left the club last night. She probably tried to get me to go home with her for a follow-up story, Angry Aidan confronted by paparazzi after a night of-"

"But you didn't do anything with her last night?" his mum interjected.

Shrugging, he waited for the kettle to boil. "Didn't want to."

"Someone else in your head? You've been like a lion with a thorn in its paw all morning, even before you read that madam's lies."

"Madam?" he teased, he was glad he and his mum were close, especially after everything that had happened over the years.

"I was thinking worse." The well-practised air of sophistication was dropping. She grinned impishly. "The girl that's in your head is it the one who was here on Friday?"

"Sophia? Why do you ask that?" Turning away casually, attempting nonchalance, he focused on the boiling kettle.

"Call it a mother's instincts. And don't you turn away from me, I can tell when you're lying whatever direction you stand in."

"Either way, it doesn't matter. She didn't trust me before, and she'll probably think I'm the devil's spawn after this crap. '*Angry Aidan wanted the sex tape made.*

He insisted we did it and liked to watch it all the time. In one scene, he made me dress as a leprechaun.' It's ludicrous. She says we had sex on the pitch at the Millennium Stadium. Apparently, she tied me to one of the goalposts. That's not possible without being caught."

"Does she know you might have Huntington's?" his mum asked.

"Bianca?"

"No, Sophia." His mum was astounding; she knew what questions to ask when his guard was low.

"She doesn't, no."

"You should tell her."

"I'll never tell."

"If you want to keep seeing her, then you should tell her. She'll find out." It was like a tennis match between them, comments back and forth like the ball.

"No, she won't. Besides we're not seeing each other, she won't talk to me." She hadn't even texted to tell him to leave her alone.

"Why not?"

"I don't know," he shrugged, but his dismay was evident. "Maybe I've said too much to her. She ran out of the club last night crying, and her phone is off."

"Find a way to reach her. This one is different."

"You barely met her."

"That was enough," she replied matter-of-factly. "Trust me."

"Mother's instincts?" Aidan asked, sarcastically.

"Maybe you're not as stupid as I thought. Now let's go for a drive so I can buy some plants for the garden." Leaning in, she pecked him on the cheek before clipping him around the back of the head. "And don't be such a cheeky brat, my instincts got you this far."

*****

Sophia dragged herself into the office. She'd avoided her colleagues all morning with offsite appointments. Mondays didn't bother her, and she enjoyed her job and spending time with children who'd suffered the heart-wrenching death of a parent had a way of minimising her insignificant issues while reminding her of the tragedies people brought themselves back from. But this Monday was different.

Her Mary Jane shoes crunched on the gravel of the car park outside her office. The stones glinted as they reflected the gold of the sun. Leaves on the trees lining the car park danced. Autumn was here. They'd transformed from emerald and shamrock to the colours of a destructive blaze. Brittle autumn leaves surrounding the greens, blood-red leaves merged with the buttercup yellows and tiger oranges creating a fire above her head. Soon they'd be drifting down from the trees, blanketing the ground and signalling the start of winter.

What will the rest of the year bring? She shivered, remembering her Sunday with Nicky. Ryan had left them to it, but not before he'd got a cold compress for Nicky, and prepared food for Sophia and Nicky while sharing his wisdom.

"Aidan is probably a typical guy whose main goal is sex," he'd said, performing stretches in the lounge. His abs rippled with each twist and flex of his body. "But that doesn't mean he's bad. Speak to him."

Ryan didn't get hangovers and had spent the rest of the day on an extreme bike ride, taking on the rough terrains of the local forest and pushing his body to its limits. Eventually, he'd found his way home, splattered with mud, the big puppy grin back on his face, and holding magazines and snacks for Nicky. The softening of her eyes proved Nicky was falling hard for her fuck buddy.

Screams of laughter had filled the house over Bianca's salacious but fabricated exclusive. The gall of the woman was astounding.

But no matter how much they laughed and deliberated, two unanswerable questions remained. Could Sophia trust Aidan, and could she trust herself when it came to him? They'd spent ages talking about it, but they didn't get far.

Eventually, Sophia turned her phone on before bed. There were over thirty messages from Aidan, but she ignored them, pushing them into a box in her mind while justifying her position to herself, unable to decide what to do about him until she saw him in the flesh.

There was a mysterious text message from Jack, the Fundraising Manager, too.

J: *Hey, babe. Hope you had a good weekend. Do me a favour and dress up smart for work tomorrow afternoon? All will become clear.*

Walking through to the office, she picked a speck of lint off her fanciest shift dress and fiddled with the gold clasp on her skinny belt. It usually made her feel sophisticated and able to achieve any goal she set herself, but not today.

I need to see Aidan. But how can I without falling for him again?

"Oh my God," Tasha bellowed from the open-plan office. "I love my job!"

As Sophia ambled into the office, a foreboding

feeling hit her. A media circus consisting of Ray, the CEO, Jack, Tasha, a newspaper photographer and a couple of rugby players confronted her. Standing in the middle, with all attention focused on him was Aidan.

Be careful what you wish for as you might just get it.

Gritting her teeth so extensively her jaw ached, she sidestepped the mob.

"Sophia, come here," Jack sang her name before rushing over and putting his arm through hers. "You have to be in the photo."

"What's going on?" she hissed.

"I think Sophia should stand next to Aidan," he shouted, forcing a space next to Aidan.

Suddenly the group shoved her next to Aidan's concrete frame. *Does he have to look so sexy?* The crimson and white material of his rugby kit gripped his biceps snugly, and his thighs swelled in his tight red shorts.

All she had to do was lean closer and touch him.

No, no, no. This is your job. At such proximity, Aidan's tropical scent flooded her senses. Her crotch twitched as if it remembered Saturday night and the last time she'd breathed him in.

"Do you have to look incredible every time I see you? That dress makes you look like a sexy secretary," he whispered in his hormone-inducing Irish accent.

Sophia snubbed him. She needed to quieten her lady bits before they gave her intentions away. The image of Bianca kissing him with her hand at his crotch had her wincing internally, but it wasn't enough.

Aidan's lips were just short of brushing against her ear. A heat was running down her spine, and her stomach was lurching again.

"Talk to me, Soph."

Sophia looked despairingly at Tasha for inspiration. She needed to be angry quickly, and that woman regularly made her blood boil. Tasha was standing on the other side of Aidan and hanging onto his upper arm. Tentacle-like fingers curled around his bicep while one of her hands travelled down. Sophia stiffened. Tasha grazed her fuchsia talons against his forearm; up and down. Was she purring?

Aidan whispered again. Hot breath teased the flesh of her neck as if he was carefully running his fingertips across her skin. "I'm sure you've seen the papers. The story wasn't true, none of it."

Sophia ignored him, but his words pressed her to do otherwise. She damned the part of her that wanted to inspect what was beneath his rugby shirt. She longed to drag her tongue and teeth against his flesh and feel his muscles strain against her.

"Are you strong enough to lift me?" Tasha asked a flirty lilt to her voice.

Aidan flexed his muscles for the head of his fan club. A sour taste filled Sophia's mouth.

*****

Aidan strained in anguish, and his hands returned to their stress response, making fists before swiftly flexing, again and again. *How can I convince her the newspaper story was all lies?*

"Everybody smile!" The photographer's sing-song voice rang out among them.

Aidan had nearly forgotten the reason he'd

fashioned to gain entry to the office, only seeing Sophia the second she'd walked into the room. The look of dread had been evident the moment she'd glanced his way.

"Sophia, for God's sake." His patience was fraying. How could he get her to believe him? "You can't keep ignoring me."

Sliding his hand down her back was a mistake, but what else could he do to get her attention? *I can feel her heat through my hand.*

"Get the fuck off me," she shot quietly between clenched teeth. Instantly Aidan dropped his hand. Smiles for the camera disappeared. "What are you doing here?"

"It's a photo opportunity because of the donation." The coconut aroma of her hair had him imagining her gorgeous bottom as she sashayed across a Hawaiian beach. *Focus, Aidan.*

"You do need the good press," she hit back.

Rambling, he ignored her irritation. *I need to fix this situation and make her happy again.* "The club is focusing their charitable efforts on the foundation this season, too. I talked them into it for you."

"I guess I should be grateful," she said without sincerity.

"I could think of ways you could pay me back." *I'm such an arsehole. What is wrong with me?*

The point of her shoe instantly connected with his shin. A stab of pain exploded through him, acid flooded up to his throat and threatened to spill into his mouth. He usually wouldn't have flinched, but 'The Destroyer' had punished him with the studs of his boot during Saturday's game.

"Sorry," he whispered, hiding his grimace. "I didn't

mean to say that. My brain is on a go slow."

"Probably tired from your weekend screwing Bianca," she snapped back.

"The article was lying. You can trust me." Once more, he attempted to put his hand on the small of her back. It was desperate measures to stop his mouth ruining him.

"I wasn't referring to the article."

He turned quickly towards her, and his fake smile dropped.

All he'd known when he'd begged Kong to persuade Jack to do an article about the donation was that he had to see her. He'd foolishly thought when she saw him it would be enough. "So, what are you talking about?"

Her volume increased. "I'm talking about you and Bianca practically fucking in the club Saturday night when I was outside. You could at least have found a room or the Millennium stadium!"

"But-"

The spiky-haired photographer sang out again, cutting him off, "I need you looking at the camera, Aidan. Show me that winning face of yours."

Aidan blanched as he turned to the photographer.

"Maybe we need to try something else," the photographer huffed. "How about you players pick up one of the women, and she lies across your arms like you're carrying her."

Aidan reached instantly for Sophia, but she pulled away.

"I'm not going to be part of your games. I've got work to do." Sophia stormed off, her body rigid with anger.

"I haven't got anything to do, I'd love to be one of

your games," Tasha laughed. "Who wants to play with me first?"

*****

Sophia stiffened at Aidan's next statement. "Come on then, Tasha, let's have some fun!"

Aidan's chuckle set her teeth on edge.

The pull to run back and rip Tasha away from him overwhelmed her. *But I don't fight battles I can't win.* Aidan wasn't hers and never would be. She wearily returned to her desk.

"Let's try this somewhere else." The photographer's melodic voice was beginning to grate. "Let's take it to the park."

"Oh, I can do it in a park," Tasha replied.

"I bet you can." Sophia looked up, pained, at Aidan's reply. The group left the room, Aidan didn't turn to look at her, let alone say goodbye. He was too busy laughing with Tasha.

Sophia's stomach spasmed as she held back the tears.

CHAPTER TEN

Sophia parked her car in the street near her home and yanked on the handbrake. *Bloody Aidan.* She slumped against the steering wheel before banging her forehead against it. *I can't even talk to Nicky.* She was doing another overnight shift at the hospital.

With one more bash of her head against the steering wheel, Sophia resigned herself to the facts. Aidan's focus was sex and where he could get it. *And that's why he's with Tasha tonight.*

The stink of sweat from Sophia's workout motivated her to get out of the car. With a shove and a slam of her car door, she left the solitude of her vehicle. Immediately she was hit by the dropping temperatures.

She gritted her teeth and pulled the hood of her jumper up with her shivering hands. A stone took the brunt of her anger as she slammed her foot into it. It took flight before smacking her front gate, but she gained no satisfaction from the crack in the wood.

"I guess I was that easy to replace," she whispered, passing through the gate that whined and struggled on its hinges. She focused on avoiding the cracks in the concrete path to her house as she lamented her situation. "And he replaced me with her."

"Talking to yourself?" Sophia heard him before she

saw him. Aidan sat on her doorstep, staring intently up at her.

She brutally shoved down her hood, causing strands of hair to come out at the follicles. But she didn't react. *Show no emotion. Not in front of him.* "Are you lost? Tasha doesn't live here," she said sarcastically.

"But you do." Aidan's eyes no longer sparkled. There was no trace of the infectious smile. Instead, a weariness that made his broad shoulders slump replaced it.

Sophia fought the longing to stroke his hair and plant kisses against his furrowed forehead. He didn't deserve anything from her.

"You keep showing up where you're not wanted. Why are you here?" The need to hurt him like he'd hurt her rose like a monster inside of her.

"Please let me talk to you. I don't have to come in. We can chat on this cold, painful, stone doorstep if you want. I will sacrifice my gorgeous bum so I can speak to you."

He's too cute for his own good. Sophia yanked up the front collar of her hoodie to hide the smile he'd drawn from her lips.

"Fine, but two minutes is all you're getting."

"Okay. Well, the newspaper article wasn't true," Aidan was rabbiting. "I never did those things. I'm not into threesomes. I have had sex outdoors, but everyone has."

"Not everyone," Sophia commented flatly.

"Really? How come?"

"I don't care about the article, Aidan. I do care that on Saturday night I saw you kissing Bianca. She had her hand on your dick!" she ranted.

"What?"

"In the club. I came back after getting some air, and you were kissing. I saw you."

Bewilderment flashed across his face. "No, no, no. Bianca launched herself at me. I stopped her and told her to get lost for good because I don't want her. You have to believe me, Soph. I should have walked away when I first realised it was her. Bianca is trouble. But I let her get close, and for that I'm sorry. Kong saw everything. I'll get him on the phone to speak to you right now. He's the most honest guy I know."

Would he tell a lie when she could prove him wrong with one phone call? Jack had told her about Kong a couple of times. Jack said he was the most genuine and truthful guy that existed.

She believed Aidan. It made sense from what she'd seen. Her fears had helped her twist what she'd witnessed. She was too scared of giving in to her wants and getting hurt again.

"What was all that about at the office? Did you come over here because Tasha was busy?" she asked. Trying to keep up the cold exterior was impossible with his little boy lost look staring back at her.

"I came to the office to see you. I had to convince you that the newspaper story was a lie. I thought if you knew that then you could base your opinion of me on truth. But when I realised how angry you were, I knew I'd made a mistake. Confronting you at work was stupid. I crossed a line. I flirted with Tasha to get your address. I'm sorry, that wasn't clever either. I don't know what I'm doing. I'm a game player when it comes to women, but you. You're not…"

"I'm not?" she asked. *I don't know what I'm doing*

either.

"You're not like anyone I've ever met before," he replied his shoulders sagging. "You're so much more."

Cracks began to show in her resolve when his head sunk to his hands. The hopelessness in front of her tore at her heart.

Desperation radiated from him. "I couldn't bear having you upset because of me. I had to make it right. I'm sorry for everything. You deserve better."

Sophia's defences were deteriorating. Perching on the step, she took his hands away from his head and held them gently in hers.

"Okay. Be better," she replied, moving Aidan's frozen hands to her lips. Her gaze fixed on him as she kissed each finger. Aidan let out a sigh of relief, but still, he struggled to look at her.

"Let's go inside before the cold step ruins that potentially award-winning arse of yours. Besides, I'm starving, and I've barely eaten all day," she said.

Standing, quietly, she turned his chin with her finger, so he looked back at her.

"What, no crappy joke or cheesy comeback? Have I broken you, Aidan?" she teased, while her nerves jangled in her chest.

The hint of a smile appeared on his face, although he still looked tired. "I hope not, but give it time and I think you might."

*****

Aidan was stunned. It had seemed like everything was lost, and now he was here, in her home.

It had been a busy two hours. Sophia had cooked,

they'd eaten bowls full of pasta, she'd tidied the house and showered. The sound of the shower blasting out hot water over her naked body had been an unexpected form of torture.

But he'd resisted his urges, and now he sat with her quietly on the sofa. Aidan rested against its worn back and pretended to watch the film. *Should I make a move or will that freak her out?* There was a tension in the room that he couldn't distil. He struggled to equate her with the woman who had instigated the intimacy of their moment outside. Affection had transformed to frostiness as she sat still as a statue beside him, her legs were concealed by skinny jeans and tucked beneath her. Did she want him to make a move? *She's nervous. But is it because she wants to be more intimate or because she hasn't forgiven me?*

Attempting a look of ambivalence, he kept his legs wide, but his brain was working overtime.

He chanced glances at her, unable to decipher her expression under the glow of the television. The semi-dark room shrouded her in mystery.

Sophia flexed her legs. It spurred him into breaking the silence. "You can sit closer."

"I don't want to crowd you." Her soft voice made her words barely audible.

"You're not crowding me."

She tugged on her lip with her teeth as she shuffled cautiously closer. Her jitters were contagious.

"How was the gym?" he asked. He moved to rest his hand on her leg. *What if that is pushing her too far?* His hand froze in mid-air.

Women in his past were like slightly subtle versions of Tasha. They commanded his attention through their confidence. They told him what they wanted and gave him the option to join in or not. Sophia was like that sometimes too. *But you broke her trust.*

"Not bad," she replied, reaching for his hand and propping it on her thigh. "It's okay for you to touch me."

"Cool. Did you run far on the treadmill?" Aidan inquired. *Don't tremble.* He was like a pilot trying to land in a tropical storm with instruments so flawed he could only rely on the instincts that twisted and pulled action from his body. Unfortunately, his instincts were broken when it came to Sophia.

"Yeah, the furthest I've run in ages. My muscles are killing me." Slowly, she inched closer.

"Maybe from too much stress?" he offered. The heat of her leg was beneath the palm of his hand. "Sophia, I can't keep doing this," he suddenly blurted out.

Sophia gasped and turned to face him, crossing her legs, straining the jeans. "Can't keep doing what?"

"I'm worried that I'm pushing you too far or not taking the lead when you want me to or maybe I'm overstaying my welcome. I don't know what you want from me, and I'm worried I've broken everything. I've broken us," Aidan explained, trying to let his heart give the words he wanted to share for a change. "This is new for me, I don't worry when I'm with women, but I don't want to do anything to hurt you."

She dipped her head and traced the rip in his jeans near his thigh. He flinched. *You need to chill out.*

"Okay, then maybe we need to try something. How about a trust game?" Sophia suggested.

Aidan laughed loudly. "Well, that broke the tension… Hold on." He looked her square in the face.

"Are you serious?"

It was another reminder that she wasn't like anyone he knew. He'd expected her to suggest anything else, even a drinking game. *I'm interested.* Every time he questioned what it was between them, she hooked him further.

"I am. You're right about the trust thing. When you're near me, I'm torn. My body is telling me to go for it, but my brain is holding me back. I'm fed up of my brain being in control and overthinking everything. I want to try something new," she explained. Her forehead furrowed in deep thought.

"Okay, let's do this. Whatever it takes," he responded, jumping up. "What do we do?"

"I have the perfect thing in my bedroom." She scampered off, shouting, "Meet me in the front garden."

She didn't give him the chance to remind her how cold it was. *What has she got planned?*

Twenty minutes later, Aidan found himself shivering in the garden while laughing so hard his chest hurt.

Sophia's eyes glinted as she waggled a water bomb in front of him. She had the balloon like object leftover from one of the events at work. Her job was sometimes about giving the children fun experiences around difficult conversations.

"I don't understand how this builds trust," he shouted to her. "Shouldn't we be having a serious conversation about feelings or something?"

Sophia's laughter was like a beautiful song he heard for the first time.

They'd started half a metre apart throwing the water bomb back and forth. Every time they caught the bomb, they took a step back. "I want to have fun, and we can chat later. If my job has taught me anything, it's that trust comes through actions as well as words. And right now you have to trust that I'm not going to lob this water bomb at your head."

She had a point. The game had taken away Aidan's fears of making the wrong move and of pushing her too far. It had also revealed her devilish side. She'd come alive. More than once he'd had to think on his feet to stop the bomb hitting him in the face. Maybe this was her payback.

With each step back, her smile grew.

"You look cold, do you think we should go in?" he asked.

"Feeling the pressure, Aidan? Scared you might get wet?" she teased. "Besides, I'm here in a nice warm hoody. You'd think the big rugby man would be able to cope in just his jumper too."

He laughed despite himself. *I can't get enough of her.*

"Whatever, Soph. I'm going to be dry as a bone by the end of this," he replied. She took another step back. She was nearly at the wall of the garden; there had to be twenty metres between them. They couldn't both come out of the game unscathed.

"You reckon, eh? How about we make this interesting unless you're not as confident as you're making out," she replied, her eyes nearly as wide as her devilish smile.

"I'll let you paint me naked if you want," he joked.

"Whoever loses has to make the first move and not

some half-assed effort. If it's you, I want your best efforts in seduction," Sophia shouted. While eyeballing him, she tossed the bomb in the air and caught it. Throw and catch, throw and catch. The movements hypnotised him.

"But that's not fair," he replied as she took a step back. "I'm a world-class rugby player, you know I'm not going to make a bad throw."

"I've seen you play, Aidan, you're not as good as you think you are," she goaded. "But I'd best limber up if this is getting serious."

Slowly she stripped off her hoody and revealed her thin white vest that he'd been aware of earlier. The vest curved and dipped seductively at her breasts.

"Are you trying to psych me out?" he asked gruffly as she turned and bent over to drop her jumper on the floor, giving him the delectable view of her bottom in her tight black jeans.

"Is it working?" she replied flirtatiously turning to look at him while still bent over. He was transfixed until she suddenly jumped up and hurled the bright orange bomb at his face.

He may not be world-class anymore, but players savvier than Sophia had attempted and failed to psych him out before. He caught it one-handed and lobbed it straight back at her chest. But it was too late, and another bomb slammed him in the chest.

BAM

Water engulfed him. She'd had a second bomb hidden in her jumper. *She outplayed me!*

At her laughter, he looked into her sparkling eyes. "I guess I win," she shouted. "But you're going to have to catch me if you think you're going to make that first move."

She bolted towards the house and rushed inside, but he was hot on her heels. Her breathless giggles made her easy to locate. She sat on the sofa, exactly where they had been before their game, he joined her before planning his next move.

It's time for seduction.

"Lay down and put your legs across mine. I want to test something." Aidan nearly laughed when her eyebrows dipped together.

Stroking his palm hand down the length of her leg caused her to shudder. "Are you ticklish, Sophia?"

"No." She had a sneaky smile. "I thought your best would be better," she teased.

Is she making jokes because she's scared? The trust game had to have helped, but she was probably still nervous.

Running his hand to the curve of her hip, he hid a groan of desire.

"So, if I touch you here?" Aidan's hand hung in the air, threatening to tickle the skin of her hip under her sheer top. The smell of her coconut shampoo intoxicated him. During the movie, he'd wanted to thread his fingers through her hair and plant kisses on her neck.

"Nothing happens wherever you touch me," she replied, but her eyes sparkled with excitement. The corner of her mouth twitched as if she wanted to smile and glare, all at once.

Confidence surged. Squeezing her hip gently, Aidan delighted in watching her buckle.

"Aidan, no!" she squealed with glee.

"You have to trust me, Sophia." Lifting an eyebrow seductively, he combined it with a deepening voice to tease her most intimate places. "Do you trust me?"

"Yes," she whispered, still breathless from her squeal.

Hunger consumed him. The rise and fall of her breasts mesmerised him. His erection twitched in his jeans. "Tell me to stop, and I will, immediately. Okay?"

Sophia nodded. Her eyes were impossibly wide as she watched him take control.

Aidan slid out from beneath her. He slowly stretched her body and eased her down so that she was lying flat on the sofa. "Close your eyes."

She complied, although uncertainty crossed her face.

"Are you ticklish here?" His lips brushed her collarbone.

Instead of a squeal, he received the greatest gift he'd ever known. A whimper of pleasure left her parted lips. He'd hit her sweetest spot.

Unable to resist the temptation of her tender lips any longer, he dropped his head.

"What about here?" Aidan whispered, pressing his full lips to hers. It was gentle at first, but need snowballed. Sophia reached up and pulled his head closer, pinning his lips to hers in an indulgent kiss. Sensuality quickly became fast and needy. Their tongues explored each other's mouths. The scent of her shampoo still tingled his senses, and he revelled in the sweetness of her taste.

Temporarily he eased back and greedily licked his lips, surveying the beauty laid beneath him.

Her eyes were on him, taking in every move, challenging him to give her more, but he refused to bend to her will. Aidan eased his body down to lay on top of her, nestling himself between her open thighs. He ran his fingertips across her cheekbones, fascinated by her beauty that grew the longer he spent with her.

Temptation eclipsed the moment, and again she reached for him. Tongues intertwined and hearts hammered as they kissed with long-held desire. Her legs gripped him before her calves pushed against his bum and pulled his erection harder against her crotch.

Pent up hunger blurred his patience. Sophia's whimpers reverberated around his body. It was as if he'd waited a lifetime rather than a few days to be close to her. Sliding a hand down from her flushing cheek to her neck, he throbbed with necessity. Aidan reached the curve of her breast. Even through the sheer material, her nipple was hard against his hand.

How wet was she? He fought the urge to undo the button of her jeans and find out. There was much to explore and discover. *Slow down.*

Sophia juddered in surprise as if she couldn't predict his actions. Gradually, his hand inched under the hem of her top.

His fingers stroked her flesh, and she quivered in response before dragging him closer with her thighs and thrusting her pelvis against his.

His hand enveloped her lace-covered breast. Its warmth and softness made his erection impossibly harder, and it pushed against the zipper of his jeans. Wincing, he flicked her nipple with his fingertip. Sophia's mouth jolted against his in surprise. The more Aidan rubbed his finger against her pert nub, the more fervent her kisses and harder her thrusts became.

Clasping her vest top he pulled it up and over her head, admiring the toll their kissing had taken on her mouth, her lips swollen and red. He dipped his head and sucked and nipped at her neck. Sophia's quivers beneath him spurred on his advances. He groaned with lust as he travelled down from her collarbone.

Anticipation was in the air. Time seemed suspended as he first grazed the top of her cleavage with his lips before hovering over her hard, lace-covered, nipple.

Sophia's eyelids fluttered closed.

He hesitated, observing her.

Her eyes shot open, and Aidan returned her suspicious gaze with a grin. *She's so beautiful. I could stare at her all night.*

He hid the stutter of fear. The importance of the moment wasn't lost on him. *For Sophia, this will mean something. It means something for me too, but what? Can I keep pretending this isn't more than a fling?* His need to reassure her reared. "Tell me what you want."

"You know what I want," she replied, her voice saturated with innocence. At her gentle tones, Aidan ground against her, satisfied when she thrust in time to his movements.

"Tell me what you want me to do," Aidan asked softly. He needed her to harness her desires. *She has to say what she wants or what she doesn't want.* She needed to own her pleasure.

"I want," she paused, worrying her lower lip with her teeth.

Aidan smiled, encouraging her to continue.

"I want you to take my nipple in your mouth and suck it." The words had barely left her mouth before he did as she asked, feasting upon her as if her request was a starting pistol.

Each lick of his tongue across her nipple was quickly replaced by a nip from his teeth before he offered a bliss-filled kiss.

She stared at him as she slipped the straps of her bra off her shoulders, revealing her breasts to his tongue. A growl left his mouth, and her rosy nipple disappeared into it. While one breast was getting all the attention that his mouth could offer, he praised the other with the pad of his thumb, twisting and pinching it before caressing it with his lips and relieving it of pain.

Beneath her veiled gaze, she witnessed each flick and suck. She closed her eyes, moaning in time with Aidan's ministrations. He rested his hand on the button of her jeans before flicking it open and sliding the zip down.

Her breath caught in her throat and she froze, her eyes tightly shut.

"It's okay, I've stopped," he reached out to her. "Soph, honey, what's wrong?"

Chapter Eleven

Aidan knew he'd lost her. Sophia had stopped grinding against him, shrinking away. His heart was heavy with disappointment. He'd made too many mistakes with her.

"You can tell me," he said softly like he was trying to coax a terrified animal from danger. He was scared, not for him, but for what was in her head. "Look at me. Tell me what's going on, please."

"I don't think I'm ready for you to have sex with me," Sophia spoke as if it was a decision she wasn't part of. But sex wasn't a deed Aidan did to any woman. It was both of them together.

"I'm sorry," she continued while he examined her. "I'll understand if you want to leave."

"Why would I? Unless you want me to. Is that what you want, Soph?"

"No!" Mild panic flickered in her eyes as she babbled. "But when guys don't get what they want, they, well, they have needs. I understand if that's what you want to do. If you want to leave, it's okay, that's all."

He sat up gently and pulled her to straddle his lap.

"What are you talking about, honey? I'm happy here with you, and I didn't expect sex."

Her cautious smile was like a ray of sunshine in the

middle of a solar eclipse. The saliva from his suckling still covered her nipples. She shivered and attempted to pull her bra straps back up.

Stilling her hands in his, he whispered, "Is it okay if I still look at your boobs? I won't if you don't want me to, but you're beautiful." He hoped his words would give her fresh confidence.

She smiled. Staring deep into his eyes, she gracefully unclasped her bra with one hand before shaking the lingerie from her body. Her breasts moved rhythmically in front of him.

"Bloody hell, you're sexy," he growled. He barely managed to resist the pull to stare in awe at her boobs. But Sophia's broadening smile encouraged him to delve into her past. "What's going on, Bambi eyes? Is this about the heartbreak you mentioned?"

There was a deliberate nod of her head.

"Will you tell me about it?"

"Okay," she said with resignation. "But can I put a top on, I'm getting a little chilly?"

"You don't have to ask me for permission, but how about this?" Aidan cupped her boobs, her nipples snug against his palms. Her soft giggles vibrated against his hands, and he smiled all over again.

"Aidan Flynn! Stop being so cheeky!"

"If you want cheeky, I can do this instead." His hands quickly reached around and grabbed her bottom, pulling her closer to him. Again, she chuckled, although this time he could taste it too as she kissed him on the lips. She took it deeper. Sophia was a sweet taste on his tongue.

"Oh, you're still hard," she replied in surprise.

"We did have a lot of fun," he replied with a shrug.

"But you still stopped? I thought you might push me to do more because of your needs. I didn't have to say anything else to make you stop."

"Of course not. I can be a prick, but I would never force myself on someone. What happened in your past?"

"Nothing as bad as what you're thinking." He was thinking the worst. "This might sound weird, but could we have this conversation while cuddling in my bed?"

"Okay..." He stretched out the word. *At least she wants to talk*. She could have told him to get lost. "Any reason for going to your bed?"

"It's more comfortable than this sofa, and although Nicky isn't due home, she might turn up unexpectedly, or Ryan might crash here."

Sophia's hand trembled in his as she led him to her bedroom. Her bra swung from her free hand as they ambled along.

The room was messy in places, but his overall impression was that it was dull. The personality that shone through her wasn't evident here. The furniture was cream, probably a mass Ikea purchase, and the walls were magnolia, which was the norm in a rented property. All the features that would have made it homely were absent, although her coconut scent lingered. He breathed it in deeply as he continued his inspection. There were only two photos propped up on the dresser, both in plain frames. In one, she was smiling next to Nicky. Nicky had been at the club, although he'd not had the opportunity to speak to her.

In the other photo, in a graduation cap and gown,

was a younger Sophia. She stood with a woman in her late thirties. Neither of their smiles looked genuine, both fixed and not reaching the eyes. The pretence of happiness was clear and recognisable. *I've experienced it often enough myself.*

His drawing of Sophia hung on the wall in a subtle yet stylish black enamel frame. He'd only drawn it four days earlier, but it seemed a lifetime ago. The drawing wasn't perfect, he'd done better, but there was something about it that captured his attention even now.

"Admiring your handiwork?" Sophia startled him. Turning, Aidan found her in bed with the duvet pulled up to her neck.

"I'm admiring you. You're beautiful."

There was a shrugged response. Sophia opened her mouth, but he cut her off. "You are beautiful, Soph, even if you don't see it."

She snapped her mouth shut.

Maybe if I tell her every day, she'll believe me.

"What are you thinking?" he asked, attempting to hide the distress in his heart. *How can I help Soph fight her demons?*

✤✤✤✤✤

"Do I have to say?" Sophia stared at Aidan.

In the time he'd been viewing her room like it was a personal exhibition, she'd managed to strip off her jeans underneath the protection of the duvet. Her unspoken request for him to join her made her feel like she was swimming against ocean swells that forced her under. *Why can't he take control of the situation and make things easier for me?*

"Yes, you do," he replied simply. "I'll help you along the way, but I don't want to always be in charge and making decisions for both of us. Tell me what scares you, what makes you pull away. I care about you Soph, I want to fix what I can, but I need you to let me. It's like the trust game. Please ask me, Bambi eyes."

Dragging in a breath, she forced her head above the water. "I want you to join me in bed… right now," she added with a shy smile.

"I love it when you tell me what to do." He dove on top of the bed and scrambled under the covers before exclaiming loudly, "Bloody hell, you took your jeans off quick!"

He swiped at her lacy knickers. "How the hell am I going to listen to you or think straight when you're this close AND naked?"

"I'm not naked," she protested.

"And yet my heart is banging in my chest. You do this to me," Aidan said softly as he pulled her closer. She shifted around so that they were spooning. He wrapped his body around hers. The aching horniness wouldn't abate, however, protected and comfy she felt.

"Don't I get to see the sexy body next to me?" Playfully he pulled the duvet away as she fought to keep hold of it.

"Hands off the duvet, Flynn. This is me telling you what to do. And keep that hard dick of yours calm!"

"What can I do?" he inquired impishly. "My cock knows what it wants, and it wants you. It must be intelligent. It can't be anything but rock-solid when you're around. Say "hard dick" again, nothing pleases it more, and you sound so sexy when you say it."

Her giggles danced between them. It was a fruitless

battle trying to be anything but elated with him.

Somehow his lips that nuzzled her neck made her crotch tingle. *I hadn't realised I was sensitive there until I met Aidan. What else could he teach me? Will he still want me after I tell him about Graham?* "Save that for later."

"Is that a promise?" he joked between kisses. He pushed Sophia hair to one side before his lips grazed her neck, his teeth gently nipping her flesh. "That was the last kiss, for now. I promise to behave."

Aidan's hands rested protectively against her stomach. *Where should I start?* She gripped the duvet tighter as her chest constricted from the panic.

Aidan's Irish timbre calmed her. "It's going to be okay, honey. You don't have to tell me anything, whatever you decide it's going to be okay."

His hands moved in soft circles against her skin. *I need to move forward.* It was time to trust Aiden with the truth. She forced the words out with a croak. "I met Graham in uni at the Graduation Ball, but I'd noticed him on campus before that. I didn't exist to him until that final week. He bought me a drink. He had this sexy geek thing going on; blonde with thick-rimmed glasses. I thought he would go on ignoring me, but that night was different, and we started dating shortly after. He was my first boyfriend."

"You didn't have a boyfriend until after university? Weren't you about twenty-one? You'd kissed other guys before that, right?"

"Yes, I was twenty-one and no I hadn't kissed other guys," Sophia said it quickly, anticipating Aidan's shock. At university, she'd been embarrassed about her lack of experience. While all her friends were bringing guys home, she was waiting for things to be different. *Aidan must want to laugh at me; he's bedded so many women.* But there was no laughter; instead, he held her tighter. If her inexperience surprised him, he wasn't making it obvious. "Anyway, Graham and I dated, although we'd only do the things he wanted. I'd spend all my time with him. I lost friends, but I didn't notice, or maybe I didn't care. He was my world and all that mattered. Nicky wouldn't let me ditch her and neither would Kelly, a friend Nicky and I lived with after university."

Breathing deeply, she sucked in Aidan's musky aroma, impressed that she'd managed to say Kelly's name without her voice shaking. *Talking about Graham is hard enough, but I'm not ready to divulge my history with Kelly.* "I stopped visiting my mum and stopped going out. All that existed for me was him and work. He was controlling. If I disagreed with his plans or what he wanted, he'd question my love for him. He threatened me and used me for my money. He was doing a Masters' degree, and I was paying for everything."

"And when you were in the bedroom, was he controlling there too?" Aidan's strong arms wrapped around her. He'd already given her more than Graham had.

"We generally did what he wanted there, too. If I didn't get him off, he'd say that I didn't love him. He was experienced and would make out that I was a failure, telling me I didn't know what I was doing and that I was shit compared to his exes."

"Did he rape you?"

"No, and we never had sex, well not the penetrative type," Sophia said it clinically. "I needed time. It sounds stupid, but I guess I never wanted him like that. I never wanted him like…"

"Like?"

"I never wanted him like I want you."

He stroked her naked skin with his thumb. She relaxed into the cocoon he'd created. "What happened?"

"The last night I refused him, something changed. At first, he tried all his usual tricks. He complained about how patient he'd been, even though he'd had numerous other offers. He said he'd do anything for me so I should do this for him if I loved him. I told him if he loved me, he wouldn't force it. He got angry. I was terrified. He shouted at me, calling me a prick tease, a frigid bitch, and worse."

Memories pummelled her, and tears blurred her vision. The story fell out of her mouth faster. Frantic shakes took hold of her body. "That night, Graham became a monster. I thought he'd hit me or worse."

Aidan's arms tightened protectively around her as the tears started to fall more rapidly, running across her cheeks.

"His rage consumed him, but before anything could happen, Nicky's boyfriend, Owen broke down the door and threw him out. Owen threatened him with the life of a eunuch if he dared to come close to me again."

"Did he?"

"Not really. Nicky and Owen barely left me alone, and at work, my calls were screened religiously. I changed my mobile number and blocked all his social media. He was in my head for a long time, and everyone was worried that I wouldn't be able to walk away, but I did. It almost broke me. Nicky saved me." Walking away should have been easy, but in those days Graham had a power over her. Sophia was used to him taking the lead in most of the aspects of her life. When she had to take control of herself, she'd lost confidence in everything, especially in who she was and what she was capable of. It took a long time to see the good parts of the relationship for what they were, more of his manipulation. *I thought it was my fault for denying him what he wanted.* She fought the memories and focused on how Nicky had helped build her up. *How can I trust my judgement when it comes to men? I was wrong before, why not again?*

Aidan turned Sophia to face him, and they lay on their sides, holding each other close under the duvet. Sophia shivered under the intensity of his gaze. Was it reckless to crave his touch as much as she did already? He leaned closer and kissed her tears away.

*****

Aidan's kissed feathered her skin. *No wonder she pulled away from getting close to me.*

"I would never want to hurt you. I'm not like Graham, and I won't push you. I know I've said it before, but you need to hear it again after that story. If it's ever too much tell me to stop. I'll always wait for consent, but I want you to be part of what we're doing, not observing. I want to support you no matter what," Aidan whispered. He knew what he was promising. He was the guy who refused long term, but he meant what he said. He'd work out the details later. *Sophia needs to know who she is and what she wants. Am I thinking this because I'm horny or because I know I'm damaged by my past?*

The first hints of a Sophia smile appeared. Joy jolted

inside him, extinguishing the anxiety from her story.

"I want this. I don't want to be an observer. But I'm still a little scared," she responded. Her eyes held him captive, glossy from the tears that had now subsided.

Somehow, she was more beautiful now that he knew more about her. The need to capture the moment tore at his insides, but soon it would run, like sand, through his hands as he tried to grip it, especially if she learnt the truth about him.

"Then what do you want me to do, Soph? What do you need from me?"

A tightness gripped him as he waited for her to speak. It was as if she held a wire that bound his heart, and with every moment that words stuck in her mouth, she pulled it tighter. She had the power to rip him in two. If she wanted him to go, he would, although the agony of losing this moment with her would be like losing a part of himself.

Sophia's soft lips parted, and the wire constricted his heart further. "I want you to make me come."

He froze.

"It's just..." She trembled. Languishing breaths caressed his face. "I don't want sex, that sort of sex, yet." Her hair fell in strands against her face, and the combination of fear and excitement crossed her features.

He cocked his head to one side. She was still a mystery to him. Waiting, struggling with his patience, he ached for her to be confident enough to speak her desires. He'd been rock hard since her supple lips had uttered, "make me come". But, still, he waited.

"And well..." The pause had him teetering on edge. "No one has ever made me come before; it's only been via my own hands and toys."

His shock was blistering. "How long were you with Graham?"

"Less than a year."

"And he never made you come?" Aidan's disbelief was palpable. "There is more to sex than penetration. What about other stuff? What about when he went down on you?"

"He never did. Everything between us was about him. He told me that the problem must be me. I presumed he was right."

The softness of her reply and the pain behind her words made him want to take Graham down, but it was Sophia that needed his attention.

"And with other guys, since Graham?" He'd guessed her answer before she spoke.

"There haven't been any other guys. Being on my own was kind of easier." Over the last half hour, Sophia had given him a lot of information to take in. Processing it would take him time, but yet it was the way she said her final sentence that threw him off balance. "I guess it's obvious. I'm a virgin."

CHAPTER TWELVE

Sophia waited. Relief washed over her. The battle was in saying it; accepting her needs and sharing them with someone who held her hopes in his hands. *Do I look at him? Why isn't he saying anything?* Relief disappeared, replaced by a new fear.

I've said too much. Aidan didn't speak, not a word. Her head dropped. *What must he think of me?* She'd never shared her past with anyone before, and only Nicky came close to knowing it all. *I should ask him to leave. I'm best off alone.*

His arms tugged at her so that she was on her back. The power of his lips against hers wrenched the words from her mouth. Aidan's kiss was that of a ravenous animal. Her thin layer of lace was a sensual torment against her skin as he ground against her. Aidan's tongue penetrated her mouth. Flares of desire combusted inside her.

She exhaled a soft moan. In an expression of surrender, she closed her eyes and moved her hands up and next to her head. The back of her hands rested against the pillow where he intertwined his fingers with hers. The intimacy of the act shocked her but didn't make her any less aroused. She wanted the satisfaction that wouldn't come from grinding alone. Desperately she pushed her pelvis up to meet his.

The strokes of his tongue against hers became longer and deeper. Scared of what she'd find on his face, Sophia opened her eyes slowly.

His eyes had transformed into a deep dark blue, like clouds over an ocean the second before a wild storm shatters the atmosphere. Raindrops were thundering down before being swallowed by the waves.

He lifted his head. "And you're sure you want it to be me? Because I'd be the luckiest guy in the world to watch you come for the first time," he said, a grin on his face.

"Yes, please you," she replied breathlessly.

Aidan growled her name. "Good. And do you know what? I'm going to make you come harder than you thought possible. Your toys will be obsolete after this, although I can think of a few things I'd like to do with them in the future."

"But what if I can't come?" she asked fearfully.

"Trust me, you will. The real question is how many times will you come?" he replied with a growl.

Before she dared disagree, his lips sucked and teased the sensitive skin of her neck. Aidan's hands still held hers, gripping and squeezing while his mouth brought her to thrilling heights. Their heartbeats thundered together.

His lips continued to move down her collar bone to the valley between her breasts, nipping and sucking. *I want more*. Sophia wrapped her legs around him. Her eyes closed, and she rubbed her body against his.

Thrusting her breasts forward, Sophia met his lips as his mouth enveloped her nipple. The way he nipped at it, lavishing it with attention, caused unexpected sensations of pain and pleasure to radiate through her. He twisted and tweaked her other bud between his thumb and finger.

Aidan continued to nibble down her body. Teeth grazed her stomach until his mouth hovered over her most sensitive area. His hot breath tickled her pussy lips through the fragile lace of her knickers.

"Fuck Soph, you're soaking wet. I'm going to enjoy tasting you," he said, voice low. She drove her hips up to meet his mouth, but Aidan had other plans. He travelled lower, brushing her inner thighs with his thumbs before sucking at the skin and grazing it with his teeth. Her moans turned to guttural cries.

His hands reached up to the waistband of her knickers. Sophia's stomach lurched with a nervous thrill when he pulled the lace down her legs before tossing the knickers to one side.

The sudden lick to her sex brought a jolt of pleasure deep inside her core. Aidan's tongue stretched widely, sweeping from the bottom of her lips up until it reached her clit.

"Oh God," she uttered breathlessly.

Aidan's movements stilled, his face consumed by his greedy smile.

"Watch me. I want you to see how much I'll love making you come." He devoured her. Desire scorched her body.

Pleasure surged through her as his mouth alternated between sucking her clit and thrusting his tongue deep inside her.

Sophia's moans rose, and she bucked her hips against his mouth. Every muscle in his tongue worked her with perfection. The scent of her juices filled the air, and lust burned. Aidan changed his technique with each lick to raise her loudest moans.

Her pleasure was his ultimate pleasure.

Every cry and whimper heralded her advancing orgasm.

Aidan pulled back and grinned at her. He was enjoying this as much as she was. It wasn't some painful sacrifice or selfish act; this was both of them together. Sex could be a mutual experience. Suddenly, Aidan gripped her arse and rammed his tongue deeper into her pussy before biting softly on her clit and pushing her over the edge.

Sophia's orgasm erupted, and the world exploded in her head. It was as he'd pumped a thousand volts of electricity into her body at once. Everything shook, and her cheeks burnt with fire.

"Yes," she screamed. Her skin was suddenly so sensitive that even a whisper of air across her form brought pleasure and pain together. He wasn't just inside her body; he was inside her head. Lighting crackled through her brain, and her emotions went off the charts. Did she want to cry, laugh or bask in the warmth exploding from her belly and flowing around her veins? It was the most powerful orgasm she'd experienced. Aidan held her tightly as it washed over her.

Continuing to suckle her clit and lick her sex brought aftershocks. His hands rubbed against her thighs as the high of the orgasm faded. Sophia's breathing transformed from shallow pants to deeper and longer breaths.

Unexpectedly, his mouth was against hers, kissing her softly. Aidan's grin was unmistakable against her lips. The taste of her juices was new, but not unpleasant.

"Well done," he whispered against her lips.

"Shouldn't I be saying that?" Sophia uttered between slowing breaths. "Thank you."

"You can thank me when I've finished."

Before she could consider what he meant, he pressed his thumb against her clit. She craved him again. Giving in to her impulses, she rotated her hips and moved against his thumb.

"That's right, honey. Let your orgasm take you. Don't hold back. You've needed this for too long. When you say yes I'm going to put my fingers inside you."

Sophia moaned a yes, but he knocked the words out of her head when he thrust one then two fingers deep inside her. Her whimpers were loud and needy as he continued to move his digits inside her. They penetrated her faster and faster as his thumb endured against her sensitive nub.

"That's right. Let go." His teeth nibbled at the flesh of her ear, and his hand worked her body with skill.

He pumped a third finger inside her and her pussy clamped hard onto him as he grazed her G-spot.

Aidan had her climaxing before she could contemplate her building orgasm. Overwhelming bliss turned her body into a writhing spectacle. The warmth from her first orgasm turned into a ball of fire that filled every limb. She lifted her body, demanding his lips on her, desperate to share the intensity of the moment. Satiation coursed through her and after being rigid for so long, she collapsed. Aidan smothered her body with wide-grinned kisses while she shook around his hand. Slowly her body unclenched, her climax edging away.

"Fucking hell," she said breathlessly, tingling as his kisses rained down on her.

"So wet, so sexy." He growled.

Aidan moved to touch her again, but she took his hand and kissed it softly instead, sucking the wetness of her climax from his fingers. His eyes were wide, and his pupils dilated.

"You are incredible," she whispered. Joy flooded her body when he smiled back. "But no more, my body can't take it tonight. I think you've ruined me."

Affectionately, he wrapped them both in the duvet. Pulling her closer while continuing to kiss her softly, he replied, "Then sleep, Bambi eyes. We'll have plenty more time for you to orgasm like that in the future. I was lucky to have experienced it."

Tenderly she brushed her fingers against his cheek. Exhaustion crept up on her.

"But surely you need to come too?" The hard kiss, combined with the delicate stroking of her hair brought more smiles.

"Tonight was about you, Soph. Don't get me wrong I'm harder than concrete watching you orgasm like that. God, I want to rip my clothes off and fuck you until I forget everything I've ever known. But let's sleep tonight."

A smile played on her lips. "Okay, but this isn't over. I'll make you come, too."

"I don't doubt that." Cuddling up to her, he held her gently.

Drifting into sleep, she caught Aidan's words. "I really should take you on a date. I'm an arse sometimes. I've got no sense of romance."

Too close to sleep to reply, a wry smile rested on her lips, and she fell quickly into a satisfied slumber.

HEAD OVER FEELS

✶ ✶ ✶ ✶ ✶

The next morning, as the sun came up, Aidan sat at the kitchen table, hands wrapped around a mug of tea. He rubbed the tip of his tongue around the inside of his mouth. *I can still taste her.* His erection shuddered in his tight boxers.

Sophia, her body creamy white in her most intimate places, had been asleep next to him. Her curves had cried out for his hands and lips while her chest had risen with every breath. His twitching cock had willed him to wake her and make her virginity a thing of the past.

But Sophia deserved more than a quick fuck. She needed every nugget of pleasure drawn out and gratified. He wanted her in control of her pleasure, not have it provided like a meaningless token or ignored as her ex had.

Aidan's anger about her past hadn't dissipated. How could anyone treat her like that?

Being the first person to take Sophia to orgasm had been a privilege but witnessing her fulfil her basic wants and desires was mind-blowing. He'd woken just as hard and throbbing as he'd gone to bed. Desperately, he tried to focus on anything but the naked woman in her bed that he was developing feelings for. The tea scalded his mouth, but he continued to force it down, attempting to dull other sensations.

She reached the parts of him that he'd kept hidden for so long. Being vulnerable with his emotions was new, but she brought that out of him. Could he trust her? What if she learnt about his possible illness?

Swirls of steam rose from his tea, turning into images of their possible future. *I'll hurt her, however hard I try not to.* Fingers still tingled from the memory of touching her. His cock jolted for the umpteenth time that morning as he remembered her grinding against him.

Was it already too late to walk away?

An indecipherable sigh startled him from his musings. Sophia watched him, framed by the kitchen doorway and barely covered by a large, blue t-shirt.

"Morning, honey, been staring at me long?" He meant it light-heartedly, but she didn't smile.

"I wondered where you were. I thought you might have left." She shuffled from one foot to another.

Aidan's gaze swept slowly down her body. The hem of her baggy t-shirt rested casually against her thighs. Was she wearing any underwear? His dick lurched.

"I was thirsty, and I didn't want to wake you." Nervously, she nibbled on her lower lip. If only she knew what that did to him. "Please come here, Sophia."

He didn't mean for his request to sound like a command, but his focus was hazy, only fixed on his desire for her to blossom. Tentatively, she stepped closer, her movements unsure and skittish. With other women, this behaviour would have aggravated his patience, he hated to be manipulated, but Sophia's fears were real. Aidan wanted to kiss them away until she was glowing like she had when he'd kissed her tears away.

"Talk to me. What's going on in your head?" he asked.

"Nothing." Her attempt at nonchalance wasn't working. Freezing awkwardly in mid-stride, she looked towards the countertop, desperately diverting her eyes from his gaze as if she was hiding something. The kitchen's creaks held her attention, and the echoing rumbles from the boiler allegedly fascinated her. "Can I get you some breakfast?"

"Sophia." It was a soft warning tone. They were both aware that he wasn't going to let things lie. "What are you thinking?"

The responding sigh made him anxious, prickling his insides as the familiar wire tore at his heart. *Maybe she doesn't want you here.* Had he said something stupid or revealing in his sleep?

Sophia's eyes dropped to the floor, unable to meet his scrutiny. She rubbed and wrung her hands together.

Aidan waited.

Seeds of doubt about her feelings grew, and with every second of silence, his confidence was washed away.

"I wasn't sure if you'd regret last night or maybe think I had expectations because of what I told you or..." She paused as if the storm of fear was building to a hurricane inside of her. "Maybe you wouldn't want me as I'm... inexperienced."

Standing quickly, his wooden chair hit the floor noisily. Her gaze shot up from the floor tiling and fixed on him.

"Look at me. Look at my body," he said.

Sophia scanned down his form. "When did you take your jeans off?"

That wasn't what he was referring to. "In the middle of the night."

The memory of how she'd looked lying next to him clouded his thoughts. His straining erection from watching her sleep, her wavy hair resting upon her breasts, had been agony in the tightness of his jeans. Jeans gone, she'd curled up into his near-naked body. He'd missed having a woman sleeping peacefully in his arms. Although no woman had brought him joy like Sophia had when she snuggled against him.

Watching her eyes dip below his waistband and stop at his now obvious erection had his cock twitching and her face flushing red. Impossibly, her spying eyes widened further. A charge of heat and excitement replaced the awkwardness in the room. It resembled the buzz of a music festival, deep in the night, the music sultry and people pushing against each other's bodies as they moved to the sounds enveloping them.

Sophia sucked the whole of her bottom lip into her mouth. The tiniest finger of restraint holding him together crumbled.

His thighs rippled as he strode towards her. He was like a tempest ready to encompass every part of her into his storm. Aidan picked her up; his hands clenched her hips tightly. Lust controlled him, surging when her naked legs wrapped around him. He perched her on the kitchen table; his desires were savage, ripping him apart.

Her legs gripped him tighter, and her ankles pulled his body into her. *I'll never get her out of my system.* Sex with Sophia would be life-changing and only serve to make him greedy for more. Aidan was heading down a path to destruction, but he didn't care. He was choosing to sprint down it with his eyes open, immersing himself in the certainty of danger and relishing every moment.

As she trembled against him, his lips met hers, nipping at her. Aidan hoped his jawline gave her a scratch, leaving his mark for all to see.

"Do you feel that?" Aidan's swelling erection pressed hard against her.

"Yes," she replied with a yearning whimper.

"Do you realise how much I want you?"

"I'm not entirely sure," she teased, enjoying her effect on him. It was a level of control she'd probably never encountered let alone harnessed.

With one hand he gripped her naked thigh, holding it against his hip as his other hand cupped her back under the t-shirt. There were no knickers in the way this time. She clasped at his shoulders as if she was hanging on for dear life. *We both are.*

"Do you realise now?" he asked, sliding forward to cup her breast that was still hidden from his view. Flicking the pebble-like nipple was just the start of his plans. The wetness from her lips soaked through his boxers. He would sell his soul to take her on the kitchen table.

"Yes, and I want you too. I've never wanted anyone like this," Sophia uttered between kisses. "I want to have sex with you. I want you inside me."

Groaning in anguish, he contemplated fucking her right there. There was still the opportunity to make it satisfying for her, giving her what she needed and what she'd asked. Lifting her t-shirt, Aidan was mesmerised by the roundness of her breasts; they seem to cry out for his mouth.

A key scratching against the lock of the front door brought them smacking down to earth. Quickly, he lifted Sophia off the table while she yanked her t-shirt down. She stood in front of him. He wondered if it was to hide his obvious erection. They didn't need everyone to know what they'd been doing. Nicky entered the kitchen in her nurse's uniform. Unfortunately, his cock hadn't got the news that playtime was over; it swelled, fighting to press hard against Sophia.

Nicky stopped, stared, and then burst into laughter.

"And here I thought I'd seen enough nakedness today at work! Morning, guys. I trust you're both well?" she asked amused.

"Yes, thanks." Sophia grabbed Aidan's arms and wrapped them around her like she was proudly wearing him. "How about you?"

"Not bad. Not as happy as you two. You're grinning like I've caught you getting hot and heavy on the kitchen table." As one, they glanced at the table. The earlier action had pushed Aidan's cup to the edge and pages of a newspaper fluttered to the floor.

Aidan's laugh surprised him.

Sophia turned sheepishly. He couldn't resist giving her a quick peck on the lips.

"Shouldn't you be leaving for work right now? It's nearly eight," Nicky asked.

"Shit! I need a shower," Sophia said, dashing from the room and dragging him behind her.

"Me too!" he hollered. *We'll have a lot of fun in the shower.*

"Don't even think about it. I need to get to work." Depositing him in her room, he caught her suggestive smile as she bounded towards the shower without him.

He sighed, his erection painful and slowly fading, but his grin remained. *She's got me right where she wants me, and I can't go back to being the guy I was before I met her. But I'm not ready to share my secret with her either.* How much longer could he keep everything from her?

Chapter Thirteen

Sophia bounced towards the meeting place for her date with Aidan. The day had dragged until Tasha had let her go early. Tasha had been busy regaling the office with stories of her photoshoot with the rugby players.

Sophia reread Aidan's message, looking for clues on what their date might entail.

A: *Meet me outside the fast food place at 3.15. Bring your fighting spirit and your sexy bum. I'll bring the rest x*

There were no hints of his plans, not even a suggestion of what to wear. She'd dragged her skinny jeans from her bedroom floor and shoved them on before they'd dashed from her place that morning.

Sophia looked up at the bright yellow and red of the fast-food joint. *Is he going to take me to a drive-through for dinner?* Although it didn't scream romantic first date she wasn't bothered, she'd go anywhere with him. Their previous night's exploits had her considering the possibilities of his promises.

Was she being rash and falling too quickly for him? She'd offered her body and mind to him that morning. If it hadn't been for Nicky, she'd have lost her virginity on the kitchen table. The smell of the mouldy kitchen tried to stink up her memories. Her mum's lecture from

Sophia's teenage years still stung. "Your virginity is a precious jewel that only a prince deserves". Would she live to regret her decisions, like her mum had regretted her past?

"If you spend too much time thinking you're going to implode." Aidan's voice in her ear had her crotch tingling with excitement.

Even though he was behind her, she melted. *I need to embrace it*. If she got hurt because of whatever it was between them, then at least she was living. It was time to grab the bull by the horns and ride by the seat of her pants, or maybe ditch the pants altogether.

"Are you going to turn around or are we going to spend the rest of the date like this?" A lone finger ran in circles against the nape of her neck. Shivers skipped up and down her spine. The last morsel of fear that taunted her about his game playing was difficult to ignore, but she batted it away. "I'm sure I can still make the date work, but I'd prefer to see your face."

Sophia spun around before pecking him on the lips. He pulled her close and pressed his mouth back to hers. The kiss had her tottering on the heels of her boots as she melted into it.

"That's much better. I am a hard-working rugby player, and a peck is never enough." Grabbing her hand, he wrapped it in his. "Let the date commence!"

His announcement had her giggling with excitement. Even if it were a meal in a fast-food restaurant, he'd make it fun.

"Don't you want to know where we're going?" he asked.

"Would you tell me if I asked?"

His deep chuckle told her he wouldn't. His hand

slipped from hers, but before she could protest, he ducked behind her and covered her eyes like he was executing one of his rugby moves.

"Do you trust me?" he whispered in her ear, reminding her of their previous night.

"Yes," she was breathless. Senses heightened at the loss of her sight and the combination of fear and excitement. The breeze ruffled her fringe. Slowly he guided her. Traffic noise blasted close by. "You're not taking me to a sex dungeon, are you?" It was an attempt at humour, but panic threaded through her voice.

"That's more of a second date activity," he joked, easing her forward, his hands still over her eyes. Occasionally, someone would pass close by, and she'd have to ignore the impulse to flinch away. Aromas of burgers and curries surrounded them. "Besides, we're not going to talk about sex. This date is about romance."

Suddenly he stopped, and his body pressed against hers. They may not be talking about sex, but their bodies were primed for it.

"Right, open your eyes!"

They flickered open and strained against the sunlight. Surely Aidan hadn't chosen this place?

"Seriously? This is romance?"

"It's romance Aidan Flynn style." The smile ate at his words as laughter escaped her lips. *He's too tempting.*

"The outfits aren't sexy."

"I never promised a sexy date. Besides, if I'm going to romance you, I need to see you as more than a gorgeous body with the power to make me as hard as a rock." Aidan flicked his tongue behind her earlobe. Her legs buckled. "Which I am nearing already, I've been watching those jeans tight against your bum."

Sophia turned, surprised he'd noticed. One of his hands grabbed hers and held it firmly while the other slapped her bottom.

"Now, come on. I've got a different sort of ass-whooping to do," Aidan hollered, walking her up the concrete steps towards the go-karting track.

*****

Aidan revelled in the warmth of Sophia's body resting against his as they lay on the picnic blanket on a local hill several hours later. *Have I ever been this happy?*

He'd worried that the karting was a stupid idea, but he'd trusted it was something they could laugh about, hoping Sophia's competitive streak would eclipse her nerves. At best, he thought he'd be lapping her several times while she rolled her eyes. His rugby coach had blasted him before about his 'cocky arsehole' behaviour. Sophia, however, was more than an opponent.

She'd hurtled around the track like a speed demon; challenging him like a warrior in an epic battle, diving into his path and refusing to surrender. Sensing her behind him, he'd readied himself to wave smugly before speeding away, but instead of pleasantries, she'd attempted to force her way past. His shock was nothing compared to the way she'd challenged him. He'd swung the kart to the left and then tugged the wheel, so he veered right to stop her. The rush that came with trying to halt her crusade had been intense. With every acceleration, she was tenacious and threatened to ram him if he didn't get out the way.

Eventually, she'd played him like a fool, pretending to submit by falling back before cutting around him on a corner. Sophia's aggressive overtaking had forced him to brake hard at the risk of smashing into her.

He should have been annoyed, especially at the laugh and coquettish wave she gave when she sped off, but it only served in adding to his fantasies. He wanted to pull her from the kart, push her against the brick wall and rip her driving suit from her body. He'd give anything to hear her scream his name in ecstasy.

The date was supposed to be about romance, but his cock hadn't got the message, preferring to stand to attention for the last couple of hours.

Aidan rubbed his hand in circles against her arse, enjoying the way she trembled against his fingers. "You're cold. We should head off."

"No." Sophia's contented voice carried on the breeze. "I'm fine. I want to see the sunset."

She wore one of his thick rugby hoodies. Watching her bring the collar to her nose and breathe in his smell made him smile so much his face ached.

"It shouldn't be much longer."

"I'm happy." She sighed and smiled. "This evening has been amazing. I feel lucky."

Aidan's heart swelled.

"Are there any chocolate brownies left?" she asked, spying the remnants of their picnic.

"I'm afraid you ate the last one, but if you open your mouth, I'll fill it with another gooey surprise."

"I doubt it would be much of a surprise," she joked with a swipe to his chest before lifting her head and presenting her lips to him.

Who am I to deny her? He kissed her lips, dipping his tongue between them.

Sophia's leg slid across his body so that she was

straddling his crotch. Slowly she rubbed against him.

"Soph," he groaned into her mouth, "this is supposed to be a romantic date."

"It is," she replied, planting kisses against his stubbled chin. "And the romance is making me horny. Very, very, horny."

He rested his hands against her thighs, encouraging her arousal as she rubbed harder against him. Sophia's mouth brushed along his jawbone and to his ear. Her lips wrapped around his earlobe and her teeth softly took hold of it and pulled. She sucked it gently before it jumped out of her mouth with a *pop* sound.

"Do you like that Aidan?" she asked flirtatiously, blowing cool air against the ear that she'd already moistened. A tingle ran from his brain to his dick. Witnessing her new-found confidence was a turn on. "The wetness of your ear is nothing compared to how wet I am right now."

Aidan's self-control snapped.

Grabbing her bottom and bolting upwards, he sat her up cowboy style. Everything ached; his gut, his cock and his heart most of all. *I want every part of her*. He'd got used to the constant longing, but her tease and touch ramped up his need of her. Pulling her against him, he fiercely pressed his lips to hers and kissed her hard. They had too many clothes on, and this wasn't the time or the place to be stripping. Golfers were crossing the green of the hill behind them. There was the occasional sweep of a golf club before the knocking sound came as it hit a ball.

Her arms wrapped tightly around his neck as if letting go would damage the bond they were developing.

"Soph." He spoke between heavy kisses, his fingers

pushing the hoody away from her neck and caressing her skin with his mouth. "You're very naughty. We're meant to be watching the sunset."

Slowly, she relaxed, and her arms eased their hold on him.

"Sorry." Pecking at the sheepish smile on her lips brought a glow to his stomach. "I can't seem to leave you alone."

"Me neither. I've been craving you all day."

They lay back down against the blanket. Aidan's cradled her before resuming the sweeping movements over her bottom. The scent of her perfume with notes of jasmine and vanilla filled the air as she snuggled up close. "Why did you pick this hill for our picnic date?"

As they stared into the golden glow washing across the sky, the sun began its descent. The orange was trying to dominate the azure blue that had held its place throughout the day. Darkness was coming. The clouds glowed with a rosy hue before reddening further as if they were blazing with fire. Throughout all the vibrancy above, there was a stillness, a beauty that lit his eyes and made it impossible to turn away.

"I love this place," he finally said. "I used to come here as a teenager when mum and I moved to England. I would bomb up the road to the hill on my bike. It had a chain that always threatened to yank off and send me flying, but I wanted space to run without anything holding me down. I think it was helpful for mum to have me out of the house, especially as I had more energy than I knew what to do with."

"How old were you when you moved here?"

"Eleven, just in time to start secondary school."

"Why did you move?" It was a simple question, but

the answers would be laden with revelations. There was too much to tell. Grains of honesty hid behind his tongue, allowing him to share some of his stories.

"Mum wanted to be with her family, and we didn't have anyone in Ireland. Her sister lived near here."

"And you would run?"

"As often as I could."

"What were you running from?" She meant when he was on the hill, but they had run from Ireland too. Sophia would leave him if she learnt the truth about his illness, and even if she didn't, he'd force her to go.

"My struggles at school, mostly. I was a poor kid with a weird accent. No one wants to stand out and be different at that age."

"What did they do to you?"

"The usual stuff; taunt me, hound me when I hid in classrooms, laugh at me, or ignore me. They'd walk into me and push me. They wanted me to react so that I'd get in trouble. I was a strong kid, but I couldn't handle it. I couldn't tell mum what was going on. She had enough to deal with. She worked all the hours of the day, taking on various jobs to keep us going." *To keep her from thinking about dad and my future*, he wanted to add, but that was a truth he wouldn't share.

Sophia hugged him closer. No woman, apart from his mum, had listened to him like this before.

"If I came up here to run, then I was less likely to beat the other kids. And I was free. I didn't have to worry about anyone. But then there came the time when the running wasn't enough."

"What happened?"

"The problems and fights at school had escalated. No one knew what to do with me. Mum was exhausted.

Then one day I met John, and my life changed. He was playing golf with one of my teachers. He saw me running night after night and managed to jump in front of me. At the time he said that nothing else was going to make me stop. We chatted, he was genuinely interested in what I had to say. No one had given a shit about me before. He told me about rugby, and I asked him to show me some of the kicks."

"John invited me to a weekly youth rugby team that he coached. I'd train with them, push myself, do everything to improve my skills and learn some much-needed discipline. I earnt my place on the team." It was a deep smile that radiated through him. The day he was told he'd made the team was one of the best of his life. "For the first time, I belonged, and there was a group of lads that liked me. They didn't care how poor I was or about my accent; they liked me for me. I performed well on the pitch, and I was able to use my excess energy while developing skills that my body had been built for. But even that wasn't enough."

"How come?"

"Well, if I hadn't discovered art, I probably would have ended up in prison."

"In prison? Tell me everything," she demanded, brushing a kiss against his jaw.

"It might not have been a prison, but I wouldn't be the fine specimen of a man you see before you," he joked. The memories were painful, and it was a struggle to revisit them, but the encouragement from Sophia kept him talking. "The fighting got worse."

Sweeping his hand against Sophia, he felt the pull to hide his skin like he'd done so many times as a teenager, fearful his mum might see the cuts and purple marks.

Terror had lived inside him that his behaviour would push her over the edge. "I was sick of the bullying, and that's when John stepped in again."

Although his hand continued stroking her bum, his mind was back there reliving the suffering. Sophia snuggled closer, reminding him that she was there and listening. There was an encouragement to continue but no judgement if he didn't. *I haven't had support like this for a long time.* He wanted to hold on to her forever.

"John started taking me to art galleries. He saved me. He was a mentor I didn't know I needed." *And a father too*, he added silently. "I'd moved to England angry against the world, and then things got worse. Discovering this gift for art and then having it encouraged changed my life.

"Once a week I'd bunk off school and get the train to London for the day, having to hide from the guard in the toilets because I didn't have any money for a ticket." He chucked, but it was a laugh bereft of soul. "In London, I'd sit in galleries for hours and admire greatness beyond the realms of my understanding. Did you know there is a painter called Caravaggio? He had this reputation for fights and drama. He killed a man and yet his paintings still leave people mesmerised. And there is another painter called Paul Nash. This one painting, *Landscape from a Dream*, it's inspired some of my work."

"Tell me more. I love hearing your passion," Sophia replied, the warmth of her body against his.

Aidan struggled to smile as he talked about other painters and paintings that had fascinated him on his travels. He didn't cherish all the memories; some were infused with pain and loss. That Sophia might want to delve further wasn't lost on him. She was the kind of person who unpacked the things she heard, processed them and went where other minds didn't.

Aidan didn't want to lie to her anymore. *But how do I form the right words?* He'd held on to his story for so long. He looked up, and the sunset stole his breath.

"It's amazing," she whispered, sitting up and looking to where his gaze was fixed. Together they watched the sun fall towards the town at the bottom of the hill. It was a town where ordinary people lived, probably unaware of the spectacle emblazoned above them. Sitting behind her, he nestled Sophia between his legs and wrapped his arms around her body. His earlier revelations unsettled him and left him empty. Sorrow rippled through him, corroding him from the inside. He pulled Sophia closer to him. *I need to know I'm not alone.*

The sky was bathed in orange. It was as if a sheet of gauze covered the expanse above them. *I'll never be able to recreate this moment.* He held Sophia tight, hoping sheer will might keep the sun from dropping. *I don't want this to end. I can't say goodbye to her.*

But hopes and dreams were not enough to keep the rosy glow above them. The sun disappeared, and the chill clawed at his bones, joining with his sadness from retelling his story. Sophia was the warmth he needed, and he didn't want to take her home yet.

"Aidan?" Sophia whispered.

The sound of his name on her lips was already something he loved. He breathed his reply while hugging her close, "Yes?"

"Can we go to your house?"

Her nervous swallow and trembling made it clear

that it wasn't a throwaway question but laden with intentions.

"If we go back to mine, I can't promise to stay away from you. Don't get me wrong, I'm not going to force myself on you, but I can't get enough of you."

"Good because I don't want you to stay away from me." Her hand slid back between their bodies. Gently she rubbed his hardening dick. "I want this."

It was his turn to swallow noisily. Aidan considered picking her up and sprinting down the hill with the enthusiasm of a teenage boy, but he was a man and had to make this special. Based on what she'd told him the previous night, she had to be terrified. It made her confident handling of him even more alluring.

"Okay," he responded awkwardly.

They drove to his house in silence. Darkness settled around them as his four by four rambled through the countryside. The celestial colours of the sky had gone, and the night obscured Sophia's face, her thoughts shrouded from him

The clock had barely struck seven when Aidan parked the car in the driveway. They sat in the stillness. The hairs on his arms rose. It was as if it was going to be his first time, not hers. Fear of ruining the moment prickled his nerves as pressure laid heavily on his chest.

"Aidan?"

He couldn't look at her. She wanted an experienced man, not a timid useless creature. "Yes?"

"Are we going into your house? If you don't want to sleep with me, it's okay." Sophia's voice betrayed her truth. In the solitude of the moment, she proclaimed her fears. "I've had a lovely day. Whatever happens, I'm happy."

Sparks of electricity somersaulted through him. He jumped out the car, slowly walked round to her door and pulled it open. She was beautiful. He couldn't help but stare.

Sophia's dark brows came close to touching as if she was questioning him. He held out his hand, and she entwined hers with it before sliding off the seat, her feet crunching on the gravel.

They headed to his front door; Aidan's palms sweaty against her trembling hands. *How can I help us both relax?* Tonight, in the next couple of hours, she might lose her virginity. He wasn't an overthinker, but the responsibility settled on his shoulders. *I need to make this good for her.*

"Please say something," she said meekly.

"I was thinking… would you make good on your promise this evening?" There was a strain in his throat as he spoke.

"Which promise?" Caution crowded her words.

"Would you pose for me?"

Chapter Fourteen

Sophia tiptoed from the bathroom, cocooned in the towel Aidan had left for her, the carpet soft against her bare feet.

Thank goodness she had sexy underwear on. It made posing for Aidan all the more exciting. It was a satin set with a white lace frill. She'd saved the set for a special event, but the occasion never arose. Instead, it had remained pristine and untouched in a drawer. This morning it had sprung out at her. It begged for attention after being overlooked so many times.

"I'm in here," Aidan called out to her from a room off the main corridor. At the growl, she trembled.

She knew what posing for him might lead to. Anticipation crept up her body. *Can I go through with this? I want him, but...* The word hung in her mind. *I'm scared.*

Sophia pushed through the wooden door into an art studio. The smell of oil paint hit her immediately. Paintings cluttered the edges of the room, pressed up against every wall. Two easels sat facing the long expanse of glass. It was the windows to what she presumed was the garden. Looking out she couldn't see anything of the world outside; it had been swallowed by night. It was only the two of them now.

Torn and tattered scraps of paper hid the top of one table. Pots, brushes and a wide array of paints covered another. The wood was splattered as if small children had got hold of brushes caked in paint and run wild across the table's surface. This had to be his sanctuary, where he was free and yet in control.

A sofa in the centre of the room caught her eye. An easel had been set up in front of it. Ready and waiting, Aidan examined her from a paint splashed stool.

Sophia's heart fluttered when he stood. A scruffy grey t-shirt covered Aidan's chest, but she remembered the muscles she'd find beneath. Baggy jeans hung low on his hips, and his feet were bare against the unpolished wooden floor. They stared at each other. Her heart stopped. The charge of electricity between them jabbed at her goose pimples. Her gaze swept to the navy sofa once more.

"I thought maybe you'd like to pose on it," he offered cautiously. "Is that okay?"

"Yep." As she walked towards it, lust pricked her skin. She licked her lips. Aidan stepped a little closer, the air heavy with anticipation.

"Shall I take the towel off now? I'm not naked," she added quickly as a disclaimer.

He rubbed the backs of his knuckles against his jaw, and she longed for his fingers to stroke her inner thighs. The heat in his eyes was like crackling flames licking at her towel and trying to burn it off her semi-naked body.

"Please take the towel off." The depth of his Irish accent combined with blue eyes that refused to leave her form. Her crotch pulsated. "I'm sure whatever is under the towel is... fine."

The towel that she'd clenched so tightly slipped

from her trembling fingers. Sliding down her body, it brushed against her flesh until it reached the ground. Time froze, and his gaze followed the trail of the towel. It was as if she was bearing her fears and her skin to him.

Aidan stood still, his eyes branding her with heat. Hers settled on his crotch, which swelled and twitched before her.

"What do you think?" Sophia asked. It was the first time in her adult life that she hadn't been ashamed of her body.

Slow, purpose-filled steps brought him closer. His hands brushed across her arms, caressing them slowly, up and down. Sophia's legs trembled.

"You're beautiful," he whispered.

"Aren't you meant to be posing me?" she teased.

"I don't want to paint you, not right now." His fingers against her arms made her entire body quiver. "I want to show you something." Aidan's emphasis on 'something' made her stomach lurch with excitement.

Smiling, she offered him a challenge. "Go on then. I dare you."

Lips dove to hers. Aidan kissed her like a hungry man who'd survived on bland morsels for too long and had finally tasted the sumptuous banquet he'd longed for. The confidence that had radiated through her since she'd overtaken him at karting exploded into a force that flooded her body.

Their mouths met hard and fast. Tongues entwined, and Sophia's hands roamed under his t-shirt before she lightly scraped her nails down his back. He pulled her closer, deepening the kiss. Aidan's tongue explored her mouth with the passion she'd craved since their first meeting.

Sophia gripped the back of his t-shirt and yanked it off. Recklessness met with lust and captured her completely.

Instead of returning to her mouth, his lips touched her throat and suckled against her pulse point.

"Aidan," she cried out in pleasure. Her fingertips raked over his scalp as he kissed her collarbone.

Lifting his head, she forcibly kissed him on the mouth. Lack of experience limited her actions, and her frustration bubbled. As if sensing her unease, he directed her to the sofa, while they kissed.

Shifting as if to sit, she held on to him.

"Your jeans." Words were wrestled from her mouth. Arousal consumed her.

Greedily she flicked open his top button. Her nails tore at the remaining two buttons before shoving the waistband down and dragging his jeans to the floor. Gasping loudly, she stared at how hard he was.

"You were commando."

"Yes." He grunted, his basic needs revealed in one noise.

"Can I touch it?"

His face was pained, but he nodded.

Sophia pushed him to sit down on the sofa. The thick erection that had brought pleasure to her clit and enraptured her imagination continued to captivate her, and she knelt between his legs.

As if she was under a spell, Sophia stretched a fingertip towards the seven inches in front of her. Rubbing her digit roughly around the tip, pre-cum spilt out and coated her skin. It lubricated both of them with every flick. His shaft twitched against her.

Aidan grimaced, declaring, "Oh God, Soph, I want

you so much."

I've never known power like this.

She playfully popped her coated digit in her mouth. Their eyes locked on each other, and she sucked hard. At the agony across Aidan's face and the jump of his cock, she sucked harder. Swirling her tongue around her finger, she continued to fix her dark eyes on Aidan's. She'd never enjoyed sucking Graham off, but the idea of taking Aidan in her mouth brought fervour to her movements. *I want to give him the pleasure he gives me. I want to see him come.* Leaning forward, she opened her mouth. Aidan reached for her, stopping her as her tongue teetered closer to the prize. Fear and confusion replaced her confident mood.

"I won't last much longer if you do that, and I desperately want to be inside you," Aidan growled.

Sophia gave her consent with a moaned, "Then do it now. Please."

Aidan tore her knickers down her legs before propping her on his lap. Yanking her bra straps down, he released her breasts to his mouth before massaging her bum cheeks and pulling her quickly against his erection. Sophia unclipped her bra and flung it across the room in wanton delight.

His firmness against her clit brought waves of desire, and she ground harder against him.

Each slow rub made his grin more fiendish. Moaning, Sophia rubbed her soaking sex back and forth across his swelled erection. Her body was ready for him.

Lust saturated the air.

He flicked her nipples with his tongue while his thumb found her clit. Without hesitation, he rubbed it skilfully, causing more moans to erupt.

With his last morsel of patience, he retrieved a condom from his jeans that lay on the floor. Ripping the foil between his teeth, he pulled the condom between his fingers before sliding the rubber down his shaft. Even the way he wrapped himself fascinated her.

Lying down, Sophia shamelessly opened her legs in wait, beckoning him closer with her smile. Privilege filled his face as he knelt between her thighs and examined the rise and fall of her body.

Aidan rubbed her with his erection. Arching her back, she thrust towards him.

"Are you sure about this, Soph?"

How can he think of me when he's like this? He was taut with hunger. Smiling back, she tried to communicate her certainty.

"Then tell me what you want me to do."

"I want you deep inside me. I want to make you come so hard that if I weren't screaming your name, you'd forget it," she said, now familiar with his need to have her as an equal partner in their experiences.

Without a breath, Aidan pushed his cock inch after inch inside of her. Wincing slightly, she smiled at him, encouraging him to continue.

"You'll tell me if you're in pain," he requested.

She nodded, and he continued to fill her. She'd expected pain, although her hymen was long gone, but it was more like a new sensation, uncomfortable at first. *I can't let him stop. I need this, and I want this.* Sophia fought the need to push him away or shift to rid herself of the temporary pain, focusing instead on the bursts of arousal that continued inside her.

"I'll wait for your body to adjust," he said. Carefully he watched, holding himself still inside her. His face softened as he stared at her.

"Keep going," she whispered, and he filled her with his length, stretching her and bringing fresh satisfaction.

"I can't believe how tight you are," he exclaimed.

Sophia's moans drowned out his words. Aidan pulled back, and she wanted to cry in anguish at the loss, but before she could utter a noise, he thrust inside her again, quickly setting a slow, smooth rhythm.

"I need you to move with me, Soph."

Using the sofa to push herself up, she met every plunge he made with a drive of her body. A haze of arousal blinded her. His hard kiss surprised her.

Aidan bobbed, sucking her nipples and bringing her closer to the eagerly anticipated climax. Her craving for him surged with every thrust, and she scraped at his scalp with her nails.

"Don't stop," she pleaded between moans.

"I'm not going to. I want you to come with me inside you." The depths of his thrusts brought noises from her mouth that she'd never heard before.

Her urges pulled him tighter, digging her heels into him and speeding up the rhythm. Breaths were shallow as she gasped for air. Her vision spun.

"Let go. Stop thinking and let go," Aidan whispered.

They moved together as days of need were finally met. It hurt, but the pleasure smothered and swallowed the pain with each movement of their bodies.

"Rub your clit, it will help, and best of all, it will turn you on. You know your body better than me at the moment. I would love to watch you come, but it's okay if you don't. There's no pressure."

"There's lots of pressure," she managed to joke as

he reached for her hand and guided it down to her clit. She rubbed her swollen nub fervently, while Aidan kept up his rhythm, pushing into her repeatedly.

Having him inside her was taking her to the highest climax she'd encountered, but she needed something more.

"I'm getting closer," she screamed. "Keep talking; it's helping."

"Come on, honey. Come for me. You're beautiful." He thrust harder than she thought possible. Lust flooded her system. "You're incredible, Soph. I've never had anyone like you."

His voice silenced the part of her brain that fought to control her body. Somehow the combination of his words and her finger against her clit pushed her over the edge.

Her pussy walls clenched around him. Contractions took hold, bringing vigorous shakes and darkness teased her vision.

"Oh God. I'm coming." Her voice rose dramatically.

The mind-blowing climax released the days of culminating arousal. It transformed into a torrent of blissful energy that never seemed to end. Sophia couldn't breathe or think, so overwhelmed by the ecstasy ripping through her veins. Trying to savour every sensation until they swallowed her up, she basked in the passion thundering through her body.

Her orgasm pushed him over the edge until he shook inside her. His cock pulsed, it blew her mind that she felt that. His face was pure relief and ecstasy in one. Joy became a tornado of pleasure rotating around the core of her being.

Long satisfied grunts replaced words, and they held each other, allowing the intimacy of the moment to bring them closer.

Tenderly he kissed and stroked her still trembling form until her heart rate slowed. As she came down from their combining orgasms relief ran through her.

"That was amazing," he whispered, resting against her as he continued to caress her slowly. "And you came. Bloody hell did you come!"

Small surges of energy, remnants of their experience together, pulsated through her as they cuddled. He fluttered kisses to her lips. They held on to each other, as adrenaline fettered away, broad smiles covering their faces.

"I did, and you did too. I don't know what to say. Thank you sounds stupid, but I can't remember any other words."

Aidan smoothed a kiss against her forehead. *I can feel his smile.*

"You don't need to thank me. The night isn't over either. I'm going to carry you to my bed and make you come again. This time you'll come so hard you won't be able to remember any words, including thank you. Well, maybe you'll remember just one; I like hearing you say my name."

"Aidan, Aidan, Aidan," she said, sighing with contentment when he wrapped his arms around her, his kisses covering every part of her satiated body.

Chapter Fifteen

Sophia couldn't stop smiling as she dressed. The vanilla tones from Aidan's shower gel rose from her body. It reminded her of sex. His scent had carried through the air as he ground inside her. His bedroom was how she expected. Paintings and prints adorned the walls, and the deep berry colour of his bedspread made her want to dive back in and snuggle up to his smell.

Although Aidan hadn't been there when she woke his message and the glass of water had made up for it.

I've popped out to get some breakfast. I'll be back soon. Have a shower and come and find me in the kitchen. I'll take you to work this morning. I didn't want to wake you again.

Sophia blushed as she crept into the hallway. The first time he'd woken her, it had been because his head was between her legs. *I came so hard.*

Memories of Aidan were distracting. *Where was his kitchen again?* As she passed his art room, her curiosity piqued. She hadn't had the opportunity to investigate it thoroughly the night before. *We had other things on our mind.* Sex with Aidan was more than she could have hoped for. Her body ached, but it was an ache she wanted to get used to. *I've been missing out, but I'm glad he was my first.*

Slowly she stepped into the art room and took in the surroundings. Everything was how she remembered. The paintings caught her eye. Her bare feet slapped against the floor as she crossed the room and stared at each piece of art. There were outdoor scenes, landscapes similar to his painting at the art exhibition, and paintings of a busy town. *They're so bleak*. Each image, no matter the setting, was filled with darkness. Sadness and pain were everywhere. Anxiety gnawed at her.

Something else stood out too. In the paintings, there was a scarlet figure. It was always in the background, sometimes standing away from a crowd or alone in a field. They weren't always easy to see, but Sophia was intrigued when she found them.

What does it mean?

Her stomach was hollow. Was it fear of what the paintings meant or something else?

She shook herself. *It's hunger; stop being silly*.

But the unsettled feeling stayed with her as she walked towards the kitchen, locating the room by the sound of Aidan's voice.

"I can hear you loud and clear, doctor, but I have no symptoms. I'm not depressed, and I'm running the pitch and working out better than ever. There are no issues with my performance," he barked.

"You can make the same point until you're hoarse. I'm not taking the test, and that's my final word on it." Aidan tossed his phone on the countertop at the same time he saw her in the doorway.

She froze. *What do I say? I overheard by accident. I shouldn't have sneaked into his art room either*. Aidan hadn't said she couldn't, but then they hadn't talked since the previous night. Maybe he wouldn't want her to see the scarlet figure. He'd know she'd have questions.

And what was the phone call about? Why was he talking to a doctor? If she asked would he tell her?

"Oh, you're nearly ready to go," he said, faltering a little. "You look good."

"Thanks," she blushed, standing awkwardly in the doorway. It was like yesterday; only this was his house. *And I feel different after last night.*

"Come and get breakfast," he said with a forced smile on his face. "I went out and got croissants."

They sat at the wooden dining room table, side by side, in silence.

"What are you thinking, Soph?" he asked softly, startling her.

She turned, caught out. Her face burned. "Nothing."

"Sophia," he replied. His tone suggested he didn't believe her. He pulled her chair close enough for their knees to touch. "It will stress you out more if you don't say."

"I was thinking about last night." It wasn't the right time to mention the phone call. Besides, what if he accused her of snooping?

"Go on," he replied, holding her hands between his. Hers looked tiny in comparison.

"Last night was significant for me because it was my first time. But for you, well, you've probably slept with lots of women," she said nervously,

"Is this a conversation about my number of sexual partners?"

"God, no."

"Have you got regrets about what we did?"

"No." She froze. *I can't tell him how much I like*

him. Sex sealed it for me; I don't want to be a fling; I want to be significant to him. But everything she'd read about him suggested he wasn't the commitment type.

"Because I don't. Last night meant something to me." He let go of her hands and cupped her face, planting kisses on her lips between his sentences. "I like you, Soph. I really like you. I can't explain what last night meant because I'm still processing it. But, please believe me when I say that I want to keep seeing you. I want to continue making you come. And I can't stop thinking about spending time with you. In fact—"

"Yes." She kissed him harder, slipping her tongue between his lips. The kiss went from soothing to hot.

He was breathless when she pulled away. "Would you come to my away game on Friday and spend the weekend with me? I need to chat with my boss, the coach, because we have team rules about an away game. But if I can do it, I'd love to have you there. What do you think?"

Was he nervous? There was an unexpected vulnerability in his voice. It melted her worries away.

"Of course," she replied as her lips met his again and her tongue found his. They massaged each other quickly, unable to get enough of each other. Her hand gripped his neck, pulling him closer. She forgot work as his hand freed her hair from its hairband and it fell across her shoulders in waves. Aidan gripped it between his hands as they leaned in closer. He growled in her mouth.

Her mobile began to ring. It was "Ding-Dong the Witch is Dead" from The Wizard of Oz. The ringtone was personalised to Tasha. It was time to get to work.

Aidan flipped open the top button of her jeans, ignoring the phone. His hand slipped past her waistband.

"We haven't got time," she whispered against his lips as his fingers grazed her clit. She pushed his hand into her anyway. *Fuck, I want him again.*

"We're going to make time," he replied as he pushed a finger inside her.

"Thanks, everyone for coming to the session. We've got Josie here, and she's going to get creative with you, we've got lots of projects today, including a giant papier-mache sculpture! But remember you don't have to do anything you don't want to do," Sophia smiled at the children as she introduced Josie, the art therapist. Thursday evenings were usually drop-ins, but every so often they did something different. For some children, it was a break from their daily lives and a chance to find their safe space. For others, they expressed their grief through the things they created or used the activity to remember the person close to them who'd died.

Josie introduced the activities for the evening. She'd helped many people and Sophia always benefitted from her sessions too. Dressed in an indigo silk dress with a sunshine yellow dressing gown over the top Josie looked like she'd stepped off a rainbow. Her lime green loafers and paintbrushes in her hair that kept her messy bun in place added an eccentricity to her look. Tasha wasn't a big fan of her style, but she couldn't deny her results. Tasha argued unnecessarily with all sorts of things Sophia did. *If only I could stand up to her and make her see the importance of our activities.*

But this wasn't the time to get frustrated about Tasha. There was another person in her head too. The memory of Aidan's smile, his hands and his words filled her. She hadn't stopped thinking about him all day, but now she had to care for those who needed her. Sophia mentally shook herself and scanned the room. Were the kids engaging with the activity? Tim, an eight-year-old who had been coming to the drop-ins for over six months, yawned loudly and rolled his eyes. He hadn't spoken more than a couple of words in the sessions. His mum was making him come along because his dad had died the previous year, and he was struggling to cope.

"If everyone could pick up the paintbrush in front of them," Josie called out. "We're going to do something unusual with it."

Tim scowled at Josie. His paintbrush sat untouched in front of him.

"If you don't want to pick it up then that's okay, but you might miss out if you don't," Josie said to no one in particular, although Tim was the only one without a paintbrush in his hand.

Tim picked his paintbrush up and threw it on the floor while eyeballing Josie.

"Tim, isn't it? I don't mind you not picking it up, but I would appreciate it if you didn't damage the equipment, it goes all over the country with me," she said gently.

Tim scowled and swiped the brush with his foot. It skittered across the linoleum floor, spinning haphazardly before coming to rest at Josie's feet. It was an impressive shot, but Tim had been the only one who hadn't witnessed it. He'd stormed out before it had come to a stop. Josie enthusiastically shared the instructions for the session to the other children as Sophia left the room in search of Tim.

He hadn't got far. Sophia found him slumped on a bean bag in the next workshop room.

Sophia grabbed another bean bag and pulled it up next to him before dropping into it. Silence descended, the only sound was the ticking clock sitting on the floor from where it had fallen off the wall. No one had found the time to put it back because there was always something more pressing.

Tim picked at his wristband, pulling it away from his wrist and letting it ping back with a snap. Again, and again.

What should I do? Sophia met kids who were grieving in a variety of ways, and there were no magic words, no quick solutions. Some kids worked through their pain with art, music, talking or play therapy. Others found chatting to someone else who had been through something similar helpful. But some kids, unfortunately, grew up to be damaged or angry adults. *I wish I could stop that happening. I don't want Tim to end up like that.*

Snap.

But what can I do to help? Other support workers told her she couldn't fix every kid.

Snap.

But it doesn't stop me trying. Tim might open up one day.

"Aren't you going to say anything?" he said sullenly. "Aren't you going to tell me I need to talk to you about my feelings and that when I do everything will be better?"

"I-" Sophia started.

"I don't need your help. You might as well leave me alone. I'm fine," Tim said. But the anger in his voice and the relentless snapping suggested otherwise. "My dad died, so what. Who gives a crap? I don't. I didn't love him anyway."

Sophia stilled, taking slow breaths and running her hands down her jeans. Tim wasn't going to let her in. His pain was coming off him in angry waves. *But what can I do?* Sorrow filled her as it did when kids were in this stage. Tim was suffering, and if she could take it away, she would.

"You're not going to get lost? Fine, I'm still not talking to you. I know you're not going to let me go until my mum comes," he replied. He was right. The first couple of months he'd come to the group they'd been through it again and again. The team had offered to call his mum, but he'd always grunted a 'no' back. "Don't speak to me either. I don't want to hear what you have to say. You speak then I run, and I'm a fast runner."

They continued to sit in silence. Sophia knew about his running. Tim was also a great rugby player or had been before his dad died. He'd played for one of the children's leagues. But now, he was either skipping school or sitting alone in his bedroom. His mum was terrified of what would happen if he didn't open up. *She's not the only one.*

Is there a way I can get Aidan to help? There were other thoughts of Aidan pushing up; it was as if they had been let out of her Aidan box and wanted to be seen. Tim's sigh reminded her that she needed to focus on him, even if he wasn't willing to talk.

Forty minutes later, a kind-looking woman peeked through the doorway.

"Hey Honey, how did today go?" Tim's mum asked. Dark circles ringed her watery eyes. The fear for her son was evident through the extra lines around her face and the way she pawed at her sleeves.

"Fine," Tim grunted and stomped out the room.

"I'm sorry, Sophia," his mum said.

"Don't apologise. We're here, even if it's to sit in silence," Sophia replied. "We'll be here again next week."

"Okay, I'll give you a call tomorrow," she said, wiping away the tears that hadn't yet fallen.

"Mum," Tim shouted from the corridor. "I want to go h… I want to go."

She gave a lifeless wave as she rushed off, cooing to him, fake enthusiasm in her voice. "How was school? Did you learn lots?"

Stepping out of the room, Sophia came face to face with Tasha.

"What was the proposal on my desk? You want to run an outward bound event for families? High ropes, zip wires and a nice little campfire at the end? Are you kidding me? That won't work, and we won't get funding anyway," Tasha snapped.

The turmoil from the last hour spent with Tim, and then seeing his mum in despair, weighed Sophia down. A competent boss might check in with her or perceive her torment. Either Tasha didn't see it or didn't care.

"I've explained in the proposal that our fundraising team see the merit in it. They think we can get fundi-" Sophia replied.

"Think? Oh well, if they THINK, then we're on to a winner," Tasha replied sarcastically. "I didn't bother reading past the first couple of lines. Your proposal was a waste of your time. Focus on your work and stop trying to get on a jolly. You're not here to enjoy yourself. And don't go to the funding team before you've spoken to me."

"But_" Sophia implored.

"But nothing. Haven't you got tidying up to do or have you got more pointless proposals to write?" Tasha replied, flicking her blonde hair.

Sophia sighed. *What is the point of answering back, she'll only dismiss my ideas? Besides, I'm seeing Nicky tonight. I guess I should get the workshop room tidied.*

"Well go on then, get back to work," Tasha said before walking out the door her high heels clipping the floor.

Sophia seethed quietly. A coffee with Nicky was just what she needed.

"What's bothering you?" Nicky asked an hour later. "Is it just work or something else?"

"It's work, but something else too. It's Aidan. The sex, the time we spent together, it was amazing, incredible and life-changing. But I haven't seen him since Wednesday morning and, although he's sent me messages, I'm overthinking everything." Sophia hated the whine in her voice.

"We can deal with your work another time. But Soph, don't worry about Aidan. He's been busy training for his match tomorrow night, right?" Nicky asked diplomatically.

Hot coffee trickled down their throats while they sat in their favourite local coffee shop. Flavours tickled their senses, and the seats enveloped them like a loving hug.

"Yep," she agreed reluctantly.

"And he wants you to go to the match and spend the weekend with him?"

"Yep." Her earlier whine faded when faced with Nicky's objectivity. "I'm not sure what he has planned."

"You have no reason to worry. Rugby is his job. He's got stuff going on. The fact you haven't seen him since you slept together doesn't mean anything. I forget how new and scary this is for you, but you shouldn't worry. He likes you."

"You sure?" Sophia didn't want to be another forgotten conquest of the rugby star.

"Definitely."

"I still think there's something he's not telling me," she sighed.

"From what you've said, I don't think he's the kind of guy to bare his soul early on."

"I guess. But what about the phone call I overheard him having with his doctor before he dropped me off at work?"

"What did he say?"

"I couldn't hear the doctor's half of the conversation, but before Aidan hung up, he said something about the tests being pointless and that he had no symptoms. He said that his body was performing better than ever." Sophia blushed, she could testify to his performances, the way he'd made her come in his kitchen had made being late for work worth it. *I can still feel his lips against my thighs. Get a grip, Sophia. Focus on this conversation.*

"Your eyes have this new sparkle. I love it!" Nicky laughed. "Don't worry about what you overheard. It's probably routine. The rugby players have to be at their peak. How was your doctor appointment anyway?

Everything sorted?"

"Yeah, it's all good." Sophia rested her chin in the palm of her hand and nibbled at her lips, absentmindedly raking the nails of her free hand against her scalp. "There's another thing. In the morning, when he was getting us breakfast, I took a sneaky look in his art room. I wanted to see his paintings. He's an incredible artist."

"I can believe it. The drawing Aidan did of you made me melt a little. And you know how hard-hearted I am." Nicky was often the first to insult herself. To everyone else, she was the most confident person in the room, but Sophia knew different.

"When I looked around his art room, I realised that all his paintings were full of darkness, sadness and pain." Anxiety gnawed at her.

"Oh, honey, don't worry. Maybe there has been a lot of sadness in his life, or maybe that's his artist's voice." Nicky's mum sculpted as a hobby. She'd always mentioned her artist's voice, and its need to speak. "I expect Aidan has baggage; he's human after all. If he chooses to, he'll tell you. For now, have fun and get to know each other at a pace you're both comfortable with."

Bleep-bleep.

Sophia had a text from Aidan. Happiness smothered her doubts.

A: *Evening, sexy. I hope you're ready for a fun weekend, starting with one of my excellent matches, fingers crossed. John will pick you up from work. Dress warmly. My big friend says hello too x*

Sophia's brows furrowed, but before Nicky had the opportunity to ask questions the phone beeped with another message.

Looking at the screen Sophia's face burned, and her stomach lurched with excitement.

"Your eyes are sparkling again," Nicky commented. "Has he sent you what I think he's sent you?"

Sophia's naughty grin gave away the truth. Giddiness was taking hold.

Bloody hell my life's changed. All this time she'd thought by keeping her barriers high she was staying safe. *But I was missing out.* What more would Aidan show her? *I can't wait to find out.* She stared back at the photo of a naked Aidan lingering on her phone as butterflies fluttered in her belly.

*****

Aidan checked his phone expectantly. *I wish I could see her face when she looks at this. I hope she has a devilish smile like she did the other night.*

"What are you up to?" He'd sent the message before joining his mum in the kitchen. The stone floors were chilly under his bare feet and helped take the edge off the heat filling his veins.

Although his mum had her small converted barn at the bottom of the garden, she loved to pop into his house to bake and host the odd dinner party. Thankfully she hadn't called by Tuesday night.

"Nothing," he replied with a shrug, but his mum's antennas were up.

"I don't believe you for a second; I recognise that smirk. I'm glad you're happy."

"I'm always happy," he protested, checking his phone surreptitiously. Still no reply from Sophia. Had he crossed a line? They'd joked about sexting, but maybe she'd only said she liked the idea of it so not to offend him.

"Liar," Kate replied, tossing a tea towel at his head in jest. "I'm guessing it has something to do with a certain auburn-haired lady?"

"I don't know what you mean," he replied with a wide grin. "And Sophia's hair is more of a chestnut brown colour with auburn and gold tints."

"I knew it!" Quickly his mum became sombre. "I hope you're treating her well. She doesn't seem like one of your normal floozies."

"Surely, you trust your kind-hearted son?" he teased.

"Hmmm, I'm not sure." Wrinkles that betrayed years of suffering etched her face. Aidan had seen photos of her on her wedding day. She'd been a vision. To him, she still was, but she'd sacrificed some of her glow for love. *I can't let Sophia wear the same emotional scars.*

"Trust me," he stepped closer and took her flour-covered hands in his. But his words found the empty spaces in the kitchen as she refused to meet his eyes.

"You're going to damage that lovely girl. I can see it. She's not a one-night stand. She's going to want a future."

"Come on, mum." He dropped her hands, uncomfortable with the direction of the conversation. Was she worried for Sophia because she saw a little of herself in her? They were beautiful souls who worked tirelessly to bring joy to others. "We've only just started spending time together. I've told you, there won't be a future with her. There won't be a future with anyone." He'd spent years turning his heart to stone as a necessity, but his mum's sadness reached inside him. There wasn't a long-term option with Sophia, and she'd understand that eventually. Maybe he would have considered marriage and kids if the threat of Huntington's disease hadn't been hanging over him since his childhood. But that future was someone else's and not his. "I can't keep going over the same thing."

"Okay, okay." She backed down her hands raised in surrender. "I won't mention it again. But promise me that you'll think about speaking to Doctor Sampson rather than discounting any future."

"Fine. I'll promise to think about it." Aidan edged towards the door. Earlier joviality had sunk beneath the cold floor. Every season brought him closer to the future he feared. "I've got to head down south shortly".

"Okay, sweetheart." A quick pecked kiss hit his cheek before he could escape. "I hope it goes well tomorrow and make sure you beat the Chiefs. I love you."

"I love you too," he responded ducking out the room, conscious that the phone in his pocket remained silent.

CHAPTER SIXTEEN

Aidan had an easy drive to Exeter. It was a relief to make his own way down rather than get the team bus. Imploring his coach's well-hidden better nature had paid off.

The coach demanded the players chill out the night before a game, but Aidan paced the hotel room. *Why haven't I heard from Sophia?*

Suddenly his phone vibrated beside him. It was her. With one message, she electrified his body. He dived onto the duvet.

S: *Only just got home, sorry for not replying sooner. I hope the journey was smooth. When you say wear something warmer do you mean something warmer than this…?*

The notification of a second message popped up. With trembling fingers, Aidan hastily opened it.

Blood filled his cock when he glimpsed her body. Boldly she'd accepted his challenge, going further than he'd imagined. *I want to fly back up the motorway and beat down her bedroom door.*

He couldn't take in all the delights of the stunning image quickly enough. His cock juddered repeatedly. Black stockings hugged Sophia's thighs, held in place by a decadent teal suspender belt. The belt embraced her curves in a way that made his hands involuntarily squeeze in longing to touch her. Delicate lace and tiny satin bows decorated the fabric. How excited was she when she took the photo? He stared at her thong, wishing he could see beneath it.

The black bows were a feature at her breasts too. At the teal hue surrounding the lace, his tongue flicked across his lips. He needed to lick her nipples. She'd kept her face hidden in the photo. He hoped she'd worn a confident smile.

Envisaging bending her over her bed and fully appreciating her arse had his erection straining under his joggers. Instead of exhausting his need for her, Tuesday night had ramped it up further.

The pained tones of Kong's singing as he prepared for sleep were an unwelcome alternative. No other player was as conscientious as Kong, he'd already completed his pre-bed stretches and was now chilling out to some music. Sharing a room with another guy made it a lot harder to deal with an erection, especially a guy murdering the songs of Taylor Swift.

Tapping out his reply Aidan stepped into the bathroom, needing to take care of himself before bed.

A: *Maybe, if I promised to treat you very well, you could bring it with you?*

Sophia's reply came back quickly.

S: *How well are we talking? I'm packing right now.*

Chuckling to himself, he felt like a naughty teenager offered the first taste of excitement.

A: *Maybe it would be easier to pack if you took it off. And if you want to send me a picture of you without it, then it would be well received.*

Was she giggling at his cheesy lines? The grin on his face was long-lasting. Expecting a few words in reply, he almost bit his tongue to stop cheering when a photo arrived. She wouldn't dare?

Jelly-like fingers opened the image. Sophia wasn't completely naked, but she teased him, covering one breast with her arm while cupping the other with her hand. *She's exquisite.* Pulling his cock with force to relieve pressure while holding his phone with his other hand, he gazed at her body.

A: *You're gorgeous Sophia. I wish I were with you right now, my hand replacing yours before slowly moving lower.*

It was difficult to send her long messages, but he wanted to bring her pleasure. His body shook while he quickly stroked the length of his shaft. Her reply was quick. *She's as excited as me.*

S: *I'm imaging it's your hand on me. I can't believe I'm doing this. You make me so wet, Aidan.*

A: *I love your wetness. I want to stroke you slowly. Use the tips of your fingers on your clit, for me, please.*

S: *OK. I want you to imagine it's my hand on your cock too. I'm rubbing my hand up and down you, slowly at first.*

He obeyed. Sophia could make him do anything.

A: *Yes. Run your fingers around your clit. Faster and faster. Use your wetness to run circles around your nipples and imagine my tongue licking your hard nipples.*

S: *I can't stop myself. I wish you were here.*

A: *I want you to thrust your fingers inside yourself, gently at first.*

Rubbing himself slowly was agonising as he

imagined her acting out his requests.

S: *Focus on the head of your dick, squeeze it, coat yourself in your pre-cum, use that to rub yourself quicker.*

Pulling himself a little harder, he thought about her alabaster skin against his tongue. He recalled their night together; it turned him on more. It wasn't just that he was her first in all these experiences it was that she was discovering more of herself through their time together. *I'm in awe of her.* She was meeting every challenge he set her with a passion that gripped him.

A: *Thrust those fingers harder. I wish I could hear your moans. Are you close?*

S: *Yes, so close. Are you?*

A: *Yes. But I want you to come first. Watching you come again is all I've been able to think about since I saw you. Remember how it felt before. Let the heat build in your belly and thrust harder. I'm the one pushing my fingers into you. If I were there, I'd be sucking your clit. I'd smile when you screamed my name. I want you to come with me inside you.*

S: *Yes, Aidan. I'm coming. Fuck!*

The gap before she continued was brief, and he continued to pull on himself. His fist was around his cock, moving faster as he imagined her coming to his messages. It took a while for her next one to arrive. Was she basking in the afterglow?

S: *I want you to imagine your hands are on my body, on my boobs before I slip down and replace your hand on your cock with my mouth. I'm sucking hard, taking you deep. My tongue flicks over your tip before I suck down. I hear you cry out, you're close, but I keep going. I want you in my mouth as you come.*

The thought of them together had him coming quick and hard. He held back a shout. Aidan aimed for the sink and watched his cum splash against the ceramic before his body sunk to the bathroom floor. The phone buzzed with a message as Kong banged heavily on the door.

"Oi, Aidan. You better not be jacking off in there. I need a piss so hurry the hell up!"

"I'm coming."

"I bet you're "cumming", you bastard. I'll give you ten seconds, and then I'm busting the door down. Put your cock away."

Aidan speedily cleared up and pulled his joggers back up before grabbing his phone and unlocking the door.

Kong looked like he was going to tear his limbs off. Aidan bit back a witty retort as Kong shoved him aside and slammed the door.

Settling back into the bed, Aidan opened his messages quickly.

S: *Did you come? That was amazing. I can barely breathe.*

He gleaned a giddiness from her messages, and he couldn't stop smiling.

A: *Yes, I came too. You're amazing.*

S: *I can't wait to see you tomorrow. I have high hopes for what we can do then.*

A: *I will make the earth move. Promise to bring that outfit.*

S: *Hmmm, we'll see. Now go to bed. You need a good sleep before your match. I'm expecting great things.*

A: *On or off the pitch? Goodnight sexy, Sophia, see you tomorrow. X*

S: *Goodnight, Irish x*

✷✷✷✷✷

Sophia stood mesmerised with the other spectators. The outdoor stadium was big enough for thirteen thousand, and it was full tonight. Seeing a rugby game up close was a revelation. It was a spectacle of strength and skills, a momentous event for her senses to behold. The men were like gladiators in a battle for their souls. Sweat splashed from the player's bodies and the cold night air froze the spectators' bare skin. Chants and shouts flowed from the throngs of people around her, and the smell of pies had her stomach demanding a feed. It was like a carnival, a celebration of achievement. Sophia jumped up and down with every push forward of Bulls players.

"What's going on, John?" The Bulls had been playing the Chiefs for twenty minutes of the second half, and Sophia was baffled. *I might as well be an American watching cricket blindfolded.*

"They're doing a line out. One team kicked the ball out, and both teams want possession."

A Bulls player, the "hooker", slung the ball towards the two lines of men. One guy from each team tried to catch it. They sprung into the air, chucked up by teammates. It was like a cheerleader movie.

"Aidan's playing an incredible game." John's enthusiasm was infectious. Although she'd only known him as a trustee of her charity before now, it was enlightening to see him in this different context. She could understand the mentor he was for Aidan.

Occasionally, while watching the game, her protective nature kicked it, trying to drag her towards the pitch to nurse Aidan. He was battered and bruised as players took him down with the force of super trucks, but he continued to spring back up and throw himself down the pitch. Expertise and passion were never far away. Already he'd scored three tries, a couple of conversions and a penalty. His tenacity was enthralling.

"You're good for him," John said. Sophia looked at him quizzically as he continued. "I don't just mean by inspiring his playing."

"Then what do you mean?" Her stomach was unsettled. Darkness swallowed the parts of the grounds that the floodlights couldn't touch. It was inevitable for a near November evening kick-off, but it was John's ominous words that made her shiver.

"He's been through a lot. He's still going through it. But he's been different since you. Maybe you're more likely to understand him." It was like a riddle. Rugby and the pressures that came with it were alien to her. "Nobody has had such an immediate and impressive impact on him. Maybe if things work out between you two, then you can help him if things get difficult."

Questions were on the tip of her tongue, but before she could speak, John was shouting at the players.

"He's got the ball, and he's off again!" John bobbed excitedly, pushing Aidan on with the sweep of his fist. "He's magnificent!"

Sophia smiled encouragingly, but turmoil bubbled inside her. What had John meant? *I thought I'd been open with Aidan and that he trusted me.* Doubt crept in. *How is he still hiding things after everything I shared?*

Surrounded by Aidan's fans who frantically jumped with joy as their boy scored wasn't helping. The try brought proud hollers from hometown accented mouths, but she might as well have been standing alone in an empty field. The atmosphere was electric as supporters sang Aidan's praises.

John smiled reassuringly. "End of another superb game from Aidan. I'll take you to him when the team interviews and chats have finished. I need to catch up with some people first if that's okay?"

"Yep, sure. About earlier-"

John grabbed her hands, and his wrinkled eyes spied her concern. "Don't worry about what I said. I was rambling with the excitement of the game. But you know I'm here for you if anything happens or you need to chat?"

"Yes. Thank you."

He smiled at her before taking her to meet his friends. Sophia smiled politely and laughed at their reminiscing stories, told partly for her benefit, but it was a mask. She replayed what John had said, turning it over in her head. How might things get difficult? Was this related to how Aidan was adamant he wouldn't have a wife and kids or something else?

The smell of sweat lingered around the changing rooms. Damp towels littered the benches. Aidan's teammates had gone but standing in front of Sophia was a burly older man with a booming hometown accent and a smile that quickly disarmed her.

"Soph, this is my coach, aka Boss Man, Charlie. Charlie, this is my... my friend Sophia," Aidan announced.

Sophia smiled, although silently she loitered on Aidan's use of the word friend and more tellingly the way his voice had hitched when he'd said it.

Charlie's veracious hand shaking almost yanked her arm off. His voice was like a foghorn. "His good luck charm, too. I expect it's you we should thank for his recent performance. At training he's been energetic and skilful too, which is a rare combination for chicken legs here," he joked with a twinkle in his eye. "He must finally be listening to my flawless coaching too of course."

"Your coaching is truly flawless just like your sparkling wit, boss man." Aidan winked cheekily at Sophia who was basking under Charlie's attention.

"I haven't done anything. There's nothing lucky about me." She'd intended to join in the jovial atmosphere, but sadness teetered at the edge of her voice.

"Well, keep doing what you're doing. Aidan's been a different player this week. I've let him travel down on his own and not have to be at training until eleven on Sunday morning. Big allowances considering they call me the ogre behind my back."

"Surely not." Sophia smiled broadly, already warming to Charlie. "How could they?"

"I like you a lot. Now take this pain in my arse and enjoy your weekend. I'm fed up of his smug ugly mug, and I'm starting to wonder what you're doing with him. Have you considered dating an older, more handsome man?"

They both laughed heartily as Aidan glared. "Not cool, boss." His hand rested against the small of Sophia's back, and he guided her towards the door. "Come on. Let's get out of here before he exaggerates the size of his "coaching stick" or makes you his third wife."

"I heard that, Aidan," Charlie shouted as they headed for the exit. "You be careful, or I'll make you do fifty extra laps of the pitch on Sunday."

"He's not joking." Grabbing her hand in his, he warmed it instantly. "He really is an ogre. You must have brought out his rarely seen good side."

Sophia nodded absentmindedly as she continued to overthink John's words.

"What's going on, honey?" He asked seriously when they sat in the four by four. "We're not going anywhere until you explain why you're looking like your puppy has been run over."

She blurted out the first thought that wouldn't betray John. "Are we just friends messing around? I thought we were more than that?"

It had only bothered her a little. Although she enjoyed being with Aidan and wanted there to be a future between them, she wasn't sure if she was ready to define it with labels.

The car was small and crowded in the silence. Aidan stared out the windscreen and into the night. The interior light went out, and darkness enveloped them.

"I didn't know what else to call you." The words fell out of his mouth and into the suffocating air of the car. "I only met you recently. I care about you; I really do. But I'm not ready to say girlfriend."

"Okay, fair enough," Sophia lied.

"It's not okay, though is it," he replied. "I wish I could say all the right things to reassure you. I haven't felt about anyone the way I feel about you…"

Aidan's hand found hers. He clasped it tightly.

"Maybe that's enough for now," she replied,

surprising both of them. It was easy to be distracted by his touch. Even when struggling with emotions, he still turned her on. "I guess I needed to know I'm not the only one risking something. This is new and scary for me."

He brought her hand up to his lips. "I trust you more than I've trusted anyone in a long time." She believed him easily. "Do you know how important you are to me?"

Maybe it was a fresh understanding of his words, a reminder that everything was new to them. Sophia didn't need to know everything about him yet. Was this what a relationship was? Learning about someone gradually and enjoying it.

Alternatively, it could be the way his lips brushed against her knuckles, reminding her of the way they'd caressed other parts of her body. Had it only been three days since he had been inside her? *I need it again.* There will be plenty of time to talk this weekend. *I used to be ruled by my head and my judgement, but now I just want him.*

"Yes, I think I do," Sophia replied, her tongue flicking his ear. She pulled her hand away and pressed her lips hard against his. Her tongue teased open his mouth. They made out in the darkness of the chilly car. Her hand stroked his thigh, gravitating towards his thick cock.

"Now take me to where we're staying and show me how much I mean to you," she demanded, speaking between pants of breath, "And don't forget I have a surprise for you too. Maybe it will help with trust."

She pecked him quickly on the mouth as he started the engine and headed out the car park.

HEAD OVER FEELS

✻ ✻ ✻ ✻ ✻

As their feet padded along the corridor towards their hotel room, Aidan brushed Sophia's arse with his palm. The need to touch her never left him. He thought back to their conversation in the car. His emotions were like a rollercoaster when she was around. He'd known he wasn't ready to lose her, but how could he convince her of his sincerity when he was keeping his illness from her. Was time all they needed? Time had been a noose around his neck before, bringing him closer to a future filled with suffering. Might Sophia give him hope?

Her touches were disarming, and he hadn't settled on any thoughts for long. Typically, a couple of hours after a game, the adrenalin would fade, and exhaustion would sideswipe him, but the prospect of what Sophia might have in store for them obliterated it. She'd refused to drop any hints on the drive to their bayside hotel. It had been too dark to see the beauty of the ocean, but there was a peace around them as the car rolled down the hotel's driveway. It wasn't enough to quieten the hunger that pulled at him in a frenzy. When the vehicle had edged nearer the hotel, and she'd confidently told him that she had plans he'd have to abide by, his cock nearly exploded.

They sneaked down the corridor and inside their room, unable to walk more than a couple of steps without touching or kissing. The door thudded, signalling the departure of the rest of the world. The room was their sacred space. Instantly Aidan's mouth was on hers, not giving her the chance to look at the luxurious room he'd booked or the sumptuous materials in dark plum and grey that adorned their sanctuary.

"Aidan," she uttered with a sexy breathlessness between kisses, "slow down. I have plans for you."

She pushed against his muscles and wiggled her eyebrows.

"This is my night to be in charge. Do you promise to do what I say?" Diving towards her lips for another kiss, she shoved at his chest again. Strength wise she was no match, but he stepped back anyway. "Naughty. Hands-off or I may have to restrain you!"

To be tied up, by Sophia? He juddered involuntarily. "I'm not sure I can behave right now. Can't you be in charge tomorrow?"

Her pupils dilated as she stared at his crotch. "No, my rules tonight. My first demand is that you get completely naked. I want your club uniform off right now!"

Her authoritative tones increased his throbbing. If he disobeyed her, he'd never find out her plans.

"You're not going to do it for me?"

She casually eyeballed him.

"Strip, Irish."

Aidan's bespoke club tie and smart black suit fitted his body perfectly, gripping his arse muscles. Many women had enjoyed watching him from behind, and Sophia was no different. He was taut with anticipation.

He shrugged off his jacket as she gazed down his body, her eyes resembled the colour of soft earth blackened by a downpour of rain. Eagerly he spied her squeezing her thighs together, a sure sign of her arousal.

"Any preference on what you want me to take off next?" His words teased her like he wished his fingers were teasing her clit.

"Lose the trousers and then the shirt. And I want

your tie!" There was a quiver in her voice. *She's attempting confidence. I want her all the more for it.*

Sliding the zip before slipping the trousers down his legs and off, he feasted on her appetite. Shoes and socks went with his trousers. *Shit, I can't stop trembling.* He took his time to undo his crimson and white tie before tossing it towards her. Her knuckles were white as she held it. She was on the edge of taking him where he stood.

"Don't I get to see you take your clothes off?" He licked his lips. The layers that covered her during the cold rugby match hid too much of her body.

"All in good time." She spoke every word confidently. "Lose the rest, including your boxers. Then lay on the bed."

He was rock hard and desperate to touch her. Women had tried to play control games with him before, but this was different. Sophia was a woman used to submitting, but now she was harnessing power. He had to comply.

Stripping off his shirt and boxers, he attempted to be slow and seductive, but hunger blocked his moves. Aidan lay on the bed with his head raised. His eyes never left hers. Moisture clung to her freshly licked lips as she focused on his rigid member.

"And now what?" he asked gruffly.

"This." She walked to the bed, and he shot out his arm to touch her.

"Hands by your sides," she ordered. "If you break my rules, I stop, and that means no treats for you. Are we agreed?"

He nodded. Sophia straddled him, the tie in her quivering hands. The ease with which she rubbed herself against him brought pressure. How long could he hold out?

"Close your eyes," she said firmly before wrapping the club tie around his face and tying it behind his head. Aidan's world turned to black.

"You can't see anything, can you?" she asked cautiously, but still he jumped.

"No," he uttered. Her lips brushed against his. The sweetness of her taste was brief. Quickly her weight was gone from the bed.

He licked his lips, trying to hold on to her taste a little longer. Although he couldn't see her face, he wasn't nervous. She said once that sex was a challenge for her because of all it involved. Now she was embracing these challenges.

There were muffled voices in the corridor coupled with footsteps as people walked past their room, the odd close of a door and seagulls squawking outside. He focused on the noises in the room that Sophia had to be making. The shuffling of her feet, materials brushing against each other and the suggestion of clothes falling to the ground. What was she up to? He lifted his head to hear better. What would happen if she caught him moving?

The sound of a zip lowering made him freeze.

"Soph," he called out, trembling at the mirage she conjured. "Please tell me what you're doing."

There were more movements. Sophia's breath against his naked chest startled him.

"As I'm feeling kind, I'll allow you one clue and one touch." Seduction dripped from every syllable.

"Yes please," he tried not to beg, he wanted to play with her.

"I like it when you say please. Maybe two touches."

"Please, please, please."

"Nice try, Irish. Two touches are your limit, for now." Sophia's hand took hold of his shaking one. She'd built up a frenzy of excitement even though she'd barely started.

"Keen, aren't we? Try not to get too carried away." She said, amused. "But first the clue. Can you remember what I wore in the photo I sent you last night?"

"Yes," he whispered, his throat dry. "Is that what you're wearing now?"

"Why don't you feel for yourself?" She guided his hand, brushing his fingertips against the soft satin and delicate lace. Nipples, hard and erect, pushed against the fabric, pressing into his fingers.

"Is that all you're wearing?" He groaned.

"You ask astute questions." Aidan grazed her flesh and the top of her stockings. Continuing to be led his hand climbed again, brushing satin once more and then something else. A gasp sprung from his lips.

"You're soaking wet."

Sophia's intense arousal startled him. That being in control was a massive turn on for her was making his dick ache.

"That's enough for you." Her tongue found his earlobe as she spoke seductively. "It's my turn now."

Her mouth roved his torso. Her teeth grazed his nipples, making him hiss. Pleasure and pain fused, arousing him more. Anticipation seared his flesh as she closed in on his cock. The brush of her lips or the light scratch of her fingertips and nails scorched his skin. Each trick of her mouth signalled an increase of volume for his groans. It was as if she was twisting the dial control of a stereo.

Answering his silent pleas, she licked the head of his erection, softly at first. Aidan's hands shifted as if to guide her movements. Cold air replaced the heat of her tongue.

"Soph, why have you stopped? What are you doing?" he whispered into the darkness.

"Just watching." If it was possible to hear a smile, he sensed it when she spoke. "And making sure you're not going to move your hands because if you do, then I'll stop what I'm doing."

"What are you watching?" *She needs to be in control.* The guy from her past had taken her confidence, and Aidan wanted to help her get it back.

"You," she replied with a whisper that teased his nerve endings. "You're gorgeous. I don't just mean your body, but everything about you. You're handsome and beautiful and- I'm babbling now, aren't I?"

"A little but that's okay." Her laugh was like a secret only they shared. "However, I have a slightly pressing issue right now, and while I love hearing how great I am, I'd be very grateful if you'd continue with what your mouth was expertly doing. If you're okay with that? Pretty please with a cherry on top."

"You have to promise not to move your hands or blindfold."

"I promise, and if I break that promise, I'll owe you one."

"Now there's a temptation to make you break your promise," she teased.

Sophia was a force to be reckoned with, and he craved more of her because of it.

His smile died quickly when she engulfed his cock.

She sucked him into her mouth hard and fast before she moved her lips up and grazed him with her teeth. The swirling of her tongue around his tip had him begging for more.

"Fucking hell! Do that again, please?" Aidan sensed a smile behind her lips as she used her mouth, teeth and tongue. He had no idea what she was doing or what to expect. One moment her lips were barely touching him and the next her hands combined with her mouth. She sucked and licked his whole shaft and used his lubrication to slide her grip around his base or gently squeeze his balls. Sophia was trying to learn what made him moan and throb before focusing her skills there. She'd turned a simple blow job into an art form.

Defiantly she started to mouth fuck him while he thrust into her. Was he pushing her too hard? He couldn't gauge it by looking at her. *I have to believe she'll stop me if she needs to.* Wasn't that part of relenting control and learning to trust?

The noises of her eager sucking pushed him closer to coming. Aidan cried out his request, "Can I come on your boobs?"

Terrified he'd pushed her too far, he whipped his blindfold off. She'd tossed her bra across the room.

He knelt, and Sophia lay down beneath him. Wide eyes looked up at him as he grabbed his cock and pumped it. His body convulsed as cum splattered across her breasts. She was beautiful. The tightness gripping the nerves in his body eased from the climax. He looked into her eyes, unsure how she felt about the moment. She had the same look of awe that he knew was on his face. They stared at each other, sharing a moment he'd never realised was more than a selfish act.

Collapsing next to her, he graced her reddened lips with endless kisses. He'd done a lot of different things with many women, yet everything he did with Sophia was special. But why? His blood must be drifting slowly to his brain because the answer wasn't forthcoming.

Flat on their backs next to each other they gasped for breath.

"I love seeing my sperm across your breasts," he said with a massive grin.

"Your pillow talk is delightful." Her giggle made him grin wider.

"But we should clear you up. How do you fancy a nice hot shower together?"

"I'd like that," she replied breezily. "But don't forget you owe me. You took your blindfold off, naughty Aidan."

She stripped off her stockings and knickers.

"Hmmm, now what shall I do?" He mused climbing off the bed and tossing her sticky body over his shoulder. "I'm guessing you've never straddled a man's face?" Aidan didn't give her time to answer. "I think it's time you did."

Chapter Seventeen

Aidan woke, unnerved by his surroundings. As a teenager, he'd struggled to sleep in new places. As soon as he'd had enough money, he'd bought a dilapidated barn and converted it to his home. The first day he'd woken in the property was the first time he'd understood what it was to be safe.

The clock on his phone read five past four. Turning, he swallowed a gulp of surprise. Sophia was wide awake and staring through him.

"Hey, honey. What's going on?" he croaked. "I thought I'd exhausted you. You tired me out."

Her gaze was like the stroke of a feather against his skin. She was distant, unmoving.

"Talk to me, Soph. I'm not going anywhere." Patience wasn't one of his skills, but he was willing to wait as long as she needed him to.

"I had a nightmare. It sometimes happens after a tough week at work," Sophia said sadly.

"Is Tasha giving you shit? I can flex my muscles at her." He wanted to make her laugh and to fix her problems. *But she needs someone to listen.*

Light shone through the window and onto her face, her tear-stained cheeks glistened.

"I've been working with this kid. Last year his dad

died from an illness. He hasn't spoken much since he came to us. He rarely makes it through a grief workshop. I normally separate myself from work, but sometimes I have nightmares that I can't stop. The boy is going to implode. I'm scared of what might happen when he does. He's only young," she wept.

Aidan planted kisses against her hair to soothe her. "The work you do is important. I bet you don't always see the impact, but it changes lives in ways you might never understand."

"Sometimes I think it's pointless. I can't bring this boy's dad back, and that's what he needs," she said. The tears had stopped, and she was resting into him.

"No, but you can make the world better. You're giving him a safe space where the healing might start. You give a safe space to lots of people." *I could tell her the truth now. But what if she only wants to be with me to make me better? I don't want her pity.*

"Thank you for listening," she whispered against his broad chest. "I know chatting won't fix it, but sometimes my head gets so full I need a distraction. You give me that."

"I'll always listen to you," he replied. "And be the distraction you need."

She was silent for a while.

"There's another reason I can't sleep, but it's silly," she said mysteriously.

"How about I say something silly first?" he said, saved from sharing his painful past.

Sophia nodded.

"See this scar?" Aidan pointed at the tiny line on his forehead above his eyebrow. Her fingertip traced it. "I tell people it was from playing football as a kid. But the truth is that one afternoon, I was too lazy to take my boots off properly. I flicked my foot, and the boot flew up, and the studs ripped the skin on my forehead. I kind of kicked myself in the head."

Her giggles smothered his embarrassment. Her earlier sobbing had torn at his heart. *Maybe I can be her safe space.*

"What did your mum say?"

"Oh, you know mothers." His mum hadn't noticed because she was still broken over his father's death. Eventually, his mum had healed. *The jury's still out on me.* "Now it's your turn. Tell me what's wrong."

Tensing slightly, she babbled. "I didn't believe I could enjoy sex. I thought it was a sacrifice and obligation. That's what my mum suggested, and that's what it was like before."

"And now?" He waited nervously.

"With you it's incredible. I never imagined it would feel like this. I want to go into the street and shout how amazing sex can be, but then I don't want to leave the bed, and I certainly don't want to leave you. I want to have sex again and again until I'm exhausted and eat and sleep and then wake up and do it again. I can't get enough of you. I loved giving you a blowjob!"

At his deep chuckle, she spied him warily. "Possibly not as much as I loved receiving it, but anytime you want to enjoy yourself that way again, I am right here ready, always ready."

The playful swipe she gave him was nothing compared to the kiss that he planted on her lips. Gently Aidan rolled her onto her back and settled between her thighs. *I've never met anyone as beautiful as her. But is her heart big enough for my problems? I don't want to lose her.*

"But women aren't meant to enjoy blowjobs," she whispered.

"Says who?"

"Everyone, anyone," she argued. "Maybe I learnt it from those female television chat shows."

"Maybe not all women enjoy them, but some do, and that's okay. Well, it's more than okay from where I was lying last night. Sometimes it depends on the person you're with."

"I enjoy you. I never thought I'd like blowjobs, but you make it this special thing. I've never felt cheap or used by you. I want to experience more; I want everything," she explained.

"And we will. We have lots of things to share about us. I've never told anyone about the real reason for my scar. It's silly, but I used to be embarrassed. We're good together."

Aidan worshipped her body with the praise of his lips. Their lovemaking was slow and gentle. He caressed her curves while brushing kisses across her skin. They immersed themselves in each other's adoration. He wanted their closeness to continue beyond a couple of weeks. *Please let her want it, too. I don't deserve her, and if she knew the truth about me, she'd know it too.*

Aidan came with her as she moaned his name. Sophia's lips brushed his face again and again as she wrapped her legs around him. Slowly they drifted back to sleep in each other's arms. Contentment shared.

*****

Sophia spent most of Saturday laughing as she strolled

with Aidan around the seaside town. Seagulls nosedived for chips discarded on the sand, while noisy 2p machines blared out from the arcades.

The day had started as pleasurably as the previous one had ended. Continuing with her aim of embracing new experiences, Sophia had put all her efforts into trying her first 69 position experience. With flurries of excitement, she remembered laying on top of him. She didn't worry about how her body looked or rue that her belly wasn't flat. There wasn't even a worry that she might not be pleasuring Aidan in textbook fashion. She revelled in the tickle of her clit and nudge of his tongue while giving as good as she received. It was easy to have him twitching in her mouth, but the real skill was keeping him there.

"What shall we do next?" she asked.

They'd played mini-golf, visited the amusement arcade and enjoyed ice creams while shivering. Aidan had dipped his finger in his ice cream and slopped it on her nose before licking it off and reminding her how skilful he was with his tongue. Both of them were flush with joy and so absorbed in each other it was easy to ignore the strangers that glared and rolled their eyes when he tickled her hips or made her screech with laughter.

"I do have one idea. It would fulfil your plan for new experiences." His eyes sparkled.

"Go on," she replied cautiously.

"It's a surprise. You'll have to trust me," he said with a low growl. Sophia swore she felt the depth of his Irish tones in her crotch. "You do trust me, Sophia?"

Swallowing noisily, her heart hammering in her chest, she nodded.

He grabbed her hand, and they ran towards the shops. *Was he joking last week when he said sex dungeons were a second date activity?*

They dived into an underwear store, giggling like kids sneaking into a sweet shop after school. Sophia was in awe. Chiffon underwear as black as midnight surrounded her. It was accompanied by scarlet bows that reminded her of the night she'd met Aidan. Ivory corsets befriended satin in the colour of calm Spanish seas. Stretching out her hand, she let the materials fall through her fingertips. It was unlikely he'd buy her something like that as it wasn't the new experience he'd inferred. Maybe he had a fancy-dress outfit in mind or a naughty peep bra and crotchless thong.

His breath toyed with her ear, and she shivered against him. "While the underwear is beautiful and I'm imagining your curves putting on quite a show in one of those corsets, I was thinking of something a bit different."

Aidan led her to the depths of the shop. There they found a plethora of toys in different sizes and colours. Trembling in anticipation, she held his arm tightly as they wandered around a Santa's grotto for lustful adults.

Although she'd only just lost her virginity, nothing in the shop surprised her. Nicky had taken her to sex toy shops over the years, and Sophia had a little toy box. Aidan searched the array of toys before stopping close to the anal toys and strap-on dildos. *Please not one of those. I'm not ready.* His hand loitered near the vibrating anal beads, causing her to hold her breath and her face to blanch. Finally, after much inspection, he greedily swiped something from the display.

"Do you dare?" He emphasised each word.

She studied the item cushioned in his hands.

"It's for tonight, for when we go out to dinner." He paused like he was considering the feasibility of his plan. "You've brought a dress, haven't you?"

Nodding nervously, she licked her dry lips, but no amount of moisture would rescue them from the intensity of Aidan's gaze. "And yes, I accept your dare."

Pulling her head close, he, kissed her fiercely. "I won't do anything you're not comfortable with." His teeth nipped at her lips. "And I will stop when you ask."

Protection filled his words and surrounded her as the sales assistant rang the item on the till.

A Remote Egg.

"I'm going to have the remote," he whispered excitedly. "It's my turn to be in control tonight if you'll let me."

That meant giving him control of her body. She shivered, and he pulled her close. He would be her rock in all of this.

"Come on, Bambi eyes. Let's nap before dinner. I think we're both knackered after last night."

They strolled back to the hotel before stripping off and snuggling under the duvet. Sleep came quicker than she expected. Her life had been missing excitement, but also someone to cuddle her and care for her.

*****

Aidan held her close as they walked to the restaurant. To strangers, his hand was resting in his pocket, but in truth, it was clasping the remote. He was desperate to use it, but the timing was everything.

Occasionally he'd offer Sophia a reassuring smile.

She'd been trembling since he'd helped her slide the lube covered egg inside herself.

Sophia was pushing herself beyond her comfort zones, and instead of hiding under a blanket like a terrified puppy, she was instigating the acts frightening her.

"You okay?" he asked tentatively. "We don't have to do this. I'm happy spending the evening with you."

"I'm excited." Again, she surprised him. Aidan thought she was nervous, but she matched his hunger for the adventure looming in front of them.

They were seated quickly in the Indian restaurant. There were the typical groups of hens and stags, including ladies adorned with large L plates. The soon to be bride had a plastic veil balanced precariously on her head. On the other side of the restaurant, a group of stags hollered to each other. They wore matching t-shirts that stated Gary was getting married. The clattering of cutlery resonated around the restaurant as they gorged on food. Various groups of friends and couples were dotted around, which made for a busy and noisy night.

He'd heard the phrase '*the cat that had got the cream*' numerous times, but as he sat and stared at Sophia seated opposite him, he realised he was the cat that had landed the whole dairy. *I'm not good enough for her. She's looking at me like I'm some sort of king, not a man destined for suffering.* She was helping him be better. Life wasn't about what he could get out of it anymore, but instead about making it good for everyone. He'd spent time after practice helping the new players hone their skills, other days he'd spent time with his mum listening to her as she gardened. *And after listening to Sophia talk about the boy at work, I'm going to volunteer for her charity*. She'd taught him to care about others in a way he'd never considered before. She'd also shown him that sex was more than an act. He couldn't imagine his life without her. *But that will happen.*

Aidan let his fingers get acquainted with the remote, aware of the jittery Sophia pinning him with her eyes. The prospect of the next couple of hours was tantalising. He flicked the button with the tip of his finger and tested the lowest setting as Sophia spied him.

He enjoyed toying with the remote control almost as much as he relished teasing her body. Her eyes darkened.

"Having fun, are we?" She arched an eyebrow in question, but her cheeky smile betrayed her excitement.

"Just testing." Aidan's eyes dipped to the menu as bravado hit him. "Anything taking your fancy? Maybe someone right in front of you?"

Sophia made exaggerated movements as if looking at the menu was a strain, swinging it in front of her face to make a point. "The korma does look nice."

Flicking the switch again he pushed the intensity up a little.

Her doe eyes flew to him as she wriggled in her chair.

"Sorry, my finger slipped." He grinned.

Before a comeback left her mouth, the waiter arrived to take their orders. Aidan blurted his choices at speed. How long would he be able to play this game before the urge to take Sophia back to the hotel and ravage her overtook him?

While placing her order, her tongue peeked out of her mouth to moisten her lips. Only he knew what the flash of excited annoyance and nibbled lip meant as he continued to play. Sophia glared at him while politely discussing ingredients of dishes. The challenge she offered sparked his devilishness, and he increased the intensity of the vibrations again.

The waiter departed and strode to his next duty without a clue of their game.

Sophia jabbed Aidan. He reached for her leg and ran his finger up her calf. Slowly he stroked higher before stopping at the back of her knee. Waiting for her to resist and maybe pull away, he made swirling patterns with his fingertip. She welcomed him, moving closer, encouraging his caresses.

Her black strapless dress emphasised her breasts and her pert nipples reminded him she wasn't wearing a bra. It gripped her at the waist before flowing down her thighs and resting above her knees. The black brought out the tints of red in her hair and hinted at her almost faded summer tan.

"Tell me about your housemate. What's the deal with her and the guy she's kind of with?"

"Nicky and Ryan? How do you mean?"

"Are they together? One of my teammates is interested in her." Several of his friends had been talking about the enigmatic blonde.

"I don't think anyone knows, including them. Nicky likes him, and she wants a relationship, but they're 'friends with benefits'. She's scared about broaching the subject with him."

"What do you think she should do?"

"No idea. If she's scared of losing Ryan, then she might keep things as they are rather than risk saying anything."

The subtext was clear. The same was happening

between Sophia and Aidan. They refused to speak their truths for fear of the repercussions. Thankfully their awkward silence was broken by the waiter bringing their poppadoms and dips, a staple of any good Indian restaurant. He'd once heard poppadoms described as thin plate-sized crisps fried in oil. They looked like fried tortilla wraps to him. The waiter smiled pleasantly before rushing off.

Aidan let go of her leg and snapped the poppadom between both his hands. Sophia's impish grin formed quickly. With both hands on his food, there was a reprieve from her torture.

Something moved gingerly against his trouser covered member. Arousal jolted through him when her foot slowly stroked him. She'd ditched her heels.

"Sophia," he warned between the snapping and crunching.

Pushing against him more confidently, she used her toes to goad his hardening dick.

"Oh, you want to play, Bambi eyes?"

The smile of burgeoning delight was irresistible. Half the fun of the remote was in Sophia's lack of control. When would he use it and in what way? *I can't get enough of her.*

Aidan dived for the black remote, quickly flicking on the button and pushing the intensity up high, hoping the vibrations would ravage her.

Sophia's head lolled slightly to the side, and her hands gripped their table. Teeth pulled at her plump bottom lip. Eyes closed tightly. Her forehead creased as each vibration stimulated her already aroused body. Watching her writhe made his erection press painfully against the zip of his trousers.

Holding her foot against him, he delighted in feeling the sensations she was experiencing. Sliding his hand up her leg and stroking her inner thigh, he communicated what her climbing orgasm was doing to him. Pushing the button again, he tried to pull higher intensity from the little machine. She brazenly embraced her body's reactions. He was mesmerised. The restaurant was busy, and the patrons were oblivious to her quiet moans falling like raindrops from her mouth.

She twisted in her seat, rubbing the palm of her hand against her forehead. Every breath that left her mouth was erratic, and she was practically panting. Imagining the pulsation of the egg inside her his fingers continued to control her ecstasy. Aidan longed to see the sparks fly when she gave in to the pleasure throbbing through her. Her quiet moans were like a tongue flicking the head of his erection before her throat sucked it hard and deep like she'd done the previous night.

"Sophia." He demanded her attention. "I need to have you now. The hotel is down the street, and we need to go, right now."

"Yes," she uttered. Her need came out in waves.

Aidan tossed down money before they sped out of the restaurant. Their footsteps smacked quickly against the pavement. There was no time to waste. Desire consumed them.

Aidan kept pressing the button on the remote, increasing the intensity until Sophia could barely walk. The way she shook as she hung on to him was an aphrodisiac he hadn't anticipated.

They flew into the lift at the hotel, but her dress remained on due to the unavoidable presence of other hotel guests. Aidan's back was against the wall. Pulling her against him, he continued to finger the remote button. She convulsed against him, her bum rubbing his cock.

The lift doors finally opened, and he dragged her near climaxing body to their suite. They barely made it through the opening before he slammed it shut with Sophia against it.

Aidan tore at her knickers, and she grabbed at the button and zip on his trousers. Desperately, she clawed his clothes off. He pulled the egg out from inside her before grabbing her bum. His cock was thick and painfully hard, the veins pronounced. Lifting her and pushing her against the door, he let free his animalistic need to be inside her. Again, and again he slammed into her. Sophia's screams echoed around the room, and they seized gratification from each other's bodies.

"Yes, harder," she shouted as he thrust into her.

It was the hard, fast sex of two people on the brink of orgasm. All they wanted was to take the climax from each other and find release from the sexual torture that had consumed them.

"I'm coming," she shouted, although he needed no warning.

Ramming himself inside her as deep as possible one last time her walls clenched him tightly. With a cry, he filled her. He was the only thing keeping her body from collapsing as she came forcefully around him. Their climaxes powered over them at the same time. Sophia's legs wrapped around him and he held on tightly, her body taking every last drop.

Carrying her still trembling form to the bed, he eased her down to lay on top of the covers. They collapsed with exhaustion.

Aidan covered her with soft sensual kisses and slowly stripped her of her dress before removing his shirt and trousers.

Moonlight streamed through the window and flickered off the silver earrings that still dangled from her ears. Sophia's body shone keenly with a light sheen of sweat. Disarrayed hair and smeared makeup showed all the tell-tale signs of their exploits. Aidan swelled with pride. He yearned for her again. *How is this possible?* The need to make her come overwhelmed him, and casually he brushed his hand against his penis. How quickly would it get hard again?

"Shit!" Aidan suddenly roared, waking her from her slumber. "For fuck sake! We forgot about a condom!"

CHAPTER EIGHTEEN

Sophia woke with a start. The volume of Aidan's expletives sent her into a frozen state.

He stormed around the room, only stopping to pound his fist into the wall hard enough to crack the paint. She'd never seen him like this. The wrath in his eyes reminded her of the night Graham nearly attacked her. Was Aidan going to do that too? *I didn't know he was like this.*

"How could I be such a prick? This is all my fault! If something happens! Fuck." Aidan raged, his voice booming off the walls. His body shook, and his eyes flashed with uncontrollable anger. "You twat. You thick fuck."

Memories of her night with Graham returned in a flash, and a sob escaped her mouth as he moved to thump the wall again. She'd thought she could trust him, but she'd put her trust in a stranger.

Aidan whipped around to stare at her. "What's wrong with you?" Aidan shouted, stepping closer, his face tight and red. Realisation flashed across his face, and he moved towards the bed.

Sophia inched nearer the headboard pulling the duvet with her and covering herself with it.

"It's okay," he said, sitting on the edge of the bed. "I'm sorry. I didn't mean to kick off. But we did something wrong." He took a deep breath. "Not wrong as in bad, but we forgot to use a condom. I never forget to do that. Never."

She spied him. It was like an out of body experience. His lips moved, and his forehead wrinkled. He looked pained.

Sophia closed her eyes. *He isn't Graham, and he didn't do anything to you.* But she couldn't forget the moment, the anger she'd witnessed, so sudden and intense, was a trigger to a terrifying time and it was all she could do not to cower away.

Aidan continued to ramble. "To some, it's not a massive deal, but for me, it is. I will never have children. I would rather you have an abortion than have my kids."

That brought her out of her foggy state. An abortion? Was he serious? She couldn't find the words to express her shock.

Aidan's words appeared to be running away from him. "I almost had the snip this year, but stupidly I thought it would dent my masculinity. I thought I'd learnt to control my body, but with you tonight I couldn't stop. I had to be inside you. I'm not blaming you. What happened was stupid. But you have to understand that I will never have children. I'm not angry with you. I'm angry with myself. I lost control of my body so easily. I'm a fuck up." He said, traces of aggression still filled his voice.

Finally, she found the words she'd needed to say. She spoke coldly. "I'm recently on the pill. I would have told you if you'd asked."

Fearfully he reached out for her hand, frantically

trying to improve the situation, but she pulled away. "I need to sleep. Don't disturb me. Don't even touch me."

She turned to face the wall. The mattress dipped a while later when Aidan got into bed, but she didn't turn. He'd listened to her request. Soft snoring soon filled the room, but she lay awake, unsure of how to process what had happened. Who was this man she was with, and what was he capable of? *I can't be with another Graham.*

*****

Aidan woke from a fitful sleep. Panic still flamed his stomach. What if he lost Sophia? *I need to hold her, make everything better.*

He reached out, but she was gone.

Her warmth still blessed the empty side of the bed, and her coconut scent lingered on the pillow. The luminous green numbers on the clock said 01:45.

Had she left the hotel? Bile rose in his throat at the memory of his anger. He'd told her she'd need an abortion if she got pregnant. Their growing relationship was ruined, and blame lay at his feet.

Her stuff was still there; her money and phone were on the nightstand and the only things missing were her jeans and t-shirt. She had to be close. His heartbeat was out of control, and the bile continued to lurch up to his gullet. Throwing his jeans on, he headed for the lobby.

Aidan found her cradling a stiff-looking drink in the hotel bar. The barman took his whisky order as Aidan propped himself on the stool next to Sophia. He longed to pull her into his arms and whisper how much he cared about her. If only he could reverse time. Instead, he sat stoic, too scared to say anything.

Eventually, the silence broke like the first words heard on a day spent alone. He turned to face her, but she stared at the rows of spirit bottles framing the bar.

"What the hell, Aidan? What the fuck was all that about?" Her tone was quiet and calm, but the hurt behind the words cut deep in his gut.

"I'm sorry." *My anger might be a symptom of Huntington's, but what did Doctor Sampson say? It might be because of unresolved grief too. How can I explain this to her?* "Sometimes, my brain doesn't kick in before my emotions get out of control. I'm not sure how to explain it properly. Generally, I can control it. But I was livid with myself."

She sipped her drink slowly. *I need to explain myself adequately and tell her more.*

He took a deep breath and plunged into a lifetime of secrets. "Sophia, there are things I haven't told you. I'm not sure I'm ready to tell you yet, not everything. But something happened when I was younger. It nearly destroyed me. It's one of the reasons mum and I came to England, it's partly why I was angry as a teenager. I didn't think I needed help with it, but I'm starting to realise I do. My family doctor used to talk about counselling, but I thought that was for really fucked up people," he said.

"Lots of people have counselling; you'd be surprised," she replied.

"Do you think it would help with my anger?" he asked a vulnerability in his voice.

"Yes, you need it. What happened to you?"

Of course, she would ask. It was one of the reasons he'd been scared to tell her anything. *What if she wants to fix me, what if she sees me as another lost soul? I don't want her pity.*

"I'm not ready to talk about it. I will, with you one day. Will you be patient? I understand if you want to walk away, but I need to see a professional first." He was asking too much, but this would be a long journey for him. Maybe if he got counselling, he could get the test done. Perhaps he'd have help in knowing how to tell her the things in his heart.

"I'll give you time. But one day I hope you can tell me what you're scared to deal with." Sophia swivelled on her stool and stared at him. The sadness in her eyes was like a knife slicing his veins. "But if I ever see you angry like that again I will walk out of your life for good. I thought you might hit me. I've had that terror before, and I won't allow it. If this rage of yours turns you into a monster, then you need help. There are no excuses."

"Okay, I will." It was a promise he had to keep. "But please believe me when I say I will never hit you. I would destroy myself first. It's me I was angry with and no one else. I'm not Graham, and I never will be."

He'd never touch her like that. He might have bloodied and broken his own body if he hadn't calmed when he did, but his wrath wasn't directed at her. He'd get help and do whatever it took.

He leaned in to kiss her forehead, waiting for her to pull away. She didn't move.

They stayed like that for a frozen moment. Aidan's lips pressed tenderly against her and his arms wrapped around her, pulling her close.

"Let's go back to bed. We need to sleep. We've got an early start tomorrow, and you've got training," Sophia uttered.

Within minutes they were in bed. Sophia's soft

breaths of slumber carried through the room as she snuggled against him. But Aidan lay awake. He'd come to close to losing her. That couldn't happen.

*****

Sophia stifled a yawn. The countryside flew past as they travelled home. Trees were losing their leaves, and the greens of the fields were duller than several months earlier. Winter was approaching. *I wonder what it will bring.* Moisture rose off the grass, creating a mist that hung in the air. The future was inevitable. Apprehensive for the coming months it was as if the mist clung to her own body.

Aidan's rage the previous night revisited her. In the light of day, she knew he wouldn't hit her, in truth, she knew it at the time, but it hadn't stopped her terror. *I won't ignore the signs. What if his rage isn't as rare as he made it out to be?* If this is who he was, then she'd leave him. It wasn't just sex keeping her with him. *I'm falling for him quickly, too quickly. I need to see where this thing goes. I enjoy his company; I love laughing and being cared for by him.*

But what wasn't he ready to tell her? Was it an excuse? Was he playing mind games with her? *I thought I'd worked through my past.* But the toxicity of her relationship with Graham still lingered, rising it's head the closer she got to fully trusting Aidan.

Why was the prospect of having children so abhorrent? If he didn't want children, it was his choice, but at the very least she wanted a discussion rather than him freezing her out. It had sent him into a frenzied panic. The speed of the reaction suggested it was unlikely he would change, and yet her instincts told her that it was a manifestation of something more. It wasn't the first time she'd witnessed that level of desperation in someone.

But no matter the root of the anger Sophia had meant what she'd said, if he came close to behaving like that again she'd walk out of his life for good.

"You're quiet. Got lots to think about?" Aidan asked nervously.

"I'm wondering what to do with the rest of my day." It was a white lie, but still a lie. Trust was disappearing from their relationship as quickly as the mist was vanishing from the dew-covered fields around them.

"You could come to training. Although I won't be able to concentrate with you there, and boss man will chat you up." His laugh was laced with anxiety.

Leaning over, she kissed him on the cheek. Instead of bringing out a smile, he raised his eyebrows in confusion.

"I'm worried about you, Aidan."

"Me?" He gave a poor attempt at laughing her comment off. "I'm okay; you don't need to worry about me. I'm a big rugby star, no worries."

"I probably won't be able to see you tonight," she said carefully. Aidan was already shifting awkwardly in his seat. But this wasn't the inevitable brush off. *I still want him.* "I probably won't be able to see you until Wednesday. I've got to work for the next two evenings,"

"Oh, okay." His disappointment saturated the air of the car. "I'm sorry about last night."

Again, she leant over and kissed him before resting her hand affectionately on his leg.

"I know, but I do have to work. We can spend all of Wednesday evening and Thursday evening together. I'll cook you dinner." His leg relaxed. "Who are you playing next Saturday?"

"Leicester, at home. It's going to be a tough game. Training will be painful today." He rested his hand on top of hers. "Can I ask you something?"

"Yep." It was her turn to be nervous.

"The photo in your room of your graduation, are you with your mum?"

"Yep," she repeated. Sophia was uncomfortable with his question and unsure where it was leading, but if she was going to get to the bottom of Aidan's mysteries, she had to be willing to share her secrets, too.

"You don't talk about her or your dad. I'm guessing you don't have any siblings?"

"No, I don't think so. Mum had me when she was nearly seventeen. My dad was an older guy, but that's all I know. Her parents threw her out, and so she brought me up on her own. My dad didn't want to be involved." She didn't like discussing her past, but it helped explain some of who she was.

Aidan listened attentively, occasionally squeezing her hand.

"Mum instilled in me that I wasn't to make the same mistake she had, but instead work hard, achieve academically and avoid men," she said.

Watching the cars passing by Sophia thought about the people in them. They each had their own stories, regrets and experiences. Memories of lives lived or maybe not lived enough, a little like hers.

Finding her voice, she continued. "I grew up thinking I was a mistake. I was mum's biggest regret. I guess I became a little scared of men, and I worried about how to act around them. Mum used to tell me men weren't to be trusted. I thought sex was a sacrifice every woman made when she loved someone." Sophia daydreamed her teenage years for a while before continuing.

Another breath escaped her lips. It was the only noise in the silence of the car. "Mum wasn't happy when I got together with Graham. There's been a strain on our relationship ever since."

"Do you still see her?"

"Not really, she lives in Spain. She met a man about five years ago when she was working as a dental nurse. Mum worked hard when I was growing up, studying late into the night. She could have been a dentist, but she didn't have the money or the time to go to university. Work was necessary for our survival." Sophia had gone to university to please her mum. Upon reflection, she realised she'd done most things in her life to please her. "The guy mum met was very rich and had his own financial management business. It was quite a romance. He had to work hard to get her to go on a date with him, but eventually, they dated and fell in love. He retired, and two years later they were married and moving to Spain. She's happy. She's a different person, but our relationship remains fractured. She struggles to trust my opinion, especially when it comes to men. I don't think she has a lot of faith in my choices."

"But she must be proud of you? The work you do is life-changing. And you're kind, caring, well-adjusted and of course beautiful." A smile touched her lips as he lifted her hand to his mouth, and brushed a kiss to the back of it.

As she was about to ask about his family, the end of her road came into view. Revisiting her relationship with her mum had blinded her to the rest of their journey.

As she got out of the car, Aidan lifted her in the air and propped her on the bonnet.

His kiss was gentle, and his hands stroked the outside of her thighs. "Have a lovely Sunday, Bambi eyes. Maybe call your mum and tell her that you've met the most wonderful man in the world."

"And that he's the cockiest man in the world?" she teased.

Deep laughter rumbled against her breasts, and he pulled back his head to look into her eyes. The blue wasn't his typical sparkling hue, but she recognised a bit of the Aidan she knew.

"Maybe not that bit," he chuckled.

"You're going to be late for training. You might get in trouble."

"I'll blame you. Boss man loves you, so it'll be fine," he replied calmly, kissing her again. She gave in to it, relaxing into him.

"Aidan," Sophia eventually protested, slapping him on the arse. "You have to go."

"Okay, okay." Letting her go, he helped her slide off the bonnet. Her feet were hitting the ground, but her head was still in the clouds. Aidan's taste lingered on her lips.

He walked her to her door, her bags in his hands, before pecking her on the lips once more.

Sophia watched him head back down the path and drive away. Against her better judgement, she still wanted to be with him, but misgivings were settling inside her. What secrets did he hold, and would their relationship survive them?

*****

Voices carried into the hallway when Aidan stepped through his front door. It had been a painful training session and made more difficult by the extra ten laps he had to run to make up for being late. The time he'd spent with Sophia had been worth it.

A giggle wriggled its way into his ears, followed by a flirty chuckle. When had he last heard those sounds from his mum? He tiptoed silently into the kitchen, and his jaw dropped to the floor.

Leaning against the granite covered island in the middle of the kitchen was his mum, and she was in John's arms. Their lips pressed together in a kiss.

"What the hell?" he uttered as bags slipped from his hands, smacking the floor.

It was like someone had set a bomb off between them as they jumped apart and scattered.

"Aidan, I didn't hear your car," she replied anxiously.

"Probably because you were too busy getting it on with John." Aidan was shocked, but not angry.

The only other guy his mum had been with since his dad was his coach at Bath. That had ended badly, and his mum had suffered.

"It's not what it looks like," John interjected.

Aidan's response surprised all of them, including himself. He belted out a laugh that forced him to grab the countertop to stave the shaking. Tears of laughter rolled down his cheeks.

His mum joined in the merriment. Catching her

twinkling eyes had his laughter flowing faster; it showed no signs of stopping. Eventually, Aidan's breathing slowed, and he pushed the tears of joy away.

"It's exactly what it looks like." Kate turned to John. Although her giggles eased, she still wore a huge smile. "We were kissing for goodness sake. It's not like you were checking my lips for injuries, well, not like that anyway."

"Mum." Aidan was on the brink of bursting into giggles again.

"I suppose," John mumbled slinking his hands into his pockets.

"For goodness sake. You don't need to be embarrassed." She checked her watch. "Besides, aren't you meant to be at your daughter's house right now?"

John rushed out of the door although not before pecking Kate on the cheek while uncomfortably eyeing Aidan. "I'll call you later," he shouted out.

"You'd better." Aidan teased an already anxious John.

"Right, you." She spoke with a glint in her eye once John was out the door. "Stop being so cheeky and let's sit."

She made a cup of tea and pushed it in front of him.

"How long have you two been sneaking around?" he asked mischievously.

"We haven't been sneaking anywhere," her response was sheepish. "We've been close for about a month. I didn't mean for you to catch John and me kissing before I'd spoken with you."

"If I hadn't walked in, would I have caught you doing it on the countertop?" Teasing her was too appealing. It was the first time he'd heard her laugh so gaily in years.

"Aidan Liam Flynn, stop cheeking your mum or she is going to give you a good hiding. John and I started spending more time together. He's a good man, he treats me well, and I appreciate him."

"Appreciate?"

"Fine. I fancy the pants off him."

"Mum!"

"Oh dear, I've just realised what that phrase means." Suddenly she got serious. "John means a lot to you. He's one of your few confidants so if you have deep reservations about what we're doing then let's discuss it now."

It dawned on him how worried she must have been about his reaction. He grasped her trembling hands in his. Was her happiness dependent on his response?

"Mum, I'm ecstatic for you. John is the kindest man. I'm already sure that he will treat you with the love and respect you deserve. That's what I want for you." A smile was reborn on her lips. "Besides, he knows what I'm capable of. He's either brave, stupid or he really likes you."

Kate's laugh was musical.

"Would you have considered breaking things off if I'd asked?" Aidan asked.

"Yes." She nodded. Silvery blonde strands of hair fell from her messy ponytail. "You mean the world to me, and you haven't always been appreciative of my... romantic dalliances."

"But that was when you dated an arsehole who didn't treat you right."

"True, but it wasn't only him." She was forming her words carefully. "You've never been keen on me having a social life."

Aidan mulled over her comment. She was right. He'd made it difficult for her to have friends because he thought he needed to be her focus, not just as a teenager but for many years since.

"Sorry, I'd never thought about it." His words sounded selfish. Confronted by his behaviour by the one woman who'd always loved him unconditionally was akin to having the worst things he'd ever done played on a screen in front of all the people he'd ever hurt. *I've been a bastard*. Guilt pinched his insides.

"Don't get maudlin on me. The way you dealt with John shows me that my plan to tell you and not hide it was the right thing. Recently you've been a different person. You didn't get angry this afternoon, which was my biggest fear. You were my gorgeous, caring boy. Thank you."

Remembering his anger from his night with Sophia, he tried to pull his hands away, but she wouldn't let him, holding on tighter.

"What else is going on?" Her eyes softened as they examined his. It was impossible to hide his shame.

"I got angry last night." His mouth quivered. "I scared Sophia. I didn't hurt her, well, not physically." He rushed through his retelling of what had happened, giving his mum the edited highlights.

"Maybe you should get the test done. Sooner or later you're going to have to, and it might give you peace. You'll know what you have to deal with." She didn't understand, no one did. "Have there been any other symptoms?"

"No. My playing is better than ever, including in training. I'm scoring more tries, and I'm running that pitch like never before."

"I think we can both see that your playing has something to do with a certain lady you're trying to impress."

"Maybe." He dropped his eyes and blushed.

"Have you told Sophia why you got into a rage?"

"I can't, mum. I did tell her that I'm going to get counselling. I hope she can wait while I sort myself out. I'm not ready to lose her yet." But the longer they were together, the more painful it would be if he had to walk away. Walking away was inevitable if the test was positive.

"Who says you'll lose her?"

"I do. I can't bear to put Soph through what you went through. I remember when dad was getting sick. You were once so happy, but it became less and less and then was replaced by suffering that didn't stop when we left Ireland." Aidan swallowed the lump in his throat, unsure how to discuss the ghosts of their past. "What would your life have been like without dad? You could have had real happiness instead of agony. I can't put anyone through that. I can't destroy Sophia's life the way yours was destroyed."

Words tumbled from him as he released years of pain, but still he was uncomfortable with the level of honesty. Aidan moved to stand.

"I haven't finished," his mum replied.

Fearing the repercussions he'd face if he defied the piercing blue-eyed challenge he sat quickly.

"I wouldn't change the time I spent with your dad. I'm not saying it wasn't hideous at times. Sometimes I didn't think I'd survive, but I adored him. If I had to sacrifice another ten years of my life to be with him one more day, I would. Sometimes I long for it."

Aidan shifted against the chair. Goose pimples rose on his arms as her eyes turned glassy. *She'll always love dad. She'd lived through so much because of that love.* The tea had gone cold, but he sipped it anyway. He was that sad eleven-year-old all over again, getting off the plane to a country he didn't think he'd ever be able to call home, remembering watching his mum in pain.

"And if I'd never met your dad, I wouldn't have had the opportunity to be the most fortunate mother in the world. I love you, Aidan. You're not always the easiest man to manage, but you are the best, and you've taken care of me all this time, including when I wasn't there for you like I should have been."

Standing and pulling his mum into a bear hug, he squeezed her tight. His eyes misted up. His mum had been lost and alone when he was a teenager. Sophia's explanation of her mum had reminded him how lucky he was to have his. Holding her tighter, he regretted every moment he'd made her life difficult and every opportunity she'd missed because he was trying to protect them.

"Aidan, I can't breathe," she chuckled as he popped her back onto the floor. "And you're definitely okay about John?"

"Yeah, he's a good guy."

"Can I have the house Wednesday evening then? I want to cook him a special meal," she asked excitedly.

"Yeah sure, but stay safe and clear up after," he replied.

Her cheeky smile had all sorts of unwelcome thoughts attempting to infiltrate his mind.

"Not like that, mum. So gross."

A giggle carried through the kitchen as he headed to the bathroom. Even battling the idea of what his mum might be smirking about, things that mothers should never do, he managed a genuine smile. She deserved to be happy, but did he?

Chapter Nineteen

Sophia bounded towards her house with a bouquet clutched in her hands. Blossom tickled her nose as she reread the note attached.

Can't wait until I see you tonight, I can't stop thinking about you and the things you're yet to experience. Aidan xx

The bold texts Aidan had sent throughout the afternoon had added to her lust. Hunger consumed her. Sophia recalled their weekend when he'd held her softly, cupping her breast, his lips against her neck as he stroked her clit from behind. *Thank God I'm seeing him tonight.*

Hugging the flowers, she sprang into the living room and was confronted by Aidan and Ryan. Suddenly they ceased their chat and Ryan jumped up.

"You okay, Ryan?" she asked, surprised.

"Yep, just got some things to think about," he replied as he passed her and headed out the front door.

"That was weird-," she said, turning to Aidan. The heat in his eyes made her suck at the end of the word. She licked her lips.

"Nice flowers." He slowly looked her up and down.

She observed him from beneath her thick lashes. His legs were wide apart, and he fiddled with his belt just above his crotch. Was he subconsciously trying to draw her attention to his groin? She'd barely thought of anything else for days.

His gaze travelled slowly down and paused at her breasts before continuing lower. "Are you going to thank me for the flowers?" he asked, a glint in his eyes.

Raw desire overwhelmed her, and she squeezed her thighs tightly together. Her heart thundered in her chest.

"Maybe later," she teased. She wanted to be in control again, like when she'd tied him up. "I need to get changed."

Throwing off her jacket, she walked to her bedroom. The thud of Aidan's steps chased her down the corridor. She reached her bedroom, letting out a giggle as she attempted to close her door. Aidan pushed his way inside.

"You couldn't resist me," she uttered gleefully, but her words were replaced by moans when he moved her back against the door before slamming it shut with the power of his body against hers. He bit at her lips and grabbed at her wrap-around dress.

"Aidan," she pleaded for more while he grappled with the knot of her belt.

He grunted loudly. Sophia tried to release the knot herself, but in their frenzy, they were tightening it. The need for control slipped away quickly. She wanted him inside her.

A frustrated Aidan pulled up the hem. The lust from days apart was overwhelming, and they couldn't last much longer. She nipped at his shoulder. He used his leg to push hers further apart and ran his thumbs up the inside of her thighs, nearing her knickers, which were wet with her arousal.

"Sophia!" Nicky shouted through the door. "I need

the kitchen in about twenty minutes. I've got people from work coming over."

"Shit," Sophia whispered between gritted teeth. They paused temporarily, breathing deeply while waiting for their bodies to catch up to the change in tempo. "I guess I should make dinner now then."

"I'm only hungry for one thing," he growled, his tongue flicking against her ear lobe.

Need tore at her body. "But you need to eat proper food. You've been training all day."

Aidan brushed his thumb against her panty-covered lips. Waves of arousal saturated her body.

Nicky's voice was like a smoke alarm that wouldn't die. The doorbell joined in going off again and again. "Soph, I could make you dinner, but I'm not sure I've got enough food. Are you in there with Aidan? If you're going to have sex, you might want to do it quietly. Noise really carries in this place. Oh, shit. You're doing it now, aren't you? Sorry!"

Sophia pushed Aidan away and opened the door.

"No, we're just chatting," Sophia announced although her dishevelled state and loud response suggested otherwise. "I'll make dinner now before you get started."

Dragging Aidan out of her room, she expected the disruption to have curtailed the spell of desire, but as they descended the stairs, her wetness grew. Hunger for him swallowed everything else. *I want his tongue inside me.*

Nicky's friends descended in droves causing chaos in their wake. There wouldn't be a moment's peace all night. Decamping at Aidan's house was an impossibility due to his mum's date, but they needed time alone. The house was a prison cell.

Aidan stood behind her as she prepared dinner. She sensed his eyes on her body as she chopped the vegetables. Every chop highlighted the silence. The lack of speech increased her knot of need.

"You shouldn't have texted me your horny thoughts today." Words tumbled out of her mouth. Hopefully speaking her mind would ease the desires dancing around the room. "All I can think about are your hands and what they can do."

"My thumb is still wet from you. How wet could I make you if I grazed you with my tongue?" His gravelly Irish timbre seduced her in waves.

Sophia stared at the food in front of her.

"I could lift you on to the countertop and gently lick your clit until you come over and over again."

Images flashed through her mind, his tongue on her nipples, his fingers exploring her. Gripping the cold hard countertop, she hoped the heat between her thighs would ease. Her heart raced, and she took deep breaths while squeezing her legs together.

His hands grazed her hips when he came up behind her, his erection pressing into her.

Aidan growled in her ear, "Or would you prefer something else inside you? Something hard and unrelenting?"

Arousal rocketed up her spine. She wanted his fingers sliding her knickers down, and his cock inside her. Her moans filled the kitchen.

I need him now.

"Wait outside the front door. Make sure you have your car keys," Sophia demanded.

Aidan stood, confused when she pushed past him

and sprinted to her room. In less than a couple of minutes, she found him waiting outside, his brow furrowed, his member hardened and tenting his trousers.

"Get in the car," she commanded.

"But-"

"Drive to a quiet bit of countryside." Her hunger silenced any attempt at explanation.

The vibrations of the car compelled her to act on her desire. The cold leather seat beneath her skin heightened every sensation. Pulling up her hem, she slipped her mini wand out of her pocket.

Out of the corner of his eye, he watched her. She adored teasing him.

The noise of the vibrating wand had his cock twitching. A moan escaped Sophia's lips when she brushed it over her lace-covered core. Her other hand lingered near her breasts.

"Oh God," he whispered.

They sat still at the traffic lights.

"Let me help," he begged, he stroked the inside of her thighs.

"Both hands on the wheel. Road safety at all times." A devilish grin played on her lips. "And when we get somewhere quiet, I might let you replace the wand with your mouth."

The growling response brought further excitement. *He couldn't want me more.*

She increased her pressure on the wand as the vibrations of the car caressed her clit.

"Shall I take my knickers off or do you want to do it?" The question tripped off her tongue.

"Let me," he demanded.

"What's the magic word?"

"Please, please let me rip your knickers off and lick you until you scream."

Knowing he was rock hard heightened her arousal further. Her nipples pushed against her bra. Sophia's eyelids fluttered, and she bit at her lip, tearing at it.

She was lost in her sensations. Sophia was unaware that they were at their mystery destination until his fingertips ran up the inside of her thigh. When had he stopped the car?

"I want you," Aidan groaned, his lips nuzzling her neck.

Stroking her finger across his clothed cock she swelled with triumph when he juddered.

"Get in the back. I want to come on your mouth."

Together they climbed into the back seat, she lay down, satisfied by his obedience.

Greedily he took her body in, his gaze sweeping up and down her form. There was a risk they could get caught. She had no idea where they were, and it made her want him more. Excitement scorched her skin. Her pulse raced with the quivers of his form.

She weakened the knot on her dress. Undoing it slowly, she ensured Aidan's eyes feasted on her as she revealed her bra covered breasts to him.

His eyes darkened; it was as if the sight of her intoxicated him.

"Take my knickers off."

Licking his lips, his hands ran beneath her dress. Quickly he yanked her knickers down. Suddenly his tongue was lapping at her, running along the length of her sex. She gasped as it dipped inside. He fingered her nipples inside her bra.

The tip of his tongue grazed her clit, making her

shudder.

The zeal with which he indulged on her caused her to writhe, but he gripped her tightly. His head bent as if he'd bowed to her need for carnal pleasures. Sucking hard on her clit, he took her towards climax. Sophia stroked him, rubbing her hands against his hair, needing to share every sensation.

Delicately he held her nub between his teeth, licking her clit with the tip of his tongue.

"Yes," she moaned with each flick, closing in on the orgasm she'd lusted after all day. "Make me come."

Aidan's tongue took her to glorious heights before pushing her over the edge. Holding onto him, she used him as her anchor.

"Yes," she screamed, clenching him between her thighs and gripping tufts of hair between her fingers.

Trailing his tongue over her, he stroked her down from her climax.

"Now what do you want me to do?" he asked, looking up at her, his mouth wet from her juices.

"You know," Sophia replied as her gaze directed him to her mini wand.

*****

Several orgasms later, Aidan's rumbling stomach echoed in the car.

"You need to eat," Sophia whispered in his ear, caressing the dark stubble lining his jaw as he wrapped her back in her dress.

"True." He planted kisses against her forehead. He'd enjoy her all night, but his growling belly took precedence.

Aidan drove them in the direction of a country pub. Something like a glow filled him. *Is this contentment?* Their continuing closeness brought feelings he couldn't explain. "My mum is with John tonight."

Resting his hand on her thigh, he stroked her skin with his thumb. *I never want to stop touching her.*

"How do you feel about that?" she asked, her hand resting on his as they recreated their drive home from Sunday.

"Kind of weird but okay. She deserves happiness."

The silence in the car surprised him. Remembering what his mum had said about telling Sophia the real reason for his rage, he considered trusting her with his darkest secret. Courage rose weakly as words tried to form on his lips.

But she spoke before he could. "Thank you, Aidan."

He couldn't look at her, the bends in the road demanded attention. "For what?"

"For everything. For what you've shown me, but mainly for what you've helped me become." She was serene.

"Which is?"

Sophia's pulled his hand up her leg, encouraging him to caress her thigh. "Me. You've helped me be proud of what I enjoy, and you make it safe to try new things. Thank you."

She was more than sex to him, but could he grow old with her? Images of their time together played like a cinema of memories as they walked into the pub. As they settled on a sofa, her smiles filled him with light. Thinking about what their future could be brought a punch of to his gut. The blow was harder than any he'd had in his life.

A fire roared next to them. The cosy atmosphere, a creation of the homely pub fire, filled his lungs. *I'd be happy spending the rest of the winter with her curled up beside me.* Maybe long term was be a possibility. *I want it to be a possibility.* His mum had helped him see that. But if he had Huntington's disease, it would change them from the two people falling for each other into empty shells.

He barely registered the waiter coming and going. With a soft sigh, he admitted that he was in some sort of relationship. Sophia made him happy.

Looking at her, he found hollow eyes, her mouth tight.

"Soph?" he asked cautiously.

Her startled gasp coupled with the crack of the nearby fire put him on edge. He turned to see where she was staring. A fair-haired guy with a cocky half-smile caught his eye. Even across the pub, he saw something in the guy he didn't like. Was it the way he was mansplaying while sitting at a small table? Maybe it was the way his fingers reached for the bottom of the waitresses skirt every time she passed by. Aidan shifted slightly and found himself staring at the woman sat with him. She was willowy, with long blonde hair that fell like a curtain of silk across her shoulders and down her back. She turned her mouth down at all the people she looked at before brushing her long delicate fingers across her jumper and picking at lint and tossing it on the ground.

Gently Aidan placed his hand on Sophia's shivering leg. She jumped against contact with his warm flesh.

"Soph," he whispered again. "Who is it?"

She mouthed her answer. "Graham."

Hatred overcame Aidan when he stared at the guy

again. Graham had come close to destroying Sophia through sustained control and mental abuse.

"And he's with her." Sophia's whispered words confused him, but not as much as the way her voice caught when she said "her".

Grasping Sophia's hand tightly, he threaded her trembling fingers with his. "Her?"

Sophia didn't reply. Pale and unmoving, she resembled someone surrounded by the ghosts of their past, fear etched across her face. Aidan forced the anger down. *I need to be strong for her.* He tucked a finger under her chin and turned her head to face him.

"Honey, who is the woman with Graham?" he asked, imploring her to find him through her pain.

"Kelly," she replied in defeat.

The name was familiar. Rifling through his memories, he tried to reach the right one. "Your housemate after university?"

Sophia's eyes betrayed a watery sheen. She nodded with a sadness that tore at his heart. She was battling for strength and fighting back her tears.

"There was more to the story," he stated rather than questioned.

She stared through him.

"Sophia?" he pleaded, grasping her trembling hands in his. He only had comfort to offer, but he'd wrap her in a blanket of care if she let him. "Talk to me, honey, please. Tell me."

Waiting patiently, he willed her to share, believing in the inner strength of the goddess beside him.

Chapter Twenty

Sophia faltered at first, but quickly her words flowed like a river bursting free from its dam. "When we were at university, Kelly was the flaky one, but fun to be around and caring, at times. Kelly, Nicky and I were close.

"Men clamoured for her, but she only loved Adam. He brought out the best version of her. They adored each other and would sacrifice anything to make each other happy.

"After university Adam went to study in Italy for a year. Kelly changed. They'd promised to stay faithful, but barely a month passed before she was bringing other guys back to the house. Nicky and I were unsure what to do. We tried chatting to her, but it didn't work, and we were betraying Adam by not telling him. We prayed that it was a phase that she had to get out of her system. After the New Year, it stopped. Nicky and I were so relieved. We thought she was back to our Kelly, the Kelly that adored Adam."

Sophia took a deep breath. Although relieved to be sharing the full story, it was as if fresh pain bled from old wounds. The warmth from Aidan's hands reached through to her veins. It didn't stop her shaking but acted as a reminder that she wasn't alone.

"Were you wrong?" he asked astutely.

"Yep. Kelly hadn't stopped shagging around because of Adam, who she broke up with a couple of months later. She'd stopped because there was someone else."

"Graham?"

"Yes. Graham was the first guy who'd said no to her, which made him irresistible. I found out later they'd kissed at New Year. I was with mum. Graham had been angry because he'd wanted me with him at a party, and I defied him. He punished me by kissing Kelly. But it became their dirty secret, and they didn't stop. Men bowed down to Kelly, but Graham wasn't like that. He was controlling, possessive, and no one dominated him. To her, he was something to achieve.

"Ultimately, she offered the one thing I refused to give him - sex. When he was studying at home, she'd take sick days or leave work early, and they'd fuck like rabbits. Whenever they could sneak in a session they did, I had no idea."

"And they're still together?"

"I guess they fell for each other. The night Graham attempted to force himself on me, we broke up. Nicky kicked Graham out, but Kelly snuck him back into the house. He stayed the night with her. Nicky caught him leaving the next morning, and that's how I found out. After that, Kelly moved out, and I hoped I'd never see them again." Sophia attempted to sound blasé, but she wasn't even kidding herself.

"Did you see her again?"

Their last confrontation had left a cut so deep that she wasn't sure if it had healed or continued to bleed throughout her body when she got close to people. She'd stayed away from all men, until Aidan.

"Soph, you can tell me. Nothing will stop how I feel about you." As he pulled her close, his compassion enveloped her. This man had helped her embrace her identity.

"I saw her one more time," Sophia explained, "the night, she came back to the apartment with Graham to pick up the last of her stuff. Nicky was at work. I was vulnerable."

Sophia's breath was laboured. "Kelly made digs, laughing at me as she and Graham flaunted their relationship; snogging and touching. That's when she told me that Graham had been leaving my cold, sexless bed for months for her; a 'real woman'. I never told anyone the vile things she said to be, not even Nicky," Sophia dropped her head in shame.

"Please tell me," Aidan begged. "I'm here for you. It's been eating at you for too long." His warmth spread through her body. However hard she trembled he didn't let her go. A lone tear rolled down her cheek, and he brushed it away.

"She told me that Graham had found a stunning, sexy woman who knew how to take care of his needs rather than a frigid, ugly bitch whose naked body made his dick soft. These were originally his words, apparently." Sophia's shoulders sank as she released the words. Air escaped her lungs. Those words had haunted her. *But now I understand how ludicrous they were.* The whole thing had been ridiculous.

Aidan pulled her onto his lap and held her tight. A waiter strolled in their direction before clocking their intimacy and making a swift exit.

"I don't want you to think that I wanted Graham, that wasn't why I was upset. I wasn't jealous. But I couldn't understand how people I'd once considered my closest friends, my world, were so cruel," she said hurriedly.

"You don't need to explain." He held her close and ran his fingers through her hair. It was what she needed; not words or dramatic gestures, just him.

They sat like that, Sophia resting in his arms with her head tucked under his chin, for a long time. The waiter broke their spell eventually and placed their food in front of them.

Sophia was reluctant to part from Aidan, but she slipped from his lap to eat. They stayed as close as possible, their bodies touching. There was a new intimacy between them.

"Aidan?" she said softly. "There is something I need to do. I want to do it by myself, but I need to know you're here and have my back."

"Always."

"I'm going to speak with Graham and Kelly." It was time to expel her demons.

"I can come with you. If you're worried about my anger, you don't need to be. I'm okay," Aidan replied. Sophia inspected his eyes for any ounce of rage, but there was nothing. He examined her too with a softened gaze. Creases, she'd never noticed before, formed at the corners of his eyes and a smile pulled up one side of his mouth. "But I understand why you need to do this alone. I'm here, no matter what. I think it's time to close one door of your past for good."

It was the best thing he could have said. "Thank you. I won't be long."

Although he remained seated, settling the bill, she felt his eyes on her. His presence and the confidence he'd helped her find remained with her.

Sophia trembled as she neared Graham and Kelly's table.

Graham had barely changed. His hair was the same dark blonde, and he was as lean as before. There may have been a couple more wrinkles around his mouth, but it was as if time had stood still. Fear flamed her. *I don't want to be damaged anymore.*

Kelly was admiring herself in an antique compact. Her light blue eyes were like ice, cutting through the glass she stared at so intently. At nearly six foot she'd always reminded Sophia of some elven goddess, but knowing what was beneath her alabaster skin made it difficult for Sophia to recognise her beauty.

"Having a nice evening?" Sophia asked tentatively, broaching their space.

They turned to gawp at her. Kelly's eyes narrowed while Graham's face dropped. They stared, shifting uncomfortably. *I'm not running, not anymore.*

"I hope I'm not disturbing anything, I'd hate to get in the way," she said, unable to resist a dig.

"No, it's nice to see you," Graham stuttered. The way his stare roamed across her body made her skin crawl, but she refused to let him see her reaction. Her bra was missing in Aidan's car, and her cobalt wrap-around jersey dress did nothing to hide its absence. She would have never done that with Graham. Sophia pulled back her shoulders, refusing to hide her body. *I have nothing to be embarrassed by. I'm gorgeous.*

"How are you both?" Sophia inquired.

"Good, yeah," Graham answered for them.

Kelly's eyes fixed on her like those of a snake sizing up its prey. "You've put on weight, Sophia."

Sophia laughed, confident that Kelly was attempting to inflict damage to her confidence. "It has been quite a few years. But you know what it's like when you're happy."

"Or when you're comfort eating," Kelly said snidely.

"Kelly." Graham shushed her.

"It's okay. I guess our history makes it difficult to be civil, but no hard feelings, eh? We've all moved on. Life is good for me. And you two are probably married with babies now," Sophia replied.

Kelly glared.

Uh oh, I've said the wrong thing.

"Marriage isn't Graham's thing. We'll marry when he's finished studying, apparently." Kelly turned angrily in his direction. "When will that be, Graham? When will you start paying your way? I could have been with Adam. He's made a name for himself and is a company director in Italy. What are you? A perpetual student."

"You're always insulting me. Have you ever considered that you're the problem, that I can't be successful because all my energy goes into dealing with you?" Graham spat back.

Sophia cringed. *At least Kelly answers back. Maybe they both found someone they deserved.* Either way, it wasn't Sophia's problem anymore. Maybe Kelly had inadvertently saved her from the years he would have spent destroying her.

"Don't you try that emotional abuse bullshit on me. I see what you're doing, Graham. You're a sorry excuse for a man. You're on thin ice right now. Don't forget I'm your cash cow," Kelly replied.

"Cash cow? You got one of those words right. Why do you always go on about money, is it to emasculate me? I'm building us a great future." Graham sniped back.

Sophia stepped back. "I think I'll go... But—"

"Don't call me a cow and don't give me that future bullshit. I can't keep having this argument with you. I'd leave you, but your lawyer daddy would take half my house that you live in, but never contribute to. Maybe it's time you stepped up. And, while you're at it, stop being a selfish bastard who can't make a woman come!"

Sophia stifled a laugh. *Maybe I wasn't the problem after all.* When he cheated on her and crushed her world temporarily, he'd done her a favour. She wouldn't have survived long term with him. Surely their relationship couldn't last much longer? Maybe they enjoyed the drama. They were utterly animated, with glinting eyes and powerful gestures.

"That's not what Kourtney or Amber said, or should I say screamed," he replied snidely.

Kelly stood, drink in hand. "You're going to justify your prowess by bringing up the names of women you've cheated on me with? Are you fucking kidding me? Say one more thing; I dare you."

Sophia glanced at Aiden, who waved at her, a smile full of adoration. "Okay, well it looks like you've got things going on. It was great to see you both again. I'm going to get back to my date."

"Is that Aidan Flynn, the rugby player? Bloody hell you leagued up after this piece of shit here," Kelly uttered as Graham glared at them.

"Shall we get going, honey?" Aidan's whisper was

suddenly in Sophia's ear. "I want to paint you tonight if I can concentrate for long enough. I can't get enough of you. I'm so lucky to have met you."

Sophia smiled and pecked him on the cheek.

"You're with him? What did I do to deserve this shitbag?" Kelly mumbled, pointing at Graham.

"Oh, I'm a shitbag now? I thought I was a bastard. At least I'm not a haggard whore who will put out to anyone who smiles at her," Graham raised his voice.

Kelly gasped loudly before tossing her drink in Graham's face.

"Let's go. Take care, you guys," Sophia shouted as she grabbed Aidan's hand and ushered him towards his car. He squeezed her hand tightly and locked eyes with her.

"Are you okay?" he mouthed.

She squeezed back, nodded and smiled. It was like the heavy weight that had surrounded her heart for years had disintegrated and left her free.

The drive was a mystery; she didn't know where they were until Aidan turned off the engine. His converted barn rose like their sanctuary in the darkness.

"Mum texted me while we were eating. She and John went to a movie after their food. I want to paint you tonight if that's okay."

They made their way to the art room. He guided her, unable to keep any distance.

Aidan's eyes were on her as he painted, but instead of shrinking from his gaze, she basked in the look of adoration he gave as he studied her body. A scarlet wash of satin material draped across her, but Aidan looked at her like there was nothing between him and her naked skin.

He appraised her with a look of love and told her how lucky he was to be with her. Compliments about her silk waves, her flawless skin, and her beautiful body washed over her.

The flaws she'd conjured in her head over the years fell away. Her shattered heart wasn't just repaired; it became indestructible.

I think I might be the goddess he believes me to be.

"That's enough for now," he said softly, unable to mask his hunger. For two hours he'd built Sophia up while he painted her.

Sweeping the material from her body, he lifted her into his arms and carried her to his room. His hot breath grazed her neck. "I'm going to worship you tonight. I'm going to make love to you like you deserve."

Aidan was true to his word. The skills he possessed stunned her, and the intimacy of each loving act had orgasms escaping her lips throughout the night.

Chapter Twenty-One
Two Months Later

Sophia trudged up the path to her home. It was a couple of months since she'd first met Aidan, yet her life had changed beyond recognition.

A December chill clung to the only bit of uncovered skin. The touch of winter had frozen her cheeks. As she slammed her front door closed, she heard the familiar whistle of a text message. It was Aidan.

A: *I'll pick you up after 7 x*

Oh shit. There would be no rest tonight. She'd promised Aidan they'd have dinner with Kate and John. But it was the next day she was labouring over, Aidan was coming to her work to meet a couple of the kids. He'd suggested it out of the blue after one of his counselling sessions. Sophia had no idea what Aidan talked about during those hours, but every week he seemed to open up to Sophia more. He spoke about his childhood and the bullying he'd been victim to. There was the odd moment when she thought there was something he was struggling to say, but either something else happened, or he changed the subject. What more would it take to get him to share? *And will I wait around to find out?*

Giggles that accompanied secrets shared carried from the lounge. Pausing in the doorway, she was confronted by the flushed faces of Nicky and Ryan. They tickled each other between sofa snuggles.

"I can't wait for Rome. A week until we fly out!" Ryan said with a smile, his hands entwining with Nicky's. "Our first Christmas as a couple."

Sophia stepped back, not wanting to intrude on their moment.

"Hey, you," Nicky exclaimed.

"Hey." Sophia rid herself of the layers with fumbling hands.

"Long time no see," Nicky added, her eyes narrowing in concern.

Ryan bounced to his feet. "Okay, Nix, I'd best get to football, or there'll be no one to score the goals. You keep planning Rome and don't forget; I expect romance." Ryan cupped Nicky's cheek before their lips met in a gentle kiss.

"I'll be back by nine. Bye, Sophia," he added before bounding away.

"What's up?" Nicky asked, her eyebrows raised in suspicion.

"You two are a real couple now."

The girlish laugh that left Nicky's mouth was an alien sound.

"I guess so. You and I have been like ships in the night recently." Nicky's eyes sparkled. "Ryan told me a while back that he wanted to be my boyfriend. Oh my God, I'm like a teenager! We're going on a romantic holiday next week. I think he's in love with me."

Sophia tumbled onto Nicky for a hug. "It's about time you had some love in your life."

"It's kind of ridiculous for two people who started as fuck buddies," Nicky replied, helping Sophia with the scarf that was around her neck.

"What made him consider a proper relationship?" Sophia asked.

"Aidan had a word with him."

Sophia froze. The keys in her clenched fist scraped at her palm. "What?"

"Aidan said that if Ryan wasn't careful, he was going to lose me to a guy who knew how to treat me right. Several rugby players wanted to ask me out." Nicky's eyes were wide as she retold the story.

Why was Aidan giving out wisdom like that while holding back on their own relationship? She wanted to be ecstatic for Nicky, but sadness crept up on her.

Nicky plopped Sophia's keys on the coffee table. "What's going on."

"Aidan won't call me his girlfriend." Sophia rubbed her temples. Nicky held her close.

"Why not?"

"I don't know. He said having a girlfriend wasn't his thing." Her stresses came tumbling out.

"What does he call you?" Nicky asked.

"He introduces me to people as Sophia, his "friend", but there's no one else, I'm the only woman he's with." Tears spilt over, and she tucked her legs in. The last month had taken its toll. The painted smile on her face was starting to peel and flake away. "It's like he can't say the word and he can't consider the future. I say can't, maybe he doesn't want to."

"What do you want?" Nicky soothed.

"I want him and only him. I want marriage. I want to be the mother of his children. I want him to move the earth to be with me. I know it's only been a couple of months, but at some point, in the future, it's what I want."

"Have you said this to him?" Nicky was gentle in her questioning.

"I'm too scared. I know he has counselling. When he was drunk last week, he said we're going to talk about it soon. But can I rely on that? To top it off, he hasn't finished the painting of me," Sophia blurted out.

"Why is that an issue?"

"Aidan told me that it never takes longer than a fortnight to do a painting once he lays it out in his head. It's been over a month."

"I don't understand," Nicky replied.

Why would she? Why would anyone? I'm over the top.

"The painting is us. There's a barrier stopping Aidan from moving forward, and it's affecting the painting. When he paints me, he's happy, and we're in this magical world where the future doesn't exist."

"So, what now?" Nicky asked, holding Sophia closer.

Sophia was ashamed at the lack of celebration she was giving Nicky's good news. Ryan's aftershave lingered on Nicky. Her perfume fused with his masculine scent. It made a unique new fragrance, one of their love.

"Tonight, we're going to Aidan's house for dinner with his mum and John. I'll pretend I'm happy, but I'm not. But it doesn't matter. It will be fine."

Sophia gave Nicky a massive hug before jumping up, not wanting to bother her with any more of her problems. "Thank you for listening. I'm silly and self-pitying. I'm ecstatic for you and Ryan. If anyone deserves to be happy, it's you." It was time to put on her happy mask and hide her feelings and her exhausted state. She stepped away before Nicky's hand could snake around her waist.

"You deserve happiness too, Soph. You can't stop living the life you want and denying your dreams because of Aidan. Soon walking away is going to be a lot more painful than staying."

❊❊❊❊❊

Aidan shifted in his chair, one eye on Sophia. She fiddled with the ends of her hair, twisting sections of her waves around her fingers, a pained expression on her face. Was she building up to breaking it off? He was always waiting for her to end it. *It's what I deserve, but I don't want to imagine life without her.* Their time together had started as something fun but had become a constant longing to be close to her.

The journey to her work had been silent except for the odd comment about Nicky and Ryan dating, which he'd ignored. He was destroying her because he was too scared to be without her. Something had to give. Counselling was helping, and there had been numerous moments when he'd nearly told her everything, but an image of a weakened and desperate Sophia nursing his dying body shut his mouth every time. *I can't do that to her.* But that left one option, it was time to learn if he had Huntington's. His counselling sessions and Doctor Sampson had aided his decision. But once he got the test results there would be no going back. He might never have power over his life again. He'd reached for control in the only way he could. He'd delayed taking the test one more week. Eventually, he'd tell her the whole story. Then they could manage the future. But still, he hadn't taken it.

He was driving on auto-pilot. They were already at Sophia's work. He turned off the engine and reached for the door.

"Thank you, Aidan," Sophia murmured.

"For what?"

"For taking time out and coming into work. Tim, the kid you're going to chat to today, he needs this. Meeting you is the only reason he doesn't run out of workshops anymore. He doesn't talk since his dad died last year, but he has talked about you and the rugby team. You have no idea what it means," she said, pecking him on the cheek before heading out the vehicle.

But I do know. I understand the pain that kid is going through. Pain that controlled every decision I made and sat behind each ounce of rage. I never thought the agony would go away until I met you and started counselling. Why couldn't he say those things to her? But she was already out of the car. He loved her in the sexy underwear and curve-skimming dresses, but he also loved her in her "workwear"; skinny jeans, trainers and a hooded jumper. His heart swelled. *You have to tell her soon.*

*****

"You're playing Bath again, you're gonna smash them," Lottie said in awe. Sophia watched from the doorway. Aidan was a natural with the kids. They adored him, not stopping in their questions even when he threw a ball to them.

"Yeah, we're going to take them to the cleaners," Aidan replied, winking at Sophia as he tossed the ball to Tim. The Bath game had been stressing Aidan out for weeks. The LV cup draw meant that they were facing Bath at home for the second time in a couple of months. The Destroyer had dropped comments about wanting to draw blood and Aidan had told her a couple of times he wasn't relishing the prospect of facing him again.

"Sophia, a word, now." Sophia turned to find a frustrated Tasha eyeballing her. "In private."

"Sure," she replied, following Tasha to one of the small meeting rooms off the main office. All the walls were made of glass, and as she closed the door, she could see the other staff watching intently from their desks.

Tasha had been unbearable for the last couple of months. If she wasn't barking orders at Sophia, she was increasing her workload, giving her the most complex kids and stealing her ideas in meetings. What was this about?

"Why did you go to Ray with your new idea for workshop days? I am your boss, and Ray is the CEO. You should have come to me first," Tasha ranted. "Do you know how this makes me look? You should consult me on everything."

Sophia took a deep breath. "If you took the time to listen to me, rather than getting me to do all the crap jobs you don't want to do, I might have. Besides, we both know you would have stolen my idea."

"Ha! You can talk." Tasha snapped back. "Do we have a certain rugby player, that you stole off me, to thank for your recent bad attitude?"

"Are you kidding me?" Sophia shouted. *I've had enough of this.* "It's called confidence, not a bad attitude.

I have learnt to stand up for myself and not be scared of the consequences or of the threats you want to dole out on this occasion. These kids mean more to me than anything, but I'm not setting them a great example by letting you walk all over me and being too scared to confront your bad management and even worse behaviour." Tasha opened her mouth, but Sophia was on a roll. This argument had been building for months. "And another thing, the next time you want someone to practically dress up like a tart for a fundraising art exhibition think about how it impacts our reputation."

"The charity's reputation or that of our sweet innocent Sophia," Tasha guffawed.

Sophia rolled her eyes. Trying to transform Tasha into a caring boss was impossible. *But at least I'm not scared of her anymore.* "The charity's reputation. And please keep your personal opinions of my life to yourself unless it affects my job. Now I'm going to return to what I do best; giving a shit about the kids who access our charity. At least one of us knows how to do it."

Sophia stalked out the room, slamming the door in her wake. Everyone stared at her from behind their computer screens. Jack stood up and started clapping in celebration.

"About time," he shouted as another person whooped. Even Janet was cheering.

With a curtsy and a massive grin, Sophia strode out of the office and back to the activity room. She resumed her position in the doorway. Most of the kids had gone home while she'd been chatting with Tasha. The session leader was tidying up while Aidan spoke to Tim.

The boy was in tears.

Before she stepped in to deal with the situation, Tim

said, "I'm just so scared. My dad had MS, what if I get it too? I don't want to die."

That was what going on with Tim. He was grieving, and he was scared of getting ill.

Aidan and Tim sat on the floor together, like two boys at school. The innocence of Aidan's face took her breath away. "I know, buddy," Aidan replied. "I bet sometimes you want to shout at people and other times you want to cry and cry until it all goes away."

Tim nodded before replying, "I can't talk to mum because she's sad too. I catch her crying sometimes; she doesn't know I've seen her. I hide in my room because it reminds me of dad and I talk to him there and tell him about my day. I wish I wasn't alone and that all the bad stuff hadn't happened. No one knows I'm scared of getting ill. I heard the teachers say I should be kept away from my friends. They say it's because I'm naughty all the time, but I'm scared."

A tear rolled down Aidan's cheek. "Of course, you're scared. It's okay to be scared."

Tim took a deep breath and looked up shyly. "You wouldn't be scared. You're a big rugby player. I bet you'd just get over it."

"No, not really. I have people I talk to about stuff like this. The only way I deal with it is talking about it, and finding ways to manage the anger and sadness. I'm lucky, I met someone here, and they've helped me. There are lots of people here who care about you. And they want you to shout and to cry and to do whatever you need to. Have you thought about chatting to one of the team here?" Aidan looked at Sophia and beckoned her into their chat. "Sophia is amazing, and she will help you. And any time you want to kick a rugby ball on a field when it all gets too much, and you're fed up of talking then get hold of Sophia, and you and me can have a kick about? But talk to Sophia, she can help you deal with the bad stuff."

Tim looked up at her. "Can I chat to you?"

*****

Aidan held Sophia in his arms as she wept. He'd left her alone to chat with Tim while he'd gone for a walk. He'd called his mum to remind her how much he loved her and finally called Doctor Sampson and booked the test for the day before his last match of the year. Tim had been the push he needed. The results would be back a couple of days later just before Christmas, in time to share everything with Sophia when neither of them would be working.

"It nearly broke my heart when he spoke to me," Sophia said between tears. "I don't normally get this upset, but he's in so much pain."

"Let it out, honey. You don't need to explain yourself to me," Aidan said, rocking her gently. They lay in bed, skin to skin. Lovers entwined in sadness.

"It's not fair, none of this is fair. Why should Tim suffer? Sometimes the world is cruel. I don't know if I can keep doing this job. I'm exhausted all the time. Am I strong enough?" she asked.

"You're the strongest person I know. Well, you and mum. The world is shit; it breaks people, sometimes forever. But you've given him something he hasn't had in a long time. You gave him hope."

"You did too," Sophia replied, the tears slower now. "I don't know all you said to him, but you were magic tonight."

"Not magic," Aidan replied dismissively. "But I understood him. I..."

You can do this. "I was like Tim. I guess I still am," Aidan said. His chest burnt, it was as if there was a battle inside him; the words were fighting to come out, but his shame was forcing them back in. "My dad died when I was a kid too."

"I wondered," she murmured. There were no tears now.

He stared into her deep brown eyes and witnessed her love and acceptance. If she hated him because he'd hidden things from her, then he couldn't see it.

"I was a little older than Tim. That's why we came to England, mum couldn't be around the pain of the past, and she needed to be near her family. I remember the anger, the sadness, and the fear that my mum would get worse if she knew I was struggling. Tim is lucky to have you to speak to, and I'm lucky too. If I didn't have you, I don't know where I'd be right now. You've changed my life. There's hope for Tim."

"And for you too," she said with a kiss to his lips.

He kissed her back gently, yet there was a passion to it too.

Although the burning in his chest had eased there was still pressure there. *I have to wait until the test results.* But what if he had Huntington's?

"There's more, isn't there?" Sophia asked tentatively.

I will never understand her ability to read me.

"Yes," he replied simply. His head dropped. He couldn't look at her anymore, ashamed at all he'd kept from her.

Gently she kissed his forehead, then his cheeks, his eyelashes and his lips. "Aidan, you only have to tell me when you're ready, but please don't wait forever okay? You don't need to hide anything from me."

But what if his secret destroyed her?

"I will tell you soon. I promise. Before Christmas, I will share everything. I just need a little more time," he sighed, staring down.

Her finger lifted his chin and forced him to look at her. "I will give you a little more time. I know you've been sorting out a lot of stuff. You don't have to do it alone because you're not alone anymore. No more conversations about the future until Christmas, okay?"

He nodded and snuggled up, his chin against her shoulder. It would get sorted. One way or the other he would know. The anger had been better. The rage that had been his best friend for years rarely visited anymore. But seeing Tim, seeing the grief of a child nearly destroyed by fear of his future had reminded Aidan of his vow not to have children. He couldn't let that happen. He would never see his son in pain at the thought of future illness. That was the only thing that brought anger bubbling up inside him, replacing the shame instantly. Counselling had helped, it had given him techniques for coping during the moment.

Seeing Tim upset had brought out his caring side, but the anger sat, waiting. If he hadn't gone on a walk after and talked to his mum what would have happened? Had Huntington's brought that anger or was his own unresolved emotions? Only the test would tell him.

Chapter Twenty-Two

Aidan admired Sophia as she prepared for their evening drinks with Ryan and Nicky.

I've only got to get through two more days and then we can move on with our lives. The Bath game will be over, but will our relationship be over too?

She applied the mascara to her already long eyelashes. Her beauty shook him from his anxious mood.

"Are you ready yet?" he teased. He'd be happier spending a night snuggling on the sofa or sliding his hands inside her pencil skirt. His propensity for playing with her and bringing her to orgasm never ebbed.

"I want to look my best." The sweet smile reflected in the mirror did nothing to calm his hunger. Sophia had insisted on putting effort into her hair and make-up. She'd been battling tiredness and sickness all week.

"You're stunning to me.".

"Hmmm, I know that look," she giggled. "You're imaging the dirtiest things."

She was partly right, but it was more than that. The skill with which she swept each brush and flicked applicators to accentuate her features was impressive, but it was nothing compared to her true beauty which radiated from inside. She'd changed his life, and he couldn't be without her.

Silently Aidan rose to his feet. Their eyes locked via the gold-framed mirror. Light glinted off her face, highlighting her features.

"Aidan." Her cheeks flushed in anticipation as she inspected him. "We haven't got time."

Words faded into the air when his lips found her neck.

Sophia's palms flattened against the dressing table, and his hands skimmed her body as they travelled up to her jumper. The cashmere barely brushed his fingertips as he pulled it up and over her head and tossed it across the room.

"It's expensive," she teased.

"I'll buy you another," he growled. A sultry laugh ran between them. Aidan rubbed her nipples through the lace of her red bra.

"You need to behave. The taxi will be here in ten minutes." Sophia's protests were silenced by her fingers, pulling at the zip of his jeans. Easing it down, she covered his member with her palm.

"Soph," he murmured. "I don't think that will be a problem. Besides, it's cold out, and I need to warm you up."

"Then why am I losing my clothes?" she giggled.

Sliding her skirt up to her thighs, he groaned at her combination of black stilettos and hold-ups. Had she been planning to flash them while they were out in public like she'd done before? His cock twitched at the swash of bare skin above the lace.

He pushed her knickers to one side. She was wetter than he expected.

"No teasing. I want you inside me right now," Sophia demanded.

He slipped a condom on. Swiftly he thrust inside her.

"Watch us," he commanded, their eyes focusing on each other through the mirror.

She pushed back against him as he gripped her breasts, matching his thrusts. He sucked on her shoulder. Moans reverberated around the room, causing him to plunge deeper inside her. Her eyes met his in the mirror, daring him to move faster and push harder.

They were running out of time. It was a struggle not to languish at the moment, Sophia's hot flesh against his. He wanted to take all night, letting her screams deafen him. *Later.* It was a promise to himself that he wouldn't forget.

With a yank of her hips, he pulled her against him while rubbing her clit. Biting down on her neck brought a scowl from her reflection. He bound her close, and she writhed, demanding more, panting and feral in the way she stared at him through the mirror.

For a second, he paused, drawing his hips back a little, basking in her presence. The image of her in horny desperation, becoming one with him pained his heart. They were so vulnerable, and yet they sacrificed their power to be with each other at this moment. Nothing compared to this, nothing would satisfy him but her.

"Don't stop," she cried out, her voice strained. She pushed back, trying to reach him.

Suddenly he thrust hard and deep into her while pulling her into him. Sophia started shuddering, her climax hitting quicker than he expected. Helpless to the orgasm ravaging her, she made him bolster her. Her legs shook, and goose pimples covered her arms. Enraptured by the sight of her head thrown back and her mouth open in the glorious O shape, his orgasm was triggered. He came hard while she pulsated around his cock.

Aidan held on to her. He wanted her like this forever. The longing to bring her again to climax was put on hold by a text from the taxi company. Rushing to find her jumper, he paused temporarily to watch her tidy herself up.

Time is running out.

*****

The bar was quiet considering Christmas was less than a week away. Rustic tables and velvet furnishings brought to mind a plush hideaway. The fancy gin bar with booths that encouraged closeness was hidden down a back alley, away from the crowds. Flames from a fire crackled in the corner. Tinsel shined red while gold baubles projected light around the room. Warmth radiated and couples flirted as they sat poised on stools resting their drinks on taller tables.

Throughout the evening, Sophia glanced at Nicky and Ryan. They sat close. Ryan rested his hand on Nicky's leg or occasionally brushed her hair away from her face. They were breathless from their intimacy. It was Christmas drinks for the four of them before Nicky and Ryan left for a week away in Rome the next day. They were glowing.

Aidan took the bulk of Sophia's focus. It was evident from the tension in his shoulders that he had things to tell her. Sometimes she caught him studying her with a pained expression. The painting of her remained unfinished. Sophia was counting down the days until Christmas and until he told her everything. The conversation hung over them like a noose.

Aidan's palm rested against her leg, and he offered reassurance through his gaze. A part of her hated that he easily sensed her change in mood. Unknowingly she'd let herself trust him. Her defences had fallen. He gauged, maybe not what she was thinking, but that stress was churning.

"You okay?" he whispered.

She nodded, but her anxiety betrayed her. It had taken its toll on her body through sleepless nights. Stress itched at her brain. The prosecco that bubbled away in front of her sat ignored as it fizzed with an excitement she couldn't replicate.

"I'll get you another drink," he whispered, "an orange juice. Does anyone else want something?"

He strode to the bar and out of her sight.

"I'm popping to the loo." Familiar waves of nausea hit. It was unlikely to be vomit, she'd had the same sensation for days, but the fear she might be sick sent her rushing. Nicky went to stand. "It's okay. You guys stay here."

A couple of minutes later, Sophia meandered back through the bar. She was right; it was nausea. Stress always hit her stomach. *If only I knew what was going on with Aidan and what it meant for our future. Do we have a future.*

"Alright, babes?" Sophia looked up and found herself confronted by The Destroyer, Aidan's rugby nemesis. He'd chosen the nickname himself, thinking it held more of a threat than his real name, Gavin Burk.

She attempted to skirt around him, but his hand shot out. His stare was predatory.

"Leave me alone," she grimaced, convulsing at his

touch. "I have to go."

"You're leaving before we've had a friendly kiss?" Leering closer, he threatened to force his lips against hers.

Sophia shivered. The last thing she needed was for Aidan to get into a bar fight less than forty-eight hours before the game. Though Aidan had kept his head with no hint of anger since the night at that hotel, she was sure Gavin would know how to wind him up.

"Please leave me alone."

He gripped her tighter. Her heart thundered. *How can I get out of this?*

"Look, darling, you have a firm ass and a nice rack. I noticed you from across the room, and I wanted to say hi. Let's have some fun. Those red lips of yours would look great wrapped around my-."

Aidan came out of nowhere, diving between them. Anger flashed in his eyes. His presence forced Gavin's hand away from her arm, which glowed from the red finger marks imprinted on her skin.

"Look, mate, I saw her first. Get lost." Gavin's eyes pointed in the direction he wanted Aidan to go, but Aidan slipped his arm around her.

Sophia waited for Aidan to say that she was his girlfriend, but the words never came. "She's my... Sophia is with me."

Her eyes snapped angrily to his, but he was too busy staring Gavin down to notice. *What is wrong with these men?* If she hadn't been scared Aidan might do something stupid, she'd have walked out. *I deserve respect. How dare these guys treat me like I'm nothing.*

"Fuck off. There's no ring on her finger. There's plenty of pussy here for you tonight so pick one of them, this one's mine." The anger between them was escalating. Moving closer they resembled bucks battling for position. "Besides shouldn't you be out training? You're getting old and haven't got a chance at beating us Saturday."

"I'm gonna beat you down as easily as I did last time." They were so close their noses nearly touched. Shoulders lowered, and their chests puffed out. The verbal sparring was pathetic, but it was going to get physical. "What the hell are you doing here? You're a long way from Bath, and you're not playing until Saturday. Spying on us?"

"Ha," Gavin barked. "I'm here because your coaches want me here. They're making noises about next season already. Their "best" player has had his day."

Aidan chuckled as Sophia pulled him away, but it was a hollow laugh.

"Leave us alone, Gavin. You're a piece of shit." Sophia shouted. Her hand covered her mouth temporarily. *Did I say that out loud? Anger still bubbled from the altercation, but satisfaction crawled through her too.*

Her words had diverted Aidan. "What she said," he mumbled awkwardly to Gavin as they slowly moved back through the groups of spectators.

"Bet your woman thinks the best player has had his day, too," Gavin called out. "Maybe she's like your mum and wants a nice English man, not some Irish fucker. How come you never talk about your dad, Aidan?"

Aidan exploded.

He was too quick, striding to Gavin before Sophia could stop him. He pushed a finger into Gavin's face. Words were spoken low and quiet, inaudible to anyone but them. Gavin paled, Aidan had shared a threat that he'd been unprepared for. Aidan's fist clenched and unclenched by his side, his body quivering with barely controlled rage.

Aidan made their apologies to Nicky and Ryan, who offered their own excuses about needing to pack for their trip. The entire bar had witnessed the confrontation. This sort of thing had a habit of getting out of control, and Aidan wouldn't want to risk his career. Even the bouncers had been ready to act although probably unsure how to pull apart such powerful men if it had escalated.

Grabbing their coats, Nicky hugged Sophia tight enough to crush her chest. By the time they returned, Aidan would have shared his secrets. A week seemed a long time without her best friend. *What if I need her?* A sweet lilt touched her ear. "Stay safe, doe eyes, and call me no matter what. I may be in Rome until after Christmas, but I'm still on the other end of a phone."

Within moments they were heading back to his house. The silence overwhelmed the small enclosed taxi. Sophia glanced at Aidan. *Should I say something?* Aside from the anger, he was suffering from emotional torment. A watery sheen covered his eyes as they flicked nervously around the dark taxi.

What still stunned her was that even during the fight, Aidan wouldn't call her his girlfriend. Gavin was right. *I could be with someone else.* There must be a guy out there who was proud to call her his. What Aidan offered her wasn't enough anymore.

The taxi bounced down the dirt road to his house before going on its way again. They slunk through the door, and Sophia headed straight for bed. Aidan wasn't in the right place to talk, and she wasn't going to force him. She'd had enough.

"You belong to me, Sophia." His voice, the words gruff and soulless startled her. Stopping in her tracks, she remained silent. Where would she start if she tried to reply anyway?

"I didn't mean that the way it sounded. I don't mean I own you. But you're all I want. I don't want to be with anyone else, and I don't want you to be with anyone else. I want you, and only you." His vulnerability scratched at her heart.

"But I can't hold on forever waiting for you to accept this relationship. If we don't have a future, then I need to know. I want to be with someone who isn't ashamed to call me his girlfriend."

"I'm not ashamed, but please give me a couple more days. I will tell you everything."

"Why then and not now? Why are there still secrets? I love you, Aidan!" She hadn't meant to say that at that moment. She should have said it in joy, not anger. She covered her mouth before walking to the bedroom.

He gravitated to the room too, and they lay in bed, holding each other close, but their intimacy was forced. One thought settled in Sophia's heart as she struggled to sleep. *He didn't say he loved me too.*

*****

Aidan woke hours later to the sound of vomiting. He reached out, but Sophia wasn't there. Clenching the cotton sheets, he fought against the drowsiness that tried to drag him back under.

"Soph?" He croaked, his parched throat swallowed the noise. "What's wrong?"

He rushed to the en-suite, finding her slumped against the toilet.

Crouching next to Sophia, he took her hands in his. The pallor of her face matched the white ceramic. Terror clenched him, and he held her close.

"Honey, what's wrong? We need to get you to the hospital!"

"It's okay," she uttered from her trembling lips. "I think it's gone now. It must be food poisoning."

Pulling her shivering form against his chest wouldn't subside the fear. They held each other tightly. "It's okay. I need to get ready for work," she said.

Gently lifting her, not wanting to jolt her, he carried her to the bed and tucked her beneath the duvet.

"I'll call in sick for you. You're not going in today. I'll stay home, too."

"No," she replied wearily, drifting towards sleep. "You have to go. It's the Bath game tomorrow, and you need to train. I can't let you risk that. All I'll do is sleep anyway."

He stroked her cheek before tucking a lock of hair behind her ear. Love rose inside him as her eyes fluttered closed.

Turning her slightly to make sure she'd be safe in her sleep, he realised how angelic she looked against the duvet. She was his angel, rescuing him every day. *I'm not a wasted cause yet. I'm getting the test today.*

He planted a kiss against her forehead. "I want to be with you forever." Why could he only confess his truths to her when she was asleep? "By next week I'll know what we're facing. I love you, Sophia."

*****

Sophia woke in the afternoon. Aidan had left a note for her next to a glass of water.

> *I've phoned your work, and they said not to worry. Make sure you get lots of rest and if you need anything at all then call me. I'll be back after five xx*

Reaching for her phone, she had to speak to someone about her declaration of love to Aidan. Hopefully, Nicky wasn't in the air yet.

Nicky answered on the second ring. "Hey. How're tricks?"

Sophia's shoulders instantly relaxed. Life wouldn't be right without Nicky in it.

"Good, I guess."

"I don't believe you for a second. You're groggy. Aren't you at work?"

"I didn't go in. I'm at Aidan's." Chatting with Nicky brought contentment to her previously sickly state. "I was sick this morning. I've been sleeping all day."

"Sick again? Anyone would think you were pregnant," Nicky teased.

Sophia's blood ran cold. Her body trembled.

"You've gone quiet. Is everything okay? I can't stay on much longer. The plane is taking off soon."

"I can't be pregnant," Sophia rambled absentmindedly. "We always use a condom. Aidan won't risk it even though I'm on the pill."

"You use a condom every time?"

"There was only one time we didn't, but I was on the pill. I went to the doctor a couple of days before to get it, remember?"

"You'd have been on it barely two days. It might not have worked that quickly," Nicky hollered as a woman told her to turn the phone off. "The doctor should have told you."

The doctor had told her lots of stuff that day, but she hadn't been listening. Aidan had filled her mind since the day they met.

"I've got to go. The stewardess is threatening to chuck us off the plane. Don't stress, okay? I'll call you when I can." The phone went dead.

What if I'm pregnant?

With the issues at work and problems with Aidan, she'd barely noticed her missed period. She couldn't stop shaking. Fear welled up inside her, and terror hurtled her towards the toilet.

Sitting against the toilet, the chill of the ceramic cooled her feverish forehead.

A shadow crossed her legs. Aidan hovered in the doorway.

*****

"Soph." A sheen of sweat covered her ghost-white face. "I need to get you to the doctors right now."

Her wild eyes fixed on his. "What? Why?"

"You're ill, and you need a doctor. Have you been vomiting all day? You should have called me. The match doesn't matter when it comes to you; nothing does." Panic pummelled Aidan. Thank God he'd checked on her before seeing Doctor Sampson for the test.

"I'm not sick. I think I'm pregnant." The whisper left her lips like a single drop of water falling in a hurricane.

The anger that exploded inside of him was all-consuming. It was so powerful and sudden that he was unable to use the tactics he'd learnt at counselling to stop it.

"What the fuck? How can you be pregnant? We use a condom every time, no matter what. You're on the fucking pill. Or have you been lying to me?"

Although her lips moved, all he heard was his rage. It was like flames roaring in his ears and debilitating his senses.

The words "weekend away" finally made it to his brain.

"What do you mean "weekend away"?"

"I just explained." Her calm persona boiled his blood further. There were consequences to this. The fire was searing his flesh from the inside. "That's when it must have happened. I didn't realise how long I had to be on the pill before it would work. I'd only been on it two days when we had sex without a condom."

"If you hadn't been so stupid and you could have taken the morning-after pill." He ranted.

"And if you hadn't been so horny and forgotten the condom it wouldn't have mattered whether I was on the pill or not," she snapped back. "I didn't know what length of time the pill needed to work."

"Don't you dare put this on me. You must have known, don't play the innocent virgin card." She recoiled as if he'd slapped her, but it didn't cease his wrath. Fear commanded him and turned every emotion to anger. *I can't let another child suffer like I did. I can't bring that sort of pain into the world.* "Bianca tried to get pregnant to keep me. You're just like her. You're going to get an abortion. You might as well kill it now before it dies in agony."

Sophia rushed past him into the bedroom. Words surged from him and clung to her. She needed to understand his agony. *I can't have my child live that life. No life deserves that death sentence.* "Tell me you'll get an abortion."

Turning on her heel, she stepped close. She was tiny in comparison, but her wrath scared him. The closeness was unwarranted and had him stone still. Her bony finger stabbed him in the chest in rhythm with each word she spoke.

"You're a prick, Aidan." Her volume suggested calm, but she spat the words with spite she'd never unleashed on him before. "I warned you that if you ever spoke to me like this, I would be out that door and you'd never see me again. Guess what? I'm not going to sit here and put up with it."

Swiping her car keys and phone she bit, "It's over. Now get out of my way and stay the hell out of my life."

Hatred at himself burned him with the shame he deserved. The anger that had suddenly raged inside of him left just as quickly.

What have I done?

In the act of self-destruction, he reached for his phone.

"Kong, come and pick me up. I need to get wasted." *I need to stop thinking.* Sophia's stuff languished around the room as if she'd made the place her home. Kong's placating fell on deaf ears, Aidan's self-loathing kept it at bay. "I don't give a shit about the game. You owe me one."

Tonight, he was going to forget everything, no matter what it took.

CHAPTER TWENTY-THREE

Tears flowed down Sophia's cheeks. It wasn't meant to be like this. She'd once dreamed of blooming through pregnancy and cradling her firstborn with a husband beaming by her side. *It's time to grow up. I need to do a pregnancy test.*

Quickly parking the car, she hunted for her purse.

"Shit!" She banged her face against the steering wheel. Her bag was in Aidan's room.

I'm not going back now. Calling Kate wasn't an option. She was visiting the Christmas markets in Germany.

Sophia reached home and employed the only coping mechanism at her disposal. Instead of worrying about the future, she busied herself with cooking a dinner she didn't want and scrubbing the bathroom until her hands were raw. But she couldn't avoid reality forever, and soon her chest was shaking as she sat sprawled on the bathroom floor sobbing. What was she going to do?

Like every girl struggling through sickness and pain, she needed her mum. Even full of inadequacies, she knew she'd be there for her.

Their phone call was initially full of the typical niceties, but Sophia forced herself to confront the truth. Fear wasn't an option, not anymore.

"Was I a mistake, mum?" she blurted out.

"What?" her mum stuttered. "If you mean were you unplanned then yes, but you can't possibly think that I didn't want you. You don't think that do you?"

"All my life," she admitted, trying to keep fresh tears at bay.

"Sweetheart, no." Her mother's tears escalated hers. They wept together. "As soon as I knew I was carrying you, I loved you. Why would you think otherwise?"

"Because I made your life difficult. I was an accident that shouldn't have happened." Words formed between sobs so substantial that every breath felt like a battle for air. "You had expectations I couldn't match. No matter what I tried, I failed you."

"My darling, I never meant for you to feel like that. I only saw how amazing you were, and then I saw how other children at school lorded their money over you. I knew you could do anything, and I wanted you to believe it too. I thought with the right support you'd see that nothing stood in your way."

"But why did you keep me away from boys?" She wiped her sleeve across her face. Crying had blurred her vision.

"They weren't good enough to sit in your shadow," her mum's sobbed. "I'm so sorry. I was trying to do my best for you, but I didn't know what I was doing. It's a stupid excuse, but I wanted you to be happy, and I was trying to protect you from making the same mistakes I had. I wanted you to be safe."

"I'm sorry, mum. I thought you were my jailer." She gave a big sigh as she pushed her hair out of her face.

"I guess I was sometimes, but I didn't see it. I believed you'd be happy if you didn't get hurt as I did."

Her tears were easing. "Honey, why are you only saying this now? We should have discussed this years ago."

Sophia's snivels finally stilled. "I've been thinking a lot about all sorts of things recently. It might be because of this guy. I've fallen in love with him, but he's hurt me, and I'm not sure I can forgive him. I have some decisions to make."

"It's not Graham again is it? If it is-"

"No, mum," Sophia quickly interjected. "This guy is mostly loving and caring and treats me like an equal, but at the moment he doesn't deserve me."

"Okay, well, don't you dare take him back if you don't want to. You were always so strong, and there's nothing you can't achieve by yourself. Don't settle for second best. I believe in you, sweetheart, and I always have."

Sophia's heart leapt with a shared understanding that she'd always searched for but never found with her mum.

"I have to go. Derek is looking at me like I've lost my head. But don't forget you're an incredible woman. Derek and I will be popping back to England in a week, in time for New Year. We'll catch up properly, and you can tell me everything. Okay?"

"I'm looking forward to it already."

"I love you, darling, more than anything." Sophia made out her mum whispering to her husband near the phone. "Yes, I love her more than you, Derek, you silly man."

"I love you too, mum," she giggled.

Sophia's mobile battery died not long after that. Her charger was also in her bag at Aidan's house.

Tomorrow she'd raid Nicky's room for money and

take the test. Then it would be time to make difficult decisions. *But now I need to sleep.* She swallowed a herbal sleeping tablet. Her head barely touched the pillow before she drifted off.

*****

"You said you wanted to drink yourself into oblivion." Kong reasoned. "But you've been nursing that pint for the last three hours. What's happening? You should be sleeping in preparation for the game tomorrow. We both should."

Aidan clutched his pint like it was a rubber ring saving him from drowning under waves of guilt.

"Why did I speak to her like that? Why did I force her out, Kong?"

"I have no idea why you do anything when it comes to her, mate. She's made you better in every way. You used to have a lot of dickhead moments, good ones too, but I had to tolerate a lot. And stop calling me Kong. I hate that nickname. Call me Josh."

"Sorry, Josh," Aidan mumbled, focusing on the colours of his lukewarm draft that swirled and sloshed around his pint glass.

"Tell me this, do you love her?" Josh barked.

Aidan nodded sullenly.

"Then sort this shit out because you're going to lose her if you haven't already."

"I'll do it after the game tomorrow. Seeing me right now will make it worse," he rambled. "I love Sophia. I adore her, but I was a complete prick. I don't deserve her."

"Of course, you don't. You deserve a punch in the

balls, but if you love her, you need to try."

"But how do I get her back?"

"Move the earth for her, man. Do whatever it takes," Josh advised.

"Hey, sexy." The familiar fermenting scent of Bianca's sour perfume had Aidan's stomach recoiling. "I haven't seen you around recently. I've missed that arse of yours."

Sliding into the seat next to him, her hand gripped his knee under the table.

"Leave us alone. You're not welcome here." Josh declared, animosity high.

Aidan lifted his hand in her defence. "Give us a minute, Josh? I need to have a word with Bianca."

"Don't do anything stupid. I don't care how upset you are, no funny business. Okay?" Josh walked away, not waiting for an answer. Bianca giggled in Aidan's ear while her hand moved fiercely up his thigh.

"No." His hand rested over hers, stilling its journey. "That's not why I asked him to leave. I want to talk."

"We can talk later." Her fingers wriggled, and her legs pushed intrusively against his.

"Look at me and stop messing around." Her eyes shifted nervously. "I have a girlfriend, shit, now I finally say it? I can't believe I found that word so hard to say. I have a girlfriend who I love. I adore everything about her."

"But-"

He continued enthusiastically. "I love the way she blushes when I compliment her, how she watches me out the corner of her eye and even the way she never backs down when I give her shit. Sophia is the most patient, loving, sexy woman I've ever met, and I wouldn't risk not being with her for something as pathetic as this."

Bianca's mouth tightened. Foundation settled in the creases of her face. "Then where is she tonight and why are you drowning your sorrows with a sad bunch of men?"

"Because I hurt her, and she might never forgive me. She might never speak to me again, and it would be entirely my fault. But I still love her, and that won't change. If she's not with me then I don't exist, she's my world, and I can't live without her."

Aidan's head fell to his hands. It had taken him too long to get to this point. *How can I get her back?* Josh had told him to move the earth, but how?

"Why can't anyone love me like that?" Bianca whispered. Tears fell down her cheeks. "Why did you never love me like that?"

Aidan's mouth dropped open, and he slid his hands down his face. Make-up melted under Bianca's tears.

"You wanted me to love you?"

"I wanted someone to love me. That's why I tried to get pregnant." Bianca's mask fell away.

Gripping both her hands, he admitted he was protective of the trembling creature. The whole time they were together, she was never this real or vulnerable. Maybe that's what had attracted him.

"We would have destroyed each other, and the baby brought into our lives. You didn't love me." Exhaustion from a life spent pretending was reflected in her eyes. He asked her a question more profound than any he'd asked when they were together. "Do you love yourself? Who are you really?"

"I don't know. I used to say I was the fun-loving, party girl but that sounds trite now." Her silent tears were swiftly turning into weeping.

"Tell me something about yourself. Bianca isn't your real name is it?" She shook her head. After all this time, his life had been full of lies. Fakery had surrounded him until Sophia had arrived in his life. She was honest, no matter what the consequences.

Shaking Bianca's hand, he tried something. "Hi, I'm Aidan Flynn. I'm originally from Ireland. I love to paint, and I want to learn to cook. Who are you?"

Would she join in the fresh start? *I owe her. I used her as much as she used me.* Bianca deserved love, as he had, but he'd been lucky, he'd found Sophia, and she'd fought to get beneath his surface. His heart cracked when he remembered her shame when she'd said she loved him.

Bianca's voice shook, and her hand trembled. She attempted to smile. "I'm Evangeline Draper, although I liked to be called Evie. I'm from a dull village where nothing happens, and everyone judges you, and I miss it with all my heart. When I was younger, I wanted to be a ballet dancer." Aidan's laugh was warm and encouraging. Pulling her into a bear hug, he beckoned a watchful Josh over.

"Nice to meet you, Evie." He pressed a kiss to her forehead as she continued to shake. "I reckon given time and a lot of the real Evie, someone will love you very much."

She smiled back. Her makeup was smeared across her face.

"But until that time, Josh is going to take good care of you, aren't you?"

"I guess." Josh's teddy bear face was awash with confusion. "Josh, meet Evie. She needs looking after right now."

Bouncing onto his feet, Aidan declared loudly to a bored and disinterested pub, "I have to go win the heart of a woman who deserves a lot better than me, but who loves me anyway. She's my girlfriend and the only woman I'll ever love."

Offering Josh his seat, he watched Evie scooting into him. Her forlorn form needed holding up.

"You've got to be at the pitch in the morning. Don't forget." Josh called out as Aidan rushed away.

"I wouldn't miss it," he hollered, his legs sweeping him to the door with newfound energy.

"Aidan!" Evie called out. Curiously he turned back. "You're not a bad man, just a bit of a dickhead. I'm sorry for the way I treated you. If you're honest and move the earth for her, she'll have to take you back."

Maybe those two could get on after all.

✼✼✼✼✼

The jackhammering bell invaded Sophia's dreams. *What's going on? Where's the noise coming from?* Moving groggily, she blinked against the winter sun blazing into her bedroom. The bell went off again, penetrating the cocoon she'd created.

Some bastard is leaning on my doorbell!

In the time it took to reach for her phone and check the time, she remembered it was dead and in desperate need of a charge.

"Go away," she whispered to the incessant doorbell.

Suddenly the person started banging against the door.

What the hell?

Grabbing a hoody, she stomped down the stairs.

"One step at a time. Door, then shower, then pregnancy test." It was too much to deal with, and speculating on results wasn't going to help, but the stresses continued to gain a foothold.

Please don't let it be Aidan. She unlocked the door and yanked it open.

It wasn't Aidan staring back at her.

Bloody hell. The only thing moving was the wisps of Bianca's chestnut hair dancing around her in the frigid breeze. "Say something then or are you just going to stand there all afternoon?" Bianca said, rolling her eyes.

"Afternoon?" Sophia replied.

"Yes. It's one in the afternoon. Have you only just woken up?" Sophia self-consciously fiddled with the tie on her pyjama trousers. "That's why you look like that. Do you always wear those things to bed?"

Maybe it wasn't meant to be confrontational, but it had Sophia's back up immediately. "What the are you doing here, Bianca?"

"Aidan sent me."

It was the first time she'd spoken to Bianca. She was prettier than Sophia remembered, from the few times she'd seen her in the nightclubs, and she wasn't surrounded by a cloud of cigarette smoke either.

"Aidan?" Sophia gripped the doorway tightly, bringing out the whites of her knuckles.

"Yes, he needed someone he trusted," Bianca replied dismissively.

"Trusted? You?"

"Are you going to repeat me or are you going to invite me in so I can explain why I'm here?"

"You can stay on the doorstep. Say what you need

to and then get lost," Sophia replied, pulling her crimson hoody round her to keep away the cold.

"Whatever, I'm hardy. I can cope."

"I bet," Sophia said, but Bianca didn't bite. Why had Aidan trusted her of all people? Were they back together?

"Anyway," Bianca said, interrupting Sophia's thoughts, "he asked me to bring you a couple of things."

"He's sending his new girlfriend round to drop my stuff off? Of all the shitty-"

"No, it's not that at all. Aidan's at the ground for the big match, but there was some stuff he wanted you to have as soon as possible, and he didn't think you'd want to see him."

"So, he sent you?"

"I'm a messenger that wants him to be happy."

Sophia gaped.

"For fuck sake, please let me do what I promised him. I'm not here to fight with you. I thought this would be easier."

Sophia folded her arms across her chest. Even with the freezing December temperatures, she couldn't believe Christmas would be here and gone within the next week.

"He said your purse and charger are in your bag and that you need to charge your phone. It's a matter of urgency."

Sophia snorted in derision. Refusing to be helpful, she kept her arms folded as a frustrated Bianca held the bag out to her.

"Fine, I'll pop it here then." She tossed the bag on the doorstep along with a small jewellery box. "He said that you need to watch the game at three. He's made sure it will be on in all the pubs within two miles of your house."

"Is that it?" Sophia replied with a scowl. She tried to temper her anger, but it was a struggle to forget all that Bianca had done.

"You're impossible to be nice to, and I'm really trying. Why the hell he loves you is beyond me."

Loves me? Hold on, Aidan loves me?

"One more present. Wait here." Bianca sauntered down her path. Her hips no longer sashayed offensively.

Returning moments later, Bianca held what looked like a large, framed, painting wrapped in paper and tied with string. "He wanted you to have this. Aidan told me to tell you that he's sent a voice note message thing to your phone. He said you have to listen to it. There's stuff he wanted to tell you." She propped the package against the wall.

Was this a final goodbye from Aidan and an attempt to get the last word in?

"Okay," Sophia replied, defeated by Bianca's declaration of Aidan's love.

Bianca moved closer. If Sophia hadn't been standing on the step, Bianca would have leaned over her, but now they were eyeball to eyeball. "I haven't a clue what he did to you. It's none of my business, but give him a chance, for your sake. He's said he loves you and for anyone that's big, but for Aidan it's monumental. If, once you've looked at the presents and listened to the message you don't want him, then fair enough but it may be what you need to hear."

"Okay, thank you." It was the first pleasantry Sophia had offered and the closest they'd get to reconciliation.

"And for the record, I'm sorry for the way I treated

both of you. They're not empty words; I haven't been in a good place because... Well, you don't need to know why. Just sorry, okay." Bianca said before turning on her heel and heading towards her car.

"Good luck," Sophia called out to Bianca's retreating body, unsure what she wished her luck for.

"You too," Bianca replied, not turning, her trainers slapping against the cold, grey path. "You're good people."

When Bianca was gone, Sophia scooped up her bag and jewellery box before dragging the painting in behind her.

She charged her phone while she showered. With every action, she tried to cling to the normality that was ebbing further and further away. At least now she had the money to get the pregnancy test.

For the first time in days, she wasn't fighting nausea. Maybe the signs were a false alarm, and she wasn't pregnant. She clung to her last remaining hopes. *But if I am pregnant, there's no way I'm letting anyone take this baby away from me.*

Glancing at her phone, she saw it was only 20% charged. It needed more juice.

There were several texts on it. Most were from Nicky and spanned the last fifteen hours.

N: *We've landed safely, and my phone is now working. How are you?* x

N: *Sophia, what's going on? You'd better not be ignoring me* x

N: *Talk to me!* X

N: *I can't get hold of Aidan either. Are you okay??!?!!?*

N: *Have you taken the test???*

The kisses had disappeared from the end of the messages in the early hours replaced, instead, by angry punctuation.

N: *If I don't hear from you by Saturday morning, I'm calling your mother, that's the biggest threat I know!!!*

N: *I'm calling your mum right now!!!!*

N: *Right, I've talked to your mum, she said she spoke to you last night and that you were okay. Please message me.*

N: *SOPHIA!!!!!xxxxx*

Tapping a message back as quickly as possible, she feared what Nicky would be considering next. The police might be on their way.

S: *I'm sorry. My phone died, and I didn't have my charger. Everything is okay. I haven't taken the test yet, but I will. I'll message in a bit. Go and enjoy yourself. Love you x*

The response was immediate.

N: *Glad you're okay. I can't believe you spoke to your mum. Message me after the test. We're off to the Colosseum. Ryan says hi, and he's glad you're ok. Love you back xx*

There was a text from Aidan too, she read it with a scowl already in position.

A: *You don't owe me anything, but please listen to the voice note I've sent you and watch the game. I love you. I'll spend my life telling you and saying sorry because I am, more than you'll ever understand. I'm not good with words but please watch the game and listen to the message.*

Sophia threw some clothes on and headed to the pharmacy, bag and phone in hand. How dare he tell her he loved her. The great Aidan Flynn was very sure that he could get her to do what he wanted.

✷✷✷✷✷

Aidan said a silent prayer. Everything had worked as planned, so far. He'd moved heaven and earth to be with Sophia. It was now resting on her willingness to watch the rugby match and listen to his messages. Would she forgive him, or was it too late?

"Please," he begged, staring at the blue sky that held his hopes within its frosty expanse. Darkness would fall soon. "Please give me this. I can't live without her."

"Come on, Aidan. We need to get on the pitch for warm-up. You ready, buddy?" Josh asked.

"I hope she sees it. I hope she forgives me." His heart froze, it daren't hope. By the end of the day, it might be in fragments.

"We all do. There are thousands on your side out there. You certainly know how to say sorry. Let's go."

But it was the opinion of only one person that counted.

"Please forgive me, Sophia," he whispered the mantra over and over again as he ran onto the pitch to thousands of cheering fans.

✷✷✷✷✷

Sophia gripped the pregnancy test box as she stood outside her local pharmacy. Her future was in the box. *Can I do this by myself?* Was she as strong as her mum believed? Nicky would be back in less than a week. *Then we can do it together.*

"No," she said aloud, scaring the pigeon that ferreted around her feet. "I am strong. I can do this."

The vibration against her leg signalled her ringing phone. Jack's name popped up on the screen.

"Hello?" Her voice wobbled.

"Babe, how're things? You over your sickness bug?"

"Kind of." The pregnancy test box was like a lead weight in her hand. "What are you up to?"

"Oh, nothing special." *He's acting weird, even for Jack.* "I called to ask you something. You know how you owe me one?"

"Do I?"

"Yes. I've made your life much easier at work, especially with Tasha," he joked.

"That I can believe. How would you like to collect?" She turned the box over and over in her hand.

"Go to the nearest pub and watch the rugby."

"This is about Aidan? He's been on to you, too?" she replied angrily.

"Honey, this is about you. For me, this has always been about you and your happiness. Trust me and go into a pub."

Looking up, she realised she was standing outside The Tavern, her local. Fate was conspiring against her.

"Jack, you don't know what happened between us." Why should Aidan be allowed to get away with what he did? What if she took him back and he behaved like that again? This wasn't some playground break up.

"Please go into the pub and look at the screen. That's all I'm asking."

I could put the test off for a bit longer.

"Who is this Sophia woman?" She heard from inside the pub. Curiosity niggled her.

"I'll think about it."

"Okay, babe. I love you. You know that?"

"Yes, I know," she replied with a sigh. "I love you too. Catch you later."

Sophia stepped into the worn, rundown pub. The smells of spilt beer and elderly men lingered around her. The tables looked like they'd been victim to a drive-by creosoting. The psychedelic pattern of blue and burgundy circles on the carpet drew the eyes but battled against the dark brown diamonds on the frayed upholstered chairs. Nausea reared its head again. Grey-haired and balding men decked out in their crimson and white rugby shirts were dotted around the pub.

No one noticed her even though she didn't fit in with her wavy ponytail and skinny jeans. At least her hoody was the right crimson red. The 65-inch HD television transfixed the punters. It was the only thing in the place that looked like it had seen the current decade. The television transfixed the harsh looking barmaid that fitted every stereotype with her massive pendulous boobs and beehive hair. Everyone locally knew the pub had crap customer service, but Sophia had expected a little better.

"He's going to be in so much trouble," a bushy-bearded man uttered loudly.

"She must be important, though. He's got the whole team involved," another commented.

"He's got the whole bloody crowd involved!" the first guy replied.

"He must love her," the barmaid said wistfully. Her raspy voice revealed decades of smoking, hiding the sentiment a little.

"What gave it away, the pitch or the t-shirts?" the

bearded one asked sarcastically.

Finally, Sophia forced herself to look at the television screen. She covered her mouth before a gasp slipped free.

On the screen the Bulls rugby players were warming up, their t-shirts adorned with one slogan. Everywhere the camera panned fans wore t-shirts with the same words.

Suddenly the camera focused on the pitch where someone had plastered the same slogan across the green grass. The glossy white words shone brightly, reflecting the winter sun.

"Aidan loves his girlfriend Sophia."

Everywhere the camera panned she saw the same thing. *How did Aidan make all this happen? And why?* A chill ran the length of her body and sank into the flesh of her cheeks.

Somebody pushed a chair under her bottom, and she grabbed the wooden table in front of her. The eyes of the raspy-voiced barmaid were on her. From their tired appearance Sophia imagined the barmaid had seen too much torment in her life. She'd probably caused her fair share too, but her gaze displayed a kindness that warmed Sophia's body and chased the chill away.

"Can I get you something, love?"

Sophia barely nodded, her eyes trying to communicate for her.

"Whisky?"

She fingered the test in her pocket. "Can I have a glass of mineral water?"

"Of course, darlin'." The barmaid brought the glass to the table, giving Sophia's hand a little squeeze as she popped it down. "It's on the house."

"Why don't *we* get table service?" an old guy, who looked like Captain Birdseye, shouted. He had a bushy white beard and a shoulder made for a parrot.

"Shut up and watch the rugby. The game is about to start," she snapped back.

Sophia whispered a thank you before looking back at the screen as the Bulls players jogged back onto the pitch. They wore their proper kit now, but many in the crowd still had her name on their chests. The writing on the turf didn't look like it would ever fade.

Girlfriend, it said girlfriend. He said he loves me.

Was it enough to forgive him?

It wasn't.

There had been too many lies and months of things yet to be explained. *Aidan told me to get an abortion.* Had anything changed? Maybe he wanted her back and was willing to say whatever it took.

The phone burned in her pocket. Everything in front of her wasn't enough for her to take him back, but was it enough for her to listen to the voice note?

Chapter Twenty-Four

There was nothing he could say that would win her back. But Sophia still slipped on her headphones and pressed play as Aidan and his team battled on the television screen. Maybe she didn't owe him anything, but there was a possibility she was carrying his child. She couldn't ignore him forever.

"*Sophia, my Sophia.*" His voice nearly brought tears. She missed him already. But she was determined to keep a steel heart where he was concerned.

"*I want to start by telling you how sorry I am. What I said was the result of pain from my past, pain that never went away. I've kept secrets from you. But in no way does that excuse my behaviour. What I said to you, the way I treated you was unforgivable. The things I need to tell you are not so you'll forgive me. I should have told you these things before, but I can't change that. I can only make decisions about the present.*"

Aidan's voice stopped. It was more than a pause. Would he speak again or was the secret too hideous to share? Their stars aligned once more, and he appeared on the television. The camera focused on his weary face. He'd got a conversion off his kick. It was one of his best, but he appeared dejected. Within moments his Irish accent filled her ears.

"I was born in Ireland to two parents who adored each other. They told people they'd been blessed with the greatest gift; a child to love. We were the happiest family in the world. My dad had lost his parents in a car accident when he was young. Suddenly he had his own family, and it was full of unconditional love. They thought nothing could destroy it. But something did.

"*Things started to change when my dad was thirty-five. I was a year old. At first, he had bouts of anger and displayed signs of depression. Over time his body started to spasm and jerk. Mum was nervous about leaving him alone with me because of his unpredictable behaviour. Over the next years, he tried to control the uncontrollable and hide what was happening, but eventually, he admitted everything to our doctor. After various tests, he was diagnosed with Huntington's disease. It was a hereditary disease. One of his parents must have had it, but they died when they were young. Dad cried when he explained he wouldn't have had a biological child, he wouldn't have had me, had he known.*

"*Over the next eight years, I watched him die a slow and cruel death. I only saw him at his worst. I never experienced him full of life and love, but mum did.*" There was bitterness in his voice, but his words continued to stream like a river that refused to dry. "*The love of her life became a shadow of himself. She never gave up on him. She cared for him and was always there for him. She sacrificed so much of her life in his last years. She loved him beyond the day he died and still carries the emotional scars from those years.*"

Aidan's spoke with a detachment. A tear slipped down her cheek for the poor little boy who brutally lost his dad and part of his mum before his life barely started. The action continued on screen. Aidan was playing another incredible game, and in response, the Bath players were playing increasingly dirty; stamping on them when they went down, elbows in the face. The referee repeatedly missed it. The game was dangerous.

"When I was eleven, mum and I moved to England. Although our past was in Ireland, the memories and pain travelled with us. Mum worked two jobs so we could survive, but that was all it was, survival. She was barely coping, and I was drowning in my anger, conscious of that noose around my neck. Before he died, my dad made me promise not to have children. When someone with Huntington's disease has a child, that child has a 50% chance of having the disease. I had a 50% chance of developing the slow, debilitating illness I'd watched slaughter my dad. That's a lot for anyone to deal with. It was too much for a scared and lonely eleven-year-old boy. My death sentence was signed; did it matter what I did? I got into fights and hurt whoever I could until rugby found me. That stuff I told you about my teenage years was all true. Maybe it makes more sense now."

The pauses in his story were getting longer. More than once, Sophia questioned if he'd come to the end of what he was saying only for him to continue.

"I was terrified of the future. The grim reaper has followed me around all my life. I vowed two things. The first was that I'd never get the test done. That way, I could live my life to the full and do what I wanted with who I wanted. My second was never to let anyone experience what my mum went through. I refused to fall in love. Girlfriends wouldn't be part of my life, and I would only have flings. After that, things were fine, and

life seemed in my control. I wasn't getting hurt or hurting anyone around me, just coasting along. But then I met you and all my vows meant nothing because you changed everything."

Silently she willed his speech forward.

"I love you. You're my whole world, beautiful, kind Sophia. You've made me the sort of man I'm not ashamed of. Until you, I didn't know how to care for others, but you taught me. I long to be a better man so that I can deserve your love although I'll never deserve you, in any way."

Her tears were pouring now, hitting the table with tiny splashes.

The game was in its second half. She'd missed half time.

Aidan played as if his life depended on it. It was like he was alone against the world. Maybe that was how it had always been for him. A pack of tissues had appeared in front of her. Pausing the message, she looked up to find the barmaid watching her, sadness reflected in her eyes. Sophia managing the smallest of grateful smiles.

She took a couple of deep breaths, willing the tears to subside. Aidan had kept so much hidden. How had he survived all that time holding it inside? No wonder the closer they got, the more he pushed her away.

But her thoughts were fleeting and quickly she returned to the recording. Her phone's battery was fading fast.

"I started caring about things that had never bothered me before. What would It be like to be in love and have a future? But the terror wouldn't go away. What if you found out about me and thought I wasn't worth the sacrifice? What if I had the disease? I didn't

want you to suffer like mum had. I could have taken the test, but I was scared. Sometimes when you don't know what you're facing it makes it easier to pretend everything is going to be okay. But the real reason I wouldn't get the test was because I'm a coward. I'm ashamed to admit that to my brave Sophia."

The unopened pregnancy test sitting on the table caught her eye. She'd suspected she was pregnant for about twenty-four hours, and still hadn't taken the test. They both had their gutless moments.

"In the end, I was doing the one thing I said I wouldn't. I was making you suffer. But it wasn't because of the disease; it was down to me and my secrets. I love you. I've loved you maybe since our date on the hill or earlier when you looked at me as I got out my swimming pool with those hungry eyes. Maybe I even loved you when we first met, and you called me a prick."

The rumbling laugh that carried through the headphones made her smile, although the tears continued to pour down her cheeks. There were too many to wipe away now. With glassy eyes and a soaking sleeve, she still smiled at the memory of the art exhibition and the way she'd cut him down.

"I decided to get the test done. You deserved it to be your choice rather than letting me choose for you, but I was still too scared until I met Tim. Over the last couple of months, I've had counselling, and finally, after talking about my experiences, I was learning to control my anger. Knowing how much you wanted me to be a better man helped me develop tactics for dealing with things. Once I had the test results, I could make an informed decision and map out the future a little. Yesterday I was stopping home to check on you before getting the test

done. By Christmas, we'd know the results. We'd be able to plan our future together or plan it separately, whatever you wanted.

"*After years of hiding, I was ready, but then I came home and heard the word baby, and I saw red. I can't stress enough that my words and actions were wrong and in no way justifiable. But you need to know that I wasn't angry with you. I was angry at life. It was as if all my fears were coming back to laugh at me. All that time, I'd spent suffering, and now there would be a baby living a life that I'd detested. My entire life I've been watching and waiting, wondering when I'd start developing symptoms. I'd expected to die like my dad did. Yesterday, instead of thinking rationally, I erupted. Putting a child, our child, through a life like mine, one of sadness, pain and terror was too much. It wasn't right. It wasn't fair, and so I went mad. And it was wrong, completely wrong. I was the ugliest monster and you, the woman I've loved in every way, the only woman, other than mum, who's seen the good in me saw a gruesome creature, a fucking bastard. I hurt you, terrified you, and I hate myself.*"

He was right he'd been hideous, Sophia couldn't forget it.

"*I'll understand if you never want to see me or speak to me again. But there's something you need to know. I had the test done this morning. The result should be back in less than a week. Getting the test done wasn't only about me; I did it for you, the possible baby and us. I'm ready to live and not just survive, barely survive. Soph, I want to share my life with you if you'll have me, but I'll understand if you don't. I'm sorry for how much I've hurt you. I'm sorrier than you'll ever know.*

"It's ridiculous that it's only now when we're no longer together I can say girlfriend, but I do love you, and I'm proud to say it. I can't stop saying how much I love you. I wish I'd been able to say it earlier. But I can't change the past.

"I want to face the future with you if you'll take me back. And if you don't, then I'll do whatever it takes to make sure you're okay. If there's a baby, he or she will have all they need, not only the practical stuff. We'll give them so much love. And if they have the disease, then I'll make sure they're supported for life. I'm here for both of you.

"I love you, Sophia. I can't imagine loving anyone else for the rest of my life."

Tears cascaded down her cheeks.

"I want to move the earth for you, but I don't know how to so I've given you an earth pendant because you're my world. I promise to spend the rest of my life proving it.

"And I finished the painting of you. It was my focus last night. It's my first painting that doesn't have pain and loneliness hiding in the background. I'm ready to accept my life, I love you and I always will."

Sophia sat still for several minutes in silence. There were no more words from Aidan.

But, on the television, he was bolting for the try line. Time ran out on the clock. Once more he was in combat, a warrior battling against his opponents. Whipping off her headphones, she grabbed her bag and jumped up. She had to get to the grounds and speak to him.

Glancing at the screen one last time, Aidan entered the shot. Everyone saw him. Men were shouting at him. Metres from the try line, it looked like this game was going to be one of his most significant victories. He sprinted the last section of the pitch. Gavin was heading for him, defending the line, but Aidan was going to get past him. He was going to end the match with the best try of the game.

But then the unimaginable happened.

Gavin came at Aidan. Diving low, he grabbed him by the calves before tossing him into the air and over his shoulders in an illegal rugby move, a spear tackle. It was a move that could damage or destroy, and as Aidan went down, Sophia did too.

Sophia came to. Her body was sore against the hard chair. Someone must have set her back on it after she'd blacked out. Whisky aromas from the breaths of the men crowding around her, brought her out of her grogginess.

The barmaid hollered, "Give the girl some bloody space!"

The anxious, heavily whiskered, faces eased back, and someone pressed a wet cloth against her forehead.

But what's happened to Aidan? Stretching she searched for the television screen. She nearly passed out again when a spell of wooziness hit.

"Sit back, love. You need to rest."

"But Aidan." Sophia fought the hands that attempted to still her.

On the television screen straining paramedics hunkered down on the pitch, working on an unmoving body.

"Hun." The barmaid rested her hands on Sophia's

shoulders. "Are you Sophia?"

Pain rose in the back of her head as she turned.

"How did you know?" she asked.

"I got a call this morning from an Irish guy who was very insistent that I play the game this afternoon. He said that it was for love and for a woman called Sophia. When you walked in and watched the television with those big eyes, I knew. He did all that for you?"

Bearded faces peered closer. A strange woman had collapsed in their makeshift home, and now they were learning that she was the woman who was dearly loved by their rugby hero. It would bring reminiscing stories to the pub for years.

"I guess he did, yes. How is he?"

"Honestly?" The barmaid's eyes, nearly hidden by clumpy black eyelashes, flicked towards the television. "I'm not sure. I expect they'll be taking him to the hospital. That tackle is illegal for a reason. It could be a spinal injury or worse."

"Stop upsetting the woman, Angie," a gruff local voice complained.

"Sorry, love. I'm sure it's fine." Angie attempted to coo over her, reverting to the mother hen stance. "I'm sure The Destroyer will be banned for a long time too."

"I need to get to the hospital," Sophia announced.

"You need to rest." Hands reached for her, but she pushed them away. Nausea threatened to overwhelm her as she stood.

"I don't have time for this. Please. I need to see Aidan. I need to speak to him."

Sophia focused on Angie, silently pleading with her for support. She seemed the kind of woman who could make things happen.

"Okay, but you're not driving. I'll call you a taxi."

The next thirty minutes flew by. Suddenly Sophia found herself standing in the doorway to the hospital corridor, the pregnancy test hidden in her bag. The smell of anti-bacterial hand wash hit her nostrils.

I have to take the test. She'd been hiding from her future for too long.

But what if Aidan had brain-damage or couldn't walk again? What if he had Huntington's disease? *Can I be there for him no matter what?*

It's time to face your future.

*****

The hard pillow did nothing to stop the pain shooting through his head. *Where am I?* Groggily Aidan inched his head to the side. *And why do I feel like I've had the shit kicked out of me?* He eased one eye open before working on the other. The clinical surroundings and itchy blanket gave away his location, as did the suffocating stench of sickness. He had too many bad memories of hospitals.

Shit, the tackle. Recalling the sickening grin on Gavin's face as he'd gone for Aidan brought back the crunch and snap noise that had proceeded his blackout. He wriggled his limbs. They hurt like hell, but everything moved okay.

A new noise caught his attention. It was the deep, slow breathing of someone sleeping.

Easing his head to the side, he saw his Sophia. Wavy hair framed her face, golden highlights added to her ethereal look.

She came to see me.

With a healed body, he could have jumped for joy, but suddenly anxiety gripped him. *However much she loves me, she'd have stayed away unless she has a reason to be here.* Was she going to tell him it was over for good? *Please don't get your hopes up that she wants you back.* But butterflies fluttered in his belly.

Her chest rose and fell with every breath. Aidan's groin stirred when he appraised her legs that hung off the edge of the chair arm. At least that wasn't broken. His heart stirred too. She was all he wanted; mind, body and soul. Every word of his message had been genuine. Whatever it took to make her happy he'd do it, she was his world. The trouble he'd be in, when management got hold of him, for the writing on the pitch had been worth it to tell her he loved her.

Her lips transfixed him. When she woke, the words out of her mouth could break him or give him a life he hadn't known he wanted until her. *I love her so much.*

"Stop watching me, Aidan," Sophia said. Was she annoyed or teasing him?

There had only been one occasion, since he was a teenager, that he'd felt dread like this. Several years ago, at the Rugby World Cup final, he'd kicked a ball to make the conversion. Ireland needed it to win. Having the hopes of a country rest on him was nothing compared to facing what Sophia had come to share.

"Soph," he started. *Can I make any more speeches to convince her of my regret and love?* He'd never convince her to do anything she didn't want to do. It was one of the many reasons he loved her.

"Before you say anything else," she said, devoid of emotion, "we need to get the nurse to check you over."

Stepping close, she pressed the call button. A waft

of her perfume caressed him.

He willed himself to stay calm.

The nurse arrived within seconds. Every moment she took to check his memory, understanding and movement were agonising. Sophia was taking everything in with a cold, curious stare. There was no hint of her purpose. Aidan longed for a smile, but instead, she occasionally raised an eyebrow. His anxiety climbed.

"You've been incredibly lucky," the nurse said. "You should have sustained a major injury, but aside from some bruising and stiffness, you're going to be okay. We'll keep you in for another day, but I suspect the doctor will let you go on tomorrow."

"What day is it now?" he inquired, his gaze never leaving Sophia's face.

"It's early Monday morning. You've been out for about half a day, and she has not left your side," the nurse replied, nodding her head in Sophia's direction.

His hopes were growing, but he forced them away. *I might have to watch Sophia walk away again, which she has every right to do.*

Sophia moved her chair next to the head of his bed before sitting back down.

All this time he'd thought by not getting the test done he could live his life fully when instead he was risking everything, living in a shadow of what might have been.

I'm a fucking idiot.

He'd let anger control his life. Fear of his future might have cost him everything.

"You'll need looking after when you go home, but the doctor will chat about that when he sees you. It's not the Christmas you were expecting, but as I've said you've been incredibly lucky."

Aidan managed a smile before the nurse left the room.

Flecks of hazel danced in the browns of Sophia's eyes. What was she thinking? With a deep breath, he waited.

"I thought you had another speech prepared, Aidan." Was there a trace of her signature cheeky smile?

He faltered. *My cocky attitude can't help me now.* "I think you've heard enough from me, unless… You did listen to the message? All of it?"

"Yes, I listened." She drew out every word. It was torture.

"And?" he dared to ask.

Sophia was tired; her eyes were red, and her skin pale. He'd put her through a lot in the last forty-eight hours. "And I wish you'd told me sooner."

She'd imprisoned his heart in a vice grip. Was this their ending?

"But."

"But?" His excitement brought her hand to his, holding it tenderly, skin to skin.

"But, if we're going to be boyfriend and girlfriend, then we can't have any more secrets. I can't go through this every time you bottle stuff up or freak out. I need to know what's happening. You're a difficult man, Aidan Flynn."

The smile teasing her lips had him beaming. "And if the tests come back positive and I have Huntington's disease, what will you do?"

"I'll stay," she replied as if it was obvious. "I love you with all my heart. You gave me so much, and I don't just mean sex. With you, I was able to see my true identity. You taught me to accept that and to love it, too. You're my world, and no matter what the results say I want to spend the rest of our lives together. You're mine, forever. But no more secrets."

"No more. I'll be the man you deserve. I love you with all my heart. I'm so lucky to be with you, Soph." He was a happy idiot.

"But," she stopped him once more.

"But?"

"In the new pledge of not keeping secrets, I have to tell you something."

His trembling heart was discernible only to him. He had no more secrets. Had she been hiding something all this time?

Sophia held a white plastic item gingerly in her hand. His vision cleared slowly as he battled the grogginess.

"You took the pregnancy test?" His voice shook.

"Yes."

"And?" She was like a game show presenter drawing out tension.

"And you're going to be a dad. We're going to have a baby."

His beaming smile faltered. Was it a good thing? Was it the right plan? He was surprised at his lack of anger. Had taking the test meant he could finally come to terms with things?

"You're scared, but it's going to be okay."

Aidan had no idea what the next years would hold, but they'd get through it, and they'd love that baby no matter what. Everything he'd feared was starting to happen; a baby that could have Huntington's disease. But Sophia was right; it was going to be okay because he had her by his side.

"Come here," he said, pulling the mint green blanket back a little.

Snuggling up next to her, in the bed that was barely big enough for his body, let alone for the two of them, a sudden thought made him smile.

It's three of us now.

"No funny business, though," she said, smiling. Pressing his lips to her hair, Aidan wrapped his arms tightly around her.

"I make no promises," his voice lowered, and he tried to take on the sexy gravelly tone she loved.

Aidan ran his hands across her. He didn't worry about his bruises or the tiny bed or who might walk in, instead, he focused all his attention on Sophia, a woman he'd never deserve but who loved him all the same.

Epilogue

"I can't believe I'm here." The butterflies in Sophia's stomach danced. Standing with Nicky, they listened to Aidan give a couple of details to a reporter from the local paper.

"You finished last season holding up the Premiership Cup for the Bulls and yet you no longer play professional rugby. Tell me more, Aidan," the pointy faced reporter asked.

"It was the perfect time to finish. I left on a high. I'd achieved everything I wanted, and I was lucky enough to go into my other passion, art. The backers came along, and here we are at the opening of my new art gallery." Aidan's smile eclipsed his face. Sophia grinned with him. She took in the gallery they now owned. It contained art from a variety of artists; paintings that stunned, enlightened, and confused.

"Is it true that your former coach, Charlie Owen, is not only one of your backers but has some of his work displayed?"

"You got it," Aidan replied.

Sophia giggled. He sounded like he was doing a sports television interview, not some fluff piece for the local paper. "I was scared about telling him I was leaving, but Charlie encouraged me and admitted he was a secret sculptor. He invested money and gave some of his pieces to sell. Make sure you take a look at them, they're incredibly moving. Charlie's skills have surprised everyone."

"And you found the perfect premises. The sun must be shining on you."

"I had the right friends," he nodded to Nicky. It was a revelation that Ryan, the surfer dude, worked in property. At times he resembled a puppy with an extreme sports death wish, but when he was doing business deals, he was the ultimate charmer.

"And the right lady as well. You've also become a husband and a father, it's been quite a year for you," the reporter continued.

"It has. I am the happiest and luckiest man in the world." He beamed at Sophia, who, full of blushes, smiled in return.

Soon the interview was over, and Aidan was surrounded by guests once more.

Nicky and Sophia continued their conversation, enjoying the rare chance to catch up.

"Do you think he'll miss rugby?"

Aidan chatted to the mayor, pointing out several works with all the charm Sophia remembered from their first meeting in the cathedral. The painting that had captivated her that night was nearby. Catching Aidan's eye, he gave her a wink as she recalled fondly the way they'd met.

"Maybe a bit," she replied, realising Nicky's question had been lingering in the air unanswered. "But he's going to support John by training the youth team, and he wants to help at the charity too. Besides, I think he'll be getting Patrick on the field as soon as he can walk. He's already given him a Bulls baby grow and ball. What two-month-old baby needs a rugby ball?"

Nicky laughed. "Where is Patrick tonight?"

"Kate has him until tomorrow. She dotes on him. She wept with joy when we told her we were giving him the middle name Liam, in honour of Aidan's dad. When my mum is visiting, they compete for who can be the best grandma," Sophia laughed. "He is a fortunate boy. Two grandmas madly in love with him."

"I'm glad Aidan's tests came back negative. You would have been there for him no matter what, but at least Patrick can't develop Huntington's."

Tears pricked Sophia's eyes. "What did I do to deserve this life? But let's talk about you and that diamond ring that keeps dazzling my eyes. Have you been able to set a date?"

"Yes. The wedding is July next year and then a week of sun and mountain biking. Before you ask, I have no idea how Ryan talked me into that."

Suddenly they were drawn to the doorway as Josh and Bianca, or Evie as they called her now, walked in. They looked like an odd pair, but they giggled away, sharing an exclusive world.

"When did that happen?" Nicky asked.

"It hasn't. They're just friends, but we're all waiting for them to realise how much they like each other." Sophia replied with a wry smile.

Nicky smiled knowingly. "Hopefully it will happen. Right, I've got to go. Ryan and I are up early tomorrow for my first mountain biking lesson." They hugged like it was their last goodbye. Their lives had moved on in the previous year, but their friendship would continue through everything.

Nicky whispered in her ear, "And you have the life you deserve. You're the best person, and I couldn't imagine my life without you in it. I can't wait for you to be my chief bridesmaid."

They shed a tear as they went their separate ways.

Aidan continued to network his way around the room, and Sophia offered food to all the guests like a dutiful hostess. Eventually, guests started to leave, and she was able to make a jump on clearing up.

As the gallery opening drew to a close, she stood in front of her favourite painting. It was the one that had started with a bet and ended on the day Aidan had finally said the word girlfriend. She'd had no idea that dignitaries would be looking at her near-naked body when she'd posed in Aidan's art room all that time ago. At least she'd covered her modesty with the scarlet material.

Sophia smiled as she clutched the silver earth pendant around her neck.

Suddenly Aidan's hands rested against her hips, and his musky scent enveloped her. He moved in behind her, fitting effortlessly against her body.

"So, Bambi eyes, do you like what you see?" His lips brushed her neck. Tender kisses quickly turned into sexy nips at her skin.

"The gallery is amazing. You've done an incredible job. Everyone loves you and your work." Sophia leant into him and his arms wrapped around her body. "I'm so happy."

"Me too. I love you, Mrs Flynn."

"I love you too. I do have one other thought."

"Go on," he said.

"Patrick is with your mum all night," she continued.

"And?" The deep, sexy, Irish accent rose through that one small word.

"And…" she teased, wiggling her bum.

"Are you propositioning me?" Whipping her around, he moved her back, pressing her against the solid wall next to their painting. Aidan was already hard and twitching against her. "What do you want to do?"

A giggle fell from her mouth.

"It's not just about what." Grinding her body against his, she dramatically looked over his shoulder and round the gallery to make her point. "It's also where and how many times."

"You have the best ideas," he whispered, reaching beneath the lace of her scarlet dress.

THE END

Acknowledgements

A book is rarely the result of one person sitting in a room and magically publishing it. Head Over Feels is the result of endless support from incredible writers and knowledgeable friends and family.

Thank you, Sarah Smith and Stefanie Simpson. You have been there for me every step, from the moments I got knocked down and was a breath away from giving up to the beta reading and advice. I wouldn't have self-published this story without your knowledge, encouragement and support.

Sarah Vance-Tompkins was the critique partner I needed. I wasn't always great at listening, but your advice and amendments have improved this story from the mess it was in, and I can't thank you enough for the hours you must have spent reading it.

Anne Pyle, you were there early on, and your support was the best.

To Claire, thank you for your rugby knowledge, it ironed out a lot of issues. Your patience when it came to every rugby question I could conceive was more than I can ask for.

Thank you to my sisters who inspired this story in a variety of ways and especially my eldest sister who always took the time to read whatever I'd sent her and to decipher whatever I thought I'd written.

My lovely fiancé, thank you for putting up with the many hours I've spent in coffee shops, pubs and at my desk trying to perfect a series of words and who picked me up when it all got too much.

H.A. Lynn, thank you for your editing and patience with my manuscript. You got me to a stage that I'd long thought impossible.

Thank you to the readers who have taken the time to buy and read something that brought me much joy, sadness and agony at different times. I hope the payoff has been worth it.

Finally, a massive thank you to the Twitter community who have supported my whims, offered ongoing encouragement, inspired me and always been there to cheer me on. You guys are the best community I have found.

ALSO BY REBECCA CHASE

Crave for Me: three short tales of erotic romance

Occupational Hazard: A sexy workplace anthology

REBECCA IS FEATURED IN THE FOLLOWING ANTHOLOGIES

Best Women's Erotica of the Year, Volume 4

Corrupted: Erotic Romance for the Modern Age

Erotic Teasers: a Cleis anthology

Goodbye Moderation: Lust and Gluttony

Love of the Game: Sports Stories to Make You Sweat

Working It (Sexual Expression Book 2)

About Rebecca Chase

Rebecca Chase is an English rose with a taste for drama, romance and sex. She adores writing, whether it's a short story with unexpected passion or a novel that takes you through the ups and downs of a blossoming relationship. She's always looking out for everyone's next book boyfriend. When it comes to her stories you can guarantee there will be romance, there will be lust, and most of all, there will be mind-blowing sex. You'll be desperate for more while aching for a happy ever after.

CONNECT WITH REBECCA

Website - www.rebeccahchase.com

Twitter - twitter.com/rebeccahchase

Facebook - www.facebook.com/RebeccaHChaseAuthor

Printed in Great Britain
by Amazon